Breathing

The Club Series, Book 1

Rebekkah Rogers

COFFEE CUP PRESS

BREATHING

ISBN: 978-0-9915020-1-1

Cover by Stephanie Lynn Nelson
designbystephanie.wordpress.com

PRINTED IN THE UNITED STATES OF AMERICA

10 9 8 7 6 5 4 3 2 1

Table of Contents

Prologue

I could feel them arguing on the couch. I had my earbuds in and my eyes averted because I just didn't want to see it, but they are boys, and it only takes three minutes for all hell to break loose. "Stop fighting," I yelled, although it did little good as they knew I wasn't going to do anything about it. I was elbow deep in dish suds and not really paying attention. They're aware that I'm not in my enforcement mode.

Just as I was finishing up, the door bell rang. I glanced at the boys racing to the door and did not give it a second thought it's probably the neighbor's kids. Our house was turning into a teen flop house and starting to smell like one, as well.

I felt, rather than saw, the stress on my son's body when he came in and told me that the door was for me. I could see the men as soon as I rounded the wall from the kitchen to the foyer. Uniforms…these men were in uniforms. But why? The boys were here and I just got off the phone with Marc half an hour ago. He had said that he was pulling into his office and would be a few more hours there before he came home.

"Mrs. Williams?" the older officer asked while reaching out to take my hand. Without waiting on my reply, he pulled me forward and started walking in the house. "May we come in?"

"Yes, of course, officers. How may I help you?" My always-polite work voice came out even when I didn't plan it. I motioned for them to sit.

"Ma'am, there was a shooting today."

7

I heard the ma'am, but couldn't relate the shooting to me. Did he think that I was old? He's probably my age–late thirties–with slight graying at the temples. It's kind of hot. Hey–I'm married, not dead. I really should focus more.

"A shooting? What happened? Who was hurt?" I couldn't figure out why the county sheriff would come to me, as I had no one here in this area but us. We moved here only three years ago with my husband's company.

"Mrs. Williams, do you know Sarah Thomas?" Deputy Hottie asked.

"Is she ok? She's such a sweet thing; she's my husband's secretary. She's a co-op student and can't be more than twenty. What the hell happened? Oh God…is Marc ok?" I couldn't stop the words from tumbling out. I could see the lines of stress on the younger cops face revealing that he was worried.

"It appears that her boyfriend suspected she was having an affair with a man in the office and went in to confront her and her *boyfriend*. As I understand it, it's your husband that she was having an affair with, ma'am. I'm sorry."

I chuckle because I know how this looks. "No, my husband was not seeing Sarah. She was trying to get rid of her boyfriend because he was harassing her, so she approached me and asked if it would be okay to ask Marc to play her *boyfriend*. They were not having an affair. If you ask around, it was actually one of his partner's ideas. It seemed to work for her, so I let it go. What happened?"

Deputy Hottie actually rolled his eyes. "It appears that Ms. Thomas was not at her desk, but out at your husband's truck to help him unload some boxes when Mr. Chase, her estranged boyfriend, started shooting. Both Ms. Thomas and your husband were shot. Ms. Thomas died before the first responders arrived. Your husband was taken to St Margaret's Sacred Heart. However, he did not make it. I'm sorry to tell you that he died en route."

As my hand came to my mouth, I realized my sons were standing next to the couch watching, not fighting. I could neither think nor breathe. My mind was swamped with images of how our life was supposed to be. They say before you die your life flashed before your eyes. This must be similar...I didn't die, but my life is over, stopped. The flashes are fast and cutting, our arguments, our best moments, our love. The last conversation we had was him bitching about traffic and me bitching about doing the dishes.

"What? No, no, no... I just talked to him. He was fine. We were going to go to dinner. I was doing dishes." I was trying to wrap my head around it and as I stood there and looked at the deputies. I realized, too, that my sons were looking at me. Both of them got it before I did; both of them understood the impact before I did. "Boys come here."

I held my arms open so my twin sons could curl into me like they did when they were toddlers. What was I going to do? How was I going to make them men without him? Almost as quickly as the devastation came the overwhelming fear. What was I going to do and how was I going to survive?

"Ma'am, is there anyone we can call for you?"

Oh shit; what about my mother-in-law? Who was going to tell that overbearing, pompous woman that her baby was gone? Gone...he was gone. I was never going to see him in the morning all mussed and smiling at me. I was never going to get tackled from behind while doing yoga, something he thought was hilarious. I was never going to hear him laugh that deep baritone laugh.

I shake my head. I had to call her, since she would be angry if it were anyone else. "No, no, that is okay. I want to see him." What if they are wrong,? What if it isn't my Marc? My Marc, the man that was my sunrise and sunset he was my everything.

"No mom, don't do that." Even at twelve, Peter was a solid person. Still, I had to. I had to be sure. I had to know. I wanted to be able to tell his mother with certainty.

"I have to. I will call Brittany to sit with you." I couldn't think or make sense of what was happening. I need help, I need Britt.

Standing and throwing his shoulders back, J. said, "No. We will go too. Won't we, Peter?"

Joseph got me. He always understood what I needed. I didn't want them to see me or Marc this way though. I need to be stronger; I need them to know I won't break. They are children that have just lost their father. There is no way in hell I will have them taking care of me.

"Deputy, I am sorry I didn't get your name, but can you please take us?" I didn't get his name and I didn't really care.

"Laurence, ma'am." He gestured to the older man.

"And I am Deputy McDell."

"Stop calling me ma'am. It's grating on my nerves." I took a deep breath. "Just please take us to the hospital."

Oh, no. I felt myself sliding and slipping into what my husband always lovingly called my *inner bitch mode*. The boys…I had to remember what mattered here. *Marc and the boys. Focus, focus, focus.* It became a mantra in my mind. That and the names of people I was going to have to call.

I have no idea how but I know we are going to have to get through this. I do not know what happens next but I am going to have to survive. It hurts to breathe and I don't know if I will ever be able to fill my lungs again.

Chapter 1
Beth

"Beth, you have to get out of this damned house." Britt would not let up; she was like a Chihuahua with a bone. She was tiny, feisty, and brilliant, with long blonde hair that swept her ass when she walked and blue eyes that made you think about ice. "Sweetheart, if you don't get laid, you will dry up."

"Oh god, bitch. My son is sitting here with us."

"She's right, mom." What did he just say? I think my head just exploded. "You need to get out and have some fun. Dad wouldn't have wanted you to wait to die. He loved you so much and he wanted everything for you. Go do something for yourself".

Looking at my fifteen-year-old son, I could hardly catch a breath. He looked just like his father and now he sounded like him. I could hear Marc whispering in my ear, "You're beautiful. You deserve everything; go get it." I felt the tissue being pushed into my hand as I realized I was crying, again. "No, no more tears. I can't do this and *you're* pushing too hard." I pointed my finger at my son. "Now and forever, my sex life is off the table as a discussion topic. *Got it*?" I gritted my teeth and pushed into his face. I wanted to him to know that I was serious.

Joseph leaned over the table, slid my wine glass away, and got right in my face. "As long as you are unhappy, Dad would want me to help. I will talk about your car, the house, the bills, your clothes, even your underwear, and yes, if necessary, your sex life too until I know that you are happy."

As he sits back in his chair with a smug smile across his face, I realized that he has been managing me for a while.

"Jesus, J., don't you think you should be a child? You know, maybe a fifteen-year-old boy? When are *you* going to start dating? O. M. G." I put on my best mocking tone. "Are you having sex, too? I saw that little Marcy across the street was here the other day. What's up with that?" I was trying my best to steer this conversation so he would leave.

"Mom," he said in disgust. "P. is sleeping with her. That would be too gross to sleep with my brother's girlfriend." His hand covered his mouth as he tried to physically hold in the words that he couldn't take back.

The wine I was drinking was stuck in my windpipe. I thought I might die. Sputtering and spitting wine back in my glass, I asked, "What do you mean? P.? My baby Peter is sleeping with that tramp?" Oh, that's good. Now I sound like my mother in law. Even in my own head, I knew that was the wrong approach here.

"Yes, mom. Peter has been going with her for months now and she's a nice girl."

"How did I not know this?"

Joseph drank his soda and shrugged.

"You said they are having sex? Are they using condoms?" *Huh, What, Crap.* A litany of words ran through my head.

"How would I know? Okay, I can't talk to you about this." Joseph stood to leave.

"No, you don't get to drop a bomb like that. You want to talk about my sex life and make a nonchalant comment like my fifteen-year-old baby is having sex, and then walk away? No way, sit your ass down!" Another deep breath seemed to be all that I could do. I glanced up at Britt, my best friend for six years…my life support. She was beet-red and had her hand over her mouth as if to stifle a scream; no, laughter. That bitch was trying not to laugh. I will kill her! Wait; I have two boys to kill first.

I shake my head to clear the white noise threatening to take over and ask, "Okay, so P. is having sex, are you?" I was angry at Marc again. Some days, it felt as if I was always bitter. How dare he leave this to me alone? He was supposed to teach these boys about sex. I was supposed to complain about not having time in the bathroom and dirty sweat socks.

"Aw mom, no I'm not." He didn't sit back down. Instead, he took a drink of his soda and started to turn around again.

"J. Do you know about condoms?" That stupid bitch was actually laughing out loud now. I poured her more wine and with a "Shut it bitch," I turned back to my son.

"Yes mom. I know all about safe sex. No babies here." He turned to face me. I think he was getting the gravity of the situation now. Before, sex had been something we joked about, but nothing real to discuss.

"But you know about diseases too?" Eww, I didn't want to do this.

"Yes, mom. Always wear a condom so your junk doesn't fall off." I could see him squirm. Wasn't this the kid that wanted to talk about my underwear and lack of sex life? The little shit.

"J. don't call it junk. I don't want you to treat it like junk. J., baby, do you know about waiting until you're in love? Sex should matter. It's not something to take lightly or to jump into." What was I saying? Shit was just pouring out of my mouth. "J., sex is important and the person you have sex with should be, as well. Innocent girls are going to expect things and the not-so-innocent are going to demand more." What the hell did I just say? The words continued to roll out and not even make sense to me.

"Beth, please." Britt put her hand over mine. "J., what your mom is trying to say is that she loves you and you are amazing. You should only surround yourself with other people who think you are amazing, as well. The girls will come and go, but your self-respect will be with you forever and based on your actions only. Don't ever force her; if it isn't yours let it go, don't ever let someone force you, and always ask yourself if you will respect yourself tomorrow and five years from now if you sleep with this person."

Tears ran down my eyes. Marc should have been here. In his absence, I should have been able to do this, but I couldn't. I loved my girl. She saved my ass again. "I love you, Joseph, but she's right. Sex is about respect. You respect yourself and your partner, the rest will co–" No I can't use that word. "Follow."

"I know, mom," J. said while sitting back down. "I want you to start dating. I promise to only have sex with girls I respect. Don't ask me about P. and start dating, please."

I couldn't figure out why he was pleading with me to date, but I knew that Marc would have wanted me to get out and date. We had talked about what the other expected, if they passed. I wanted him to have a nanny/housekeeper that gave him regular blowjobs. He would always roll his eyes and laugh when I would tell him that. He wanted me to wait a few years and remarry. I knew that, but what's 'a few years?' Tears came again and I felt Britt and J. staring. I knew I was breaking again, but I couldn't stop it. *Deep breath, in, out…*I could stop it. Wow, look at me. Freaking Wonder Woman!

Taking a big fortifying drink of my wine, I look at my son and say, "Okay, I will do it, but how? How, Britt? How do I get out and find something you haven't been able to find in forty years?" Yeah, that bitch was still single and raised children vicariously through me. She did a damned good job at it, as well. I have seen her claim my son as her own at his baseball game, but she was rotten at dating. She stayed at home with me and when she did date, it was always someone unavailable or she dug until she found a flaw that she could exploit.

Britt's response was automatic. "The Club."

"What club? I don't see mom clubbing."

"No absolutely not," I retorted over Joseph's words. "J., please leave the room." I knew where she was going with this and there was no way in hell that she was teaching my boys about her version of sex. Wait…didn't she just do that? She really should practice what she preaches.

Joseph just sat and stared at me. "What? Why? I think you should get an online profile."

Britt chimed in. "No, Beth, you are coming to "The Club" with me tonight."

"J., *Leave now*." Deep breath, inhale, exhale, I really want just once to not have to think about my breaths. "No Britt, I can't do that. It is not for me. J. I said leave. I was polite and asked you nicely, and I've even told you as your mother. I will punish next. Leave now." Joseph got up and walked out of the room mumbling about how fickle I was. He was right, but I was not going to have her teach him about that. Because I knew he would be at the Xbox just around the corner, I quietly added, "No, Britt. I can't. It's not me."

"Look, Beth. You don't have to do anything. Just because I like extremes, doesn't mean you have to do them. Come with me, have dinner, have a few drinks, and see if you meet someone that catches your eye."

"Yes, but Britt, he is going to be into the extremes." I couldn't believe that I was letting her think I would entertain her idea. "I don't want someone that's into the extremes, as you call them. I can't do that. I don't know how."

"Didn't you ever experiment with Marc?"

"*Lower your voice.* And yes, of course. Fifteen years of marriage requires that you invest in it, but never with another person. Never with more than the slightest amount of pain, nibbles, not bites, slight swats, not whips. I can't do it, Britt." I could feel the panic rising, mostly because I could also feel my panties getting wet.

She leaned over, slid her hand up my neck, and whispered in my ear, "Don't you want to feel someone touch

15

you again? Don't you want to know how it feels to be wanted again?" Then she kissed my cheek like she has been doing for six years. I felt that hot breath in my lower stomach. My thighs tightened and my knees came together.

"Damn, Britt. Do it again." I said on a laugh. I needed to lighten the mood.

"I am deadly serious, Beth," she spoke lowly. "You need this. I need you to have this. Your tight control is killing me and I need to see you let it go. I love you, Beth, and I want you to have someone." She took a big gulp of her wine and drew in a deep breath. "Beth, you know my idea of extreme is slightly different than others. You know I like men, but I also like women. Mostly I like both at the same time."

"Yeah. We've talked about it, at length." And it turned me on when we did!

"Sweets, I know you touch yourself after we talk. I've heard it while I was on the phone with you."

"Britt, stop!"

"Come on, Beth. I am not going to push you. I am not going to touch you. You are my best friend and I wouldn't jeopardize that for anything." Leaning even closer, she whispered, "But I do like the idea that your panties get wet when I talk to you about it. I like that I can turn you on. I can't get you off, but I sure can turn you on. Have you ever been with a woman, Beth?"

Deep breath in, deep breath out, knees together, don't fidget. Crap; I was wet just thinking about it. "No, Britt, you know that. There was one guy in high school, three in college, and then Marc. Why are you pushing me now?"

"I am pushing because you are ready Sweets. When I heard you on the phone while I told you what I was doing, I knew you were ready."

"You were testing me?" I didn't masturbate while I was on the phone with her, but she does tell me some pretty hot stuff and I might have touched myself during her latest tale.

"No, I always tell you about my weekends, but I heard you moaning. I guessed you were touching your sweet, little pussy. Tell me, Beth. Did you come?" I could feel her wine sweet breath on my cheek as she leaned into me.

"Not while we were on the phone." Thank heavens for the wine. The heat from the liquor masked the deep blush from her words. How did we get on this? Well, enough of that.

"Britt, I will go out with you once. Once! If anyone pushes, you included, I am taking my toys and going home." I slug down the rest of my liquid courage. This was going to kill me.

"Yay," Britt squealed like a little girl.

-

Okay. Hair–check. Makeup–check. Dress on and not spotted–check. Stockings–check. Heels–check. I was as good as I was going to get. The boys' looks when I stepped into the family room exacerbated my butterflies. The *wows* and *holy cows* only made me more nervous. Ironically, since their father died, they fight less.

"Boys, pause the game. Are you ok with this?" I wave my hands in front of myself.

"Um, are you asking about the dress? Because it is pretty skimpy, but you look great."

Oh, my Peter is always protecting my feelings. I knew this dress was over the top. It was one of Britt's cast-offs. Britt was always buying designer dresses and then either didn't wear them or didn't like them. I think she did it so she could dress me up because she knew I wouldn't let her buy me things. The girl had more money than she knew what to do with. "No son, I mean going out possibly to date. Auntie Britt thinks I will be able to meet a nice gentleman at this place we are going." Yeah right, I think. "Maybe it's not such a good idea. Maybe I should just stay home, order pizza, and we can rent that crazy movie about the old, dead people."

"Mom, that gave you nightmares," Joseph pointed out as he rose from the couch. "I had to sleep with you for two days. No way are you watching it again. Come on Mom; let's get you in your car. I promise P. and I are great with you dating. Mom, we know that you aren't replacing Dad. You need to have fun. Go party it up and come back later and tell us all about it."

My baby pushed me out the door with a kiss on the cheek. When did he get so grown up? I have tried to protect them and make them my focus. I didn't want to be the mom that fell apart and the kids had to take care of her, but that is what this felt like.

I turned around and punched his shoulder, just so he would remember who the parent was. "Don't go out, no girls in, and no driving because you don't have a license." Yeah, that has happened here. "Keep the doors locked and the front light on for me, as well as the kitchen light. Don't wait up. I love you J. Babe." Yelling over his shoulder, I added, "I love you P. Bear." Both gave me the requisite "*mom*" whines that I expected. The baby names were silly leftovers from when they were learning to talk. Peter was slow to talk and couldn't say his brother's name, so we called them P. and J. and they stuck. Joseph uses it at school still. P. only lets family use it.

My butterflies only got worse as I drove the belt loop to *The Club*, as Britt refers to it. I pull up to a guard gate where I had to present ID, my invitation, and was told not to take my bracelet off. A large Victorian house sat on a huge amount of acreage. This place is worth a fortune. Of course, it would be nice and on the top of high end. Britt was raised with too much money and not enough attention. She had the most exceptional taste; this place was gorgeous. The long tree-lined drive pulls up to rounded driveway. The valet takes my Jetta, which probably doesn't fit in at all, and takes it around to the back.

I walk up the step onto a wooden porch that runs the length of the house on either side. Conversation areas are set up with rocking chairs and porch swings. It's very quaint and not at all what I expected. As I look at the couple sitting to my left, it's a tall striking man turned away from me with a beautiful, petite blonde sitting with her feet in his lap. He is running his hands up her thighs, rubbing her mound and then down again. He teases her breast through her dress with his other hand, and she has her head back on the arm of the couch. A small moan escaped her lips. Obviously, her eyes are closed or she would have seen me. Standing transfixed, I am sucked into her world now and don't know if I want to get out. He raises her leg to his shoulder and bares her completely too me. As he starts to work his fingers into her, I can hear her wet slurping noises. I feel my body respond by creating my own wetness, which soaks my panties. Her rapid breath makes my breath come faster. I can feel her whole body tighten as he pulls out of her, slaps her clit, and slams his fingers back into her. Slap, a rough rub of her clit, and he is in again rubbing her clit with his thumb.

Even by the porch light, I can see she's wet and glistening. It is one of the hottest things I have ever seen. I have watched porn before with Marc and then alone since he has left. I've even seen a little soft core with Britt, but this is so much better. I can see her whole body spasm as I feel myself tighten and my cream runs down my leg. It is one of the most erotic things I have ever felt. I am so wet, and horny. I hear her breathing my name, my name? It pulls me out of my reverie and I respond on a breath as well, "Hi Britt."

Sitting up and swinging her legs around to the front, she pats the man's chest and by way of introduction. "Meet James. He is my go-to guy for the night. Aren't you sweetie?"

Her go-to guy? What is that? I can't really see him clearly he is turned away from the porch light.

He seems familiar, but I can't place him. "Um, nice to meet you James." I don't know…do I shake his hand? He just had it all over her. Maybe not, as we just walk away. She is obviously not invested.

Britt leans into me and slides a hand around my waist. My body is electric hot, her hand send shocks along my skin. "I will spend the evening here with you, but I will stay with James at the end of the night. I made my arrangements early so I don't have to worry later." We walk through the large double doors into a foyer with a large stair case and rooms off to either side. "Let's eat and get a drink."

My stomach is flipping around as she leads me to the left. Okay, nothing crazy. It's just a living room. Several large overstuffed chairs, couches and ottomans with people mingling. One couple is in a chair making out, and he has his hand up her skirt and on her ass. Okay, nothing scary here.

She leads me into what would have been the kitchen of the house. It is huge and has a full bar with two very nice looking bartenders, several tables in the center, and booths around the back. It has all the trappings of a small bar except the couple standing at the bar.

Britt leads me to a booth, but I can't keep my eyes off the couple. I know him, but I just can't place him either. She has her back to bar, right leg on a bar stool the left holding her up. He is standing next to her leg, running his hand up her inner thigh, and plunging in her open bare pussy. Mr. Nice ass has broad shoulders and looks almost lean, with strong arms and thick thighs. He is almost gray, but probably prematurely because he doesn't look old. I know because he has caught my eye in the mirror behind the bar.

Nothing slows him down; he picks up his drink with his left hand while pushing into her with his right. His thumb on her clit rubs slowly. She has her head almost on the bar. Why can't I turn away? He doesn't care about her. You can see it in his demeanor. He never drops my gaze. I hear her call out; I can almost feel her orgasm as it rocks the whole room. I can't take my eyes off him. I'm completely oblivious to my girl sitting next to me, who has apparently ordered me a drink. I feel the cold on my hands and instinctively pull the glass to my mouth. The tonic tingles on my tongue. I am aware my panties are soaked and I am rubbing my thighs together. Britt puts her hand on my leg and says, "Elizabeth Williams you need to breathe before you pass out."

Breathing; that was what I was doing. Like a broken spell, I look away from him and at Britt. Her cat-that-got-the-cream smile is going to get her killed soon. "I'm okay, Britt."

"I know, Sweets. I know you are. Would you like to meet Graham?" Is that his name? It fits him.

"I um, I don't, um...." Wow. When did I start stuttering? I don't know what to say to her.

"Beth deep breath, it's okay. Let's take our time. I ordered you soup and bread. Drink your drink. The dinner will be a couple of minutes and then we can eat and drink more. I promise there will be more floor shows. As previously agreed, you only have to talk to me and I only touch if you want me to."

Okay, I can do this. That was hot, and I was so not prepared, but I am ready enough. "Okay, I got it. We drink, we eat, we drink more, and we look at hot sex. It's kind of like when we rented smutty movies."

"Except that was frustrating and here if you want to touch yourself feel free. There are some rules though. First, you can't tell people; it's exclusive and they like to keep it that way. The bracelet you have on is yellow. Yellow means that you are a guest with full privileges. My gold bracelet means I swing both ways and I can be top or bottom. It really means that I do anything. Graham's silver." She gestured to his wrist while taking a drink. "That means he only tops and only does women."

I look around the room. "There are so many other colors." Both bartenders wore black. The woman at the bar wore white. One man across the room eying the bartenders wore pink. Okay, I can figure that one out.

"Yup, Silver is alpha, only man on top, woman on bottom. Gold is anything goes. White is woman only bottom to men. Whites can be shared with others. Yellow is guest, pink is sub man to man only. We had a couple of transvestites, so they got their own color. There are others, but really, you need only worry about what you are and what you want."

"What if I don't think I am any of those things? I can't dominate and I don't think I can bottom very well. I get a little bossy in bed and I'm not sure I know how I feel about other men or other women in my bed besides my partner. How do I know?"

"You, my darling, are going to find out. I can tell you, but I think it will be more fun for you to find o…or for Graham to tell you."

"What?" her words were just sinking into my rapidly ginned up brain.

"Hi darlin'," he said as he leaned down and placed a kiss on Britt's forehead.

Britt leaned into his kiss. "Graham, this is Elizabeth, my guest."

"Please, call me Beth." I held my hand out to shake his and then realized I didn't want to do that. I pulled it back, feeling very awkward.

Smiling, he says, "Beth, it is a pleasure to meet you. You seem very familiar. Do I know you?"

"I um, well I um, I work for a well a…." What is wrong with me? Why can't I get it out?

"Beth works for an insurance agency." Oh, that's right. I work for my husband's partner. I see it. I know him. I know how I know him.

I try to stand up. "I'm going to be sick." Britt is on her feet like lightening and pushing me out a side door, through a kitchen and outside. Blessed fresh air at last. *Breathe in, breathe out, breathe in, breathe out.* Someday I won't have to do this anymore, or so I've been told. Britt is rubbing my back and crooning to me like a child. She really would have been a good mom because nothing bothers her. She has her hands in my long auburn hair holding it out my face as I toss up all my gin and what little bit of lunch was there. I can still see his face, sitting in my living room. I can feel his warm hand as he lead me into that dark cold room that was well lit and smelled like rot. He made me tea and called Britt. Does she know who he is? I can't ask. I can't look at her. If she knew, then what, what does it matter? She probably knows him professionally and never put it together. But he called her; he waited for her to show up.

"OK, princess. Let's get you back inside and find out what is going on." That voice is silky smooth, like the scotch Britt drinks. I don't want it by me.

Then I feel his hands on my shoulders and turning me to him. "What happened? Too much to drink?" He gave Britt an assessing glare, like it was her fault I was retching in the parking lot.

"Britt, I have to go home now." I can feel the tears running. I don't want to cry. I won't cry. Breathe in, breath out I have to pull myself together. He sees me then, and I can see him register how he knows me. It was a terrible crime in a small suburb of Phoenix. If he covered our area, it is because he lives there and knows the community. My boys rose above the scandal of the cheating man who was killed by his lover's irate boyfriend. The boys are big in sports. One's into football, the other is into baseball. Both are into karate and are in the baccalaureate program. They are known; we are known. He's now aware of why he recognizes me.

"Come on, Ms. Williams. I'll drive you home." Britt flinches and takes my hand. "Sweets, let get you cleaned up, fed and see what you need." She puts her arm around my waist while still holding my hand. She is all but wrapped around me, staking a claim. I can only nod.

We walk back into the kitchen like that, with Britt holding one of my hands and her other arm around my waist. Graham follows and directs Britt, "Take her to the office." Winding up a back staircase, I can't think. What am I doing here? I am having a nervous breakdown because I met a cop? A cop that is a good and decent man, a man I saw with his fingers in a woman at the bar and then walk over to pick up on me. Circles…I am walking and thinking in circles. Where the hell are we going?

"Britt really, I am okay. You're right; I need to clean up, eat, and then go home. I have done enough for one night." All I can think is I need to get in my bed and die. I can't do this again; I can feel that thin shell I built from day one slowly cracking. It let me take care of the boys, my mother-in-law, the funeral, and the onslaught of family. Then there was the media, neighbors, and all the other million things I had to do. I couldn't break…I can't break. "Please Britt."

"There is a bathroom up here. You can clean up, eat, and settle down. Then we will talk." Britt never let her grip go or let me down. She led straight into one of the nicest bathrooms I have ever seen. Marble floors a soaking tub large enough for 4 and a snail shower in the back.

"Britt, there are clean clothes in my closet. Get her something comfortable and let her shower." His comforting, kind voice grates on my nerves. He called me Ma'am, and often. His slight southern twang makes me want to kill him. Oh God…make him go away.

Standing in front of the mirror, I could feel Britt running her hands through my hair like any good mama would. No, I didn't vomit in my hair. A cold rag pressed to my face and I feel her unzip my dress. This isn't the first time she has had to undress or dress me. She did it every day for a week to make sure I was in the right thing at the right time. Hell, I don't even know what I wore to the funeral. Britt told me I was presentable, and I trust her.

I felt the cold slide of a cotton dress shirt and then my stocking being rolled off. We were old hats at this. The knock on the door scared me. Letting out a little yelp, I jumped out of Britt's reach.

"Do you need anything, Britt? Ms. Williams?"

"Why does Graham act like he knows you? And why is he so formal with you?" Britt crawls across the floor on her knees in front of me to take off my next stocking.

"He's a first responder, Britt."

"Oh, shit. It *was* Graham, I remember now. He was the one who called me out of court. He spent all day with you, too."

More cracking…more fissures in my shell. "He made me tea and called me Ma'am."

"Want me to kill him for you?" I know that she is trying to lighten the mood.

I could still feel the tears running down my face, but I was holding the cool cloth. Maybe I was washing my face in tears, I don't really care. "Make him go away, Britt. Please…please take me home."

"Graham, go away. We don't need you here. Please have my car brought around to the back of the kitchen." I envied her easy cool. She knew how to take care of me. I would be lost without her.

"Her soup is here," he yelled through the door. "You ordered minestrone, but I changed it to noodles and broth."

Stop talking! His fine voice was smooth as scotch and filled my head.

"Graham, she is not sick," Britt answered back. "Get the minestrone since it's her favorite. I had Antoine put it on the menu especially for her."

Don't they realize I am not staying here? I can't. I have to go home. I need to pull the covers up and start again tomorrow. It will hurt then, too, but the shell will be stronger.

"No Sweets, you are eating and settling down. You are making yourself sick. Breathe and think. Nothing is going to hurt you. Marc is gone. He has been for a while and we are okay now. We are strong, we are capable, and this will not kill us.

"Strong, capable, will not die, strong, capable, will not die. I can do this, Britt." Standing in front of me, she moved out of my way of the sink so I could wash my face. She handed me some face cream to remove my makeup and a toothbrush already loaded up with paste. Was I using Graham's toothbrush? Too much; I can't think. *Just keep the mantra and focus. Strong, capable, will not die.*

Standing straight, I realized several things at once. I am mostly naked, I look like I have been tussling and just got out of bed, and my red face could easily be from passion. "Britt, where are my clothes?"

"You had gunk on your dress and your stockings didn't really go with the whole shirt thing. Your shoes are by the door, also gunked. You didn't have a bra on. You have on Graham's dress shirt, which covers more than your dress did. Oh, and you're wearing your panties. You can wear your shoes on the way out."

I am going to hell. This is a hell of my own making, what made me think I was ready for this. Okay, yes, I know I need to get laid. I know I need someone to talk to that doesn't sound well, like a fifteen-year-old boy. Fart jokes and junk jokes get old after so long. I would like someone to talk intelligently with someone of course besides Britt, because at heart, she really is a fifteen-year-old boy. Okay, I can do this. I can walk out there and be fine. I can be smart and sane…well, mostly sane. This is stupid. Why am I worried? This is Britt, the woman who cleans up after me and has been my partner in crime since I moved to Phoenix, and Graham–no, Deputy McDell–a first responder who has probably seen worse than me.

Turning to walk out the door, I lean over and kiss Britt on her cheek. "I love you bestest of all." I take her hand and walk into Graham's–no, Deputy McDell's–office. *Stupid!* I have to remember that. *Deputy!* "I am so sorry to be a bother to you. I really am okay and I will be fine. Please, go enjoy your evening and don't let my theatrics interrupt."

"Mrs. Williams, it is never a bother to help a beautiful woman."

Blushing to my toes, I can feel him taking in my appearance. I bet I do look beautiful. Disheveled, no makeup, and mostly naked. Of course, who doesn't wear black panties under a white shirt? I am such a mess.

Rebekkah Rogers

Chapter 2
Graham

She is the most beautiful creature I have ever seen. I wonder if she knows she didn't button the top several buttons and I can see the swell of her very round full breast. They're not fake and they have some freckles. She blushes; oh wow, when was the last time I saw a woman blush?

"Please, Ms. Williams, sit at my desk and eat." I have to remember this is not some woman familiar with my home and what goes on here. This is a good housewife and mother. What was Britt thinking?

"No, please, Deputy McDell. I really wouldn't feel comfortable eating in front of everyone, though I won't argue it smells great." She turns to Britt and asks, "Sweets, aren't you going to eat with me? I know you were planning dinner." She looks back at me. "Deputy McDell, we will just eat and get out of your hair."

Did she just say she wanted to get out of my hair? I think I am only getting every third word or something, I can't think with all that cleavage and sweet soft, creamy skin in front of me. What is she saying now? Damn, I was staring and I can feel Britt's knowing eyes on me. She knows me well and has never seen me so distracted. I'm still staring. Okay, focus.

"It will be right up," Britt is saying to my Princess. No, no, not mine. This is not a woman I can have. This is Ms. Williams, a mother like none I have ever seen. She is rather tall for a woman, voluptuous and soft rounded hips with breasts and an ass that would fill my very large hands. I remember that I watched her that day all but pick up not one but two teenage boys and rock them in her lap like they were babies. Tears ran... They never stopped...but she never broke down. She never let her boys think that her first priority wasn't them. That was the worst day of my life. It was like stepping into the twisted fairy tale where the Princess had the prince, kingdom, and castle, yet the evil queen–or in this case, a crazy guy–still broke the sweet princess' life and crushed her future. I have seen some terrible things in my twenty years on the force, but she stayed with me. Her hollow eyes and incredible strength never left me.

"What will be up?" I really should pay attention.

"The soup," Britt said while giving me a look like I was crazy.

Oh, thank goodness. If I had to try and listen for another moment, I was going to make a total ass of myself. Ah, soup for three. She didn't want to eat alone. I led the ladies to the small conference table in the corner I held the chair for my pr–no, Ms. Williams.

"Thank you, Deputy McDell. I really appreciate all your help."

Her voice sounded like music. My stupid cock and I needed to have a conversation. I was behaving like a school boy. I have dreamt about her voice. Flashes of her sitting in the back of the car singing to her sons had haunted my dreams. They were nonsense words and rhymes of comfort for boys that were probably too big for such things, but it obviously soothed them and her. Her tears never stopped running, but the boys' did when she started to sing.

"Of course, Ma'am," It was second nature. She is probably younger than me, but I couldn't help it. I know she hates it, but she's so much more than me.

"Don't call me Ma'am, please. Call me Beth."

"All right Beth, but only if you call me Graham." I wanted to hear her scream my name.

"Great; we are all on a first name basis," Britt announced. Man, she was bubbly tonight. Britt knew...she knew I stayed involved in the investigation to make sure the family was okay. Often, she would talk about her friend Beth and it didn't take me long to put two and two together to know it was Ms. Williams. She had even asked about security companies and ideas when the media was really bad, but never in a million years would I have thought that Britt would bring her here. Britt never brought people from her "outside" life here. She couldn't let them know what she was. She couldn't have it used against the families she represented in court. Custody cases were ugly and everything, including the attorney's proclivity to ménages and public sex, could cause her problems.

"So tell me, ladies. What was the plan for the night?" Okay, that sounded like a reasonable topic.

"Well, we saw you finger fuck our sweet Jasmine—which, I might add, was especially hot. She always sounds so sweet. Was she wet? She is always so dripping."

"Britt, you're off topic."Was she trying to kill us all? I could feel myself throbbing against my zipper.

"Oh," she said with a slight giggle. "Yeah, we were going to have some drinks with dinner and Beth was going to take a look around and see if anything appealed to her." Did she just kick me under the table? Okay. Yeah, I got it, Britt.

"Did you see anything you liked, Princess?" No, she's not my princess. I went from a grieving widow to seeing her spread out under me in a single breath. What a sight...all that hair covering the pillow, her hands above her head strapped to the headboard, her breast bouncing with each heavy breath, her knees open. Would she be shaved bare? No, she would have a small amount of dark curls. The curls would hold her sweet honey for me. I think my erection is going to tear apart my zipper if I don't stop that line of thinking.

"Um, well, it is a lovely club and so far you have a beautiful bathroom and magnificent trash cans behind the kitchen." She chuckled. At least she can laugh at herself. She must be doing better.

"That's not what I meant." I wanted to catch her eyes, but she kept them down, a blush rising from her swollen breast to the top of her hair. Beautiful!

"Oh, well I did only see a little of the entertainment." This was hard for her and she was gorgeous in her innocence. Britt was right; she was just submissive enough for me. I don't like complete submission because I want to work at it. I want a woman who can tell me what she wants and then trust me to give it to her and take care of her. I like fiery, feisty women.

"So, what did you see?" I was not going to be easy on her; if she wanted to stay she was going to have to work at it.

"Well I saw a beautiful show on the porch." She kept looking down, but turned her head to towards Britt.

"Aw Sweets, you thought it was beautiful? I am glad you liked it."

Her blush was complete. Britt just did her in. What did she see on the porch? I know Britt likes to be on the porch, since the thought of someone walking up and seeing her does it for her every time. I have myself walked up on her. She really is gorgeous in the throws, though she is nothing like my princess will be. "What did she see, Britt?" I am hoping a few details will make that blush deeper. Does it turn her nipples red?

"Oh." Yeah, she gets what I am asking. "James is such a strong man; he had me open wide and the little tease held off my orgasm until we had company. He is so good to me." Damn, she's good.

"What else did you see this evening, Princess?" Are her panties wet? I want to touch her and find out. Her nipples are rock hard and dark. Britt had to have hunted the length of my closet to find a shirt that I could see so much through. Her chest was rising at just the thought of sex. She would be so responsive.

"I, um, well, I saw you and Jasmine. That was her name…right, Britt?" She turned to Brittany, who was sitting perfectly still and taking small breathes. Was Britt worried?

"Yes, Sweets her name is Jasmine. You liked that show as well, didn't you?" Ah, Britt was not pushing, but steering. Britt was a good dominate when she wanted to be. Not usually, but with women she did it well.

"Yes, of course. It was very, well–no, it was kind of cold and distant. I could tell you didn't like her. Why were you touching her if you didn't like her?" Her gaze pierced mine.

"I well, I um…." Dear hell the woman was making me stutter. I need to regain my control here. "I don't dislike her. She is a beautiful woman with an amazing talent who uses sex to release pent up energy from her art. She is a painter. She needed to be released and requested I help her while I was at the bar having a drink. I am not attached and had no reason to say no. So I provided what she needed and nothing more." I turn to Britt because I need a reprieve from Beth's stare. "Yes, Britt. She was dripping wet. That little cunt is always ready for anyone or anything." I catch her eyes again because I want her to know me. "I prefer women who have more discerning tastes." Her eyes are a deep, dark-chocolate shade of brown, not hazel or mud. "I prefer women who will be monogamous to me. While we may bring someone to our bed, neither of us would be with anyone outside of our relationship. I prefer women who are open about their sexuality and want to explore."

I had her. She was rubbing her thighs together, lust flashing in her eyes. I had to play this just right. "I want a woman who doesn't know all that she wants but is strong enough to try." I slide my hand over hers and notice that she had the softest skin. "I want a woman who is smart enough to say no when she doesn't like it and yes when she does. What do you want, Princess?" I was not letting this small part of her go now that I had her.

In the smallest voice, I heard her say "I don't know what I want, but I want to be taught by someone kind enough to not push and strong enough to hear the word *no* yet understand its meaning."

Not pushing wasn't going to happen. I was going to push her so far that she wouldn't remember her way back.

"No pushing? But Princess, where's the fun that? If I were to push a little and let you decide if it were enough, you would never reach your full potential. If I were to push you to your potential and pull back when you determined it was too far, would you be comfortable?" What did I just say? I push, she submits. It's simple. She needs to trust me to not let her fall.

"Sweets, it's like raising children. You have to push J. in baseball because you know how good it will feel for him when he gets there. But you never push him in football, because it is not his thing." Did she just remind this woman that she had kids while we are trying to seduce her? It was a great analogy, but really?

With her eyes locked on Britt, she commented, "I love you with all my heart, Brittany, but I can't, not with you. You are incredibly sexy and you do your best to keep me turned on because you know that is helping me heal, but I...."

Britt couldn't stand to watch her flounder any more than I could. "No Sweets, not you and I. I love to tease you. I will love watching you, but wouldn't want anything to come between us. You need commitments and promises that I won't give you."

What the hell was Britt doing? She got her all worked up and talked into it and she was not finishing. That was damned near cruel and so not Britt. Catching her eye, I saw her wink at me and then the bitch kicked me again. What did she want from me? I can't make commitments and promises. I never have, and she damn well knows it.

"Point taken Britt, Princess, you are going to need Britt to hold your hand when you get scared and pour you wine when you need courage. Have you ever been with a woman?" I want to hear it. I want to hear her talking about sex. I need to get control of my cock. He is taking on a life of his own. I know Britt had her submit all the survey and medical records as we require an extensive medical and sexual history review to protect the other patrons from disease and sadists. However, I never check up on what Britt submitted for Beth. This was her club as much as it is mine, that trust goes both ways.

"Why does everyone keep asking me that?" Damn; her frustration is almost visible, and sexy. She would be a hellion and so wild.

"Because it is a fair enough question. I assume you filled out the survey to get in, but I would rather talk about you than read about you Princess." She tried to pull her hand away; she was not getting away. Stroking her hand felt too good.

"No, I have not been with another woman. I have only been with four men before my husband and I was happily married for fifteen years." Yeah, I got the happily. Everyone confirmed Mr. Williams was a good guy and would never cheat. "My husband and I experimented a little, but we were having kids and building a business and your priorities shift. Sex becomes about connecting to your spouse so you don't lose them in the shuffle, not so much about making sure you try something new. Like all couples, we had to work at making time for each other." So her husband while good and kind didn't focus on sex so much as he did satisfying her.

"Did you orgasm regularly?" I couldn't hold it in; it just came spilling out. I could picture her orgasm with her head back and her mouth open. Would she scream? Would she pant?

"*That*," she started on a huff, "is none of your business!" She pulled her hand away the tension coiling in her and I'll be damned if Britt didn't kick me again. Yeah, I need to kill her with her shoe. Alright; that probably did cross the line, but there are no lines in trust. Picturing her throwing her head back while someone else chewed on those full tits was too much. I can't picture it, especially not her loving husband, who made an effort to show everyone he was in love. What would it be like to be that in love to want to shout to world of your commitment? I have to know if she has ever been truly satisfied.

"Princess, you know as well as I do there are plenty of women in *happy marriages* and they don't get treated to the heart pounding orgasm that leaves your ears ringing and your senses shot." Yup, I am going to hell for trying to seduce this innocent widow.

"Yes, I do know women like that. I am not one of those women to be seduced by the promise of a pretty orgasm. I require more in life, because that pretty orgasm you talk about, well I can get that myself." Feisty, and so damned hot, maybe she will orgasm tonight. If she does, I may have to show her what that word really means.

"That is something I would like to see." She is going to kill me. I thought as I saw murder and mayhem flash in her eyes.

"Me too." Okay, so maybe Britt was going to hell with me.

"Fuck you both." Her blush stole up her long graceful neck

"Is that an option?" Yup, Britt was driving the hell-bound train.

I stand to walk out of the room. I had to get away from both of them. "Ladies, why don't you finish your dinners and I will go get us a booth in the bar. We can check out the entertainment and see if we can't lighten the mood." I knew exactly how far I planned to push her tonight. I had to see that orgasm pinking her cheeks and making her moan.

"I can't go like this; I don't have any pants on." There was the pretty blush again. Maybe she will let me cum on the pretty blush. I could blow my load just thinking about her opening that shirt and letting me rub my cock along that expanse of neck and cleavage lines. Maybe Britt would lick her clean. Did I just growl? Okay, it's time to get control.

"Sure you can, Sweets. You have as much clothes on as I do, and absent the stockings, as much as you did before."

"Britt, you are a shameful whore. This shirt barely covers my very large ass." My erection pounded at the thought of that sight. How can I get her to stand up so I could see that ass? "I am not walking through a scruddy bar in my bare feet." Scruddy? My bar isn't scruddy.

"Listen Princess, my bar isn't scruddy. This isn't some pay-by-the-hour seedy motel. This place is cleaner than most hospitals. You are wearing more clothes than some of the ladies you will see down there. I will get us a corner booth where you will sit between Britt and I and no one will see you, unless you want them to. Please finish your dinner, come down to the bar, and have a drink with me." Is what I said but what I really thought was put me out of my misery and please stand up and turn around. Could you please lean over the table and take this raging hard on inside your wetness? Just for an hour or so, so I can think straight. Okay, that was not helping.

"All right." She turned to Britt. "No pushing tonight. You promised me."

"Yay," came Britt's little girl squeal. How did that small woman have men cowing at her feet in court? Amazing!

Rebekkah Rogers

Chapter 3
Beth

This walk is the longest of my life because my ass is hanging out. Women with big butts should not wear thongs and then walk around in public. Okay, so my ass isn't huge, Britt tells me all the time its perfect, but still it is hanging out. I am still so wet. All I want to do is lie on a table and let Graham have his way with me. I know I should feel some shame somewhere, but my body isn't having it. I had damned near came on the porch, and again in the booth watching Graham. I vomited on myself, lost my cool, and then almost came again just from Graham touching my hand. I wonder if he would take me back to that bathroom and bang me against the shower wall. He could take all his pleasure out on my body.

How dare he ask about my sex life with Marc? I'm not talking about it with him. Maybe he was a little gentler than I wanted, and maybe I was starting to canonize him in my mind, but I love Marc. Wow, look at me. I can think about it without crying. I loved him and he is gone and fantasies are just that– fantasies. Real life never played like the fantasies did. Oh, now I'm on a tangent in my head, all because Graham was looking at my tits. It's his fault that I think I may lose my mind.

Focus, step, step, and keep the ass covered. Britt was leading me like I'm a recalcitrant child. This would not do. *Stand up straighter....* Okay, not straighter. That makes my ass hang out. *Shoulders back and next to Britt, not behind.* Britt brought my hand up to her mouth and kissed the back of it and handing it to Graham. What am I, a toy to be handed off? Watching his tongue flick out and lick up Britt's kiss left the lightening coursing and caused a mini earthquake. How do I get him to do that to my pussy?

I glance around and realize that this is the same booth. My gin and tonic with extra limes is still on the table. I saw Graham with his drink and noticed that both he and Britt were drinking the same thing. I know Britt likes them, but Graham as well? He was drinking whiskey or something dark at the bar earlier. I finally wrested my eyes from the table and the drink, knowing that I had to look.

I could hear it, but I had yet to see and take it all in. I throbbed just listening and remembering that flick of his tongue. From our corner, we could see the whole bar area. There were a couple of men sitting at the bar on barstools kissing, almost chastely. They were the easiest for my brain to absorb.

Graham followed my eye and leaned into my ear. "It won't take long. Have you ever watched a man jerk off another man's cock?" Jesus, I want to ask him to keep talking that smooth dark voice could make me come. I just shook my head; I could feel his hot breath on my neck. Britt took my right hand in hers and started stroking my hand very soothingly, very motherly.

I took in the other couple on farther side of the bar. He had her belly to the bar, her hair held tightly in his right hand. He was fully dressed but pushing his jean clad erection against her ass. Rubbing up and down, with his left hand running up her in front, I could see in the mirror when he reached her neck and pulled her face to his. He was so rough, but he didn't hurt her. So controlling, it was so erotic. He took a drink and shared it with her his mouth over hers, his body grinding against her. I could almost feel the press of his hardness against the seam of my ass.

Graham was still breathing on my neck. "He will eventually put the dick in her ass right there; see him moving her skirt up her thighs." The man was sliding her skirt up the back of her legs. I could see a small amount of pale skin that wasn't blocked by his jean clad legs. He was rubbing her ass.

Crack. I felt the slap in my chest. My heart beat skipped while my clit throbbed. *Crack.* He was pushing her head against the bar and slapping her ass. My breath coming in time with his punishing slaps. I couldn't see him jerk himself, as his back was to me, but I knew. He plunged forward with his ass clenching, his jeans around his knees and his hand in her hair as he pushed her head down to the bar. "She is dripping wet. He is going to wet his cock and then slide it deep in her ass, using her own juices to slip in. She will be so tight that she will make him lose himself." I felt myself leaning into his hot breath, wanting to feel it not on my ears, but my neck, my throat. "Look at the men, Princess. Watch him take his partner's cock in his hand. See how hard his fist is wrapped around him? He is going to come just from the pressure alone."

It was too much. I could hear her panting, as the man now slowly pushed forward and groaned in pleasure. I could see the two men, one with his back to the bar the other standing to his side with his partner's dick in his hand, slowly, tightly rubbing his fist up and down. I could see the wet pre cum dripping from the flared end. My entire body throbbed. I wanted to taste that pre cum. I wanted to feel his erection in my ass and my pussy running down my thighs. The partner started bending to his knees. I have never seen anything like it before. He took his cock in his mouth.

I could feel Graham's hot breath on my neck and across my chest and collar. He sent licks of flames that reverberated through me. I could feel Britt's hand rubbing mine up my arm and down again, softly scraping her nails sending shock waves through my body. I heard a soft groan escape. I didn't expect it but I knew it was mine. I felt Graham's hands in my hair, rubbing my scalp slowly. Britt slid closer, her body pushed against mine. Graham lifted my hair from my neck and whispered so softly, "Let it come, Princess. Feel the heat in your belly. Your clit is pulsing, your pussy is clenching." Absent any rational thought, I could feel my body start to move and my thighs rub together. "Don't take your eyes off them, Princess." Britt moved my hand to my thigh and started massaging my leg. She stayed just far enough away from me. "Are you wet?"

"Yes." I could barely breathe as I felt him lifting my leg into his lap. The cold air on my now bared wet skin sent another shock through my body. My sharp intake of air must have warned her.

"Breathe, Sweets. No pushing." Britt breathed against my ear as she lifted my other leg into her lap. Spread out under the table with my body bared to the room, I couldn't help but close my eyes and roll my head back into Graham's hand. The thought of how I looked, along with the feel of their hands on me, sent lightening and erotic heat coursing.

"We have you, Princess. Slide your hand in your panties and tell me how wet you are." Huh? What? By reflex, though, I couldn't say no. My hand, of its own volition, slid the shirt up and into my lace thong. I could feel the string pushing against my tight hole as my hand pulled on the tight lace. I wanted a hardness buried there. I wanted to feel the pounding and heat from him behind me. I didn't dare touch my clit for fear I would explode. Sliding two fingers in and out, I was so wet and it wasn't enough. It wasn't hard enough. On a moan, my head lolled back. I could feel my back arch and the hands on my thighs holding me tight, squeezing and massaging. The wet slurping sounds of my pussy, combined with the hot moaning coming from the bar, were pushing me to the precipice. Britt would never let me fall.

"Pull your hand out and give it to me. Keep your eyes on the man getting sucked. He is watching you and wants to come for you." Sliding my hand out was hard to do. I was burning and I knew I would come with very little effort. I could feel it building in me. Graham's firm grip on my wrist startled me enough to turn my head and watch him take my fingers in his mouth. The wet slide, the rough tongue, the suction had me moaning and lifting my hips again. I wanted that tongue inside me.

Letting go of my hand and leaning until I could feel his lips on my neck, he said, "Sweet like honey on my tongue. Finish it princess. Touch yourself and let me hear you scream." That was enough. My hands went to my clit, one, two, three and I was coming. Lightning exploded in my head. The pressure on my thighs tightened as I bucked against them. The tight hold only made the heat stronger. The lights in my eyes and the white hot heat in my belly were fueled by the feeling of being controlled. My groan was loud enough to fill the room. I could hear the man groan his release, the woman at the bar whimpering her release and her partner shouting all the while, I came more and more. This was the ear ringing loss of senses Graham had spoken of.

"So beautiful," he breathed into my ear. His breath stoked the prickling skin. He released my thigh and let it slide back down at the same time Britt leaned over and nibbled on my neck.

"Sweets, I knew you were hot, but holy hell that was an inferno. He's right; you are gorgeous." I could feel her breath on my neck and the slide of her tongue against me as she nipped at my neck and released my leg. I felt Graham pulling me up back into a sitting position, releasing my hair from his hold. Britt sitting up straighter and then the cold glass pressed into my hands. "Before you think, take a drink."

I take my drink and feel my blush overtake me, as my body still pulsed with the small after quakes. I couldn't think. My ears were ringing and all I could think was what had I just done? Did I just masturbate in front of a crowd? I wanted to blame Britt but I knew immediately that it was all me. She never once pushed me. Okay, Graham pushed, but I could have said no. I wanted to feel myself come stretched between the two of them.

I glanced at Graham discreetly adjusting himself. Okay, so after that larger than life orgasm, I shouldn't want to see his erection. Should I? I wanted to see him rub himself and lose himself as well. One more large drink of liquid courage and I would ask for what I wanted.

"Thank you, that was amazing," I ran my hand up Britt's leg. I felt I needed to touch her, draw my inner whore from her maybe? I felt her leg shake and I realized as much as it affected me and Graham she was probably on the edge as well. I turned my whole body to Graham, looked him right in the eyes. They were so blue I wondered if I could jump in and swim…distracted. Okay. I slid my hand up his inner thigh. "Graham, I want to see you."

"You want to see me? See me what, Princess?" Not a single twitch in his face, but I felt Britt slide closer to me to give me courage.

"I want to see you wrap your hand around yourself. I want to see you come. I want to know what you sound like. Turnabout is fair play and all." Maybe I could do this. It made me hot and tighten just thinking about it.

"You want to see me open my pants, take this raging hard cock in my large hand and rub it until I shoot my load. Are you willing to catch that load in your mouth?"

Umm, no. I didn't want to suck his dick. I wanted to watch him. Though, I bet he tasted salty and musky. Unconsciously I felt my teeth sink into my lip and my head start to nod and then move side to side. I had no control over my own body.

"Nu uh, I want to watch you do it. I want to…."

"I know what you want. But you are going to have to help." He slid the table out with one big shove until it was even with his knees. "Come here, my Princess. Stand in front of me and straddle my knees." My princess…I wanted to be his princess. I liked that. I had never been anyone's princess. It made me feel like a prized possession and damn if that wasn't just the wrong way to think. I'm supposed to be a feminist.

44

Women aren't possessions, but I wanted to be his. I wanted to belong to him. In that moment, I *did* belong to him.

"Let me help you," Britt slid over taking my hand. I felt her guiding me and then I felt his hands lift me onto the table. "Sweets, where do you want me?" Britt. Am I supposed to give her a task? I looked her in the eyes. A little of my panic must have escaped, as she asked, "Would you mind so much if I sat next him and rubbed myself as well?"

"No, Britt. God yes, please, please, Britt. Put your feet on the bench and open yourself wide."

Graham lifted Britt to the other side and pulled her leg up and draped it over his. He slid back and opened his pants. Well this was the best show on earth. Britt wasn't wearing panties, and her bare pussy was so wet that it glistened. She put her left leg on the table by my hip. I started rubbing my hand on her ankle.

"Did you know, Princess, that I have been seeing a glimpse of your breast all night?" He was drawing it out, all the while undoing his button while Britt was plucking at her nipples.

I looked down. Sure enough I had trusted Britt to dress me and I was missing the top three buttons. My cleavage was in perfect show tonight. "Did you like what you saw?" Where had this woman come from? One orgasm and I hardly recognize myself.

"No, Princess. It was just enough to drive me insane. You have great tits, but I need to see your nipples." His lust slammed into me, like something physical and tangible. He slid his zipper down and I saw he wasn't wearing underwear. I could see his line of dark hair trailing down to a large patch. I wanted to rub my face in it. It was dark and soft against his pale skin. He lifted his hips and slid his jeans down to his knees. Then he pulled Britt's bare thigh up against his again. Her bare thigh rubbing the soft hair on his thigh must feel good. The erection was intimidating. I needed to take in everything else first. He was huge; he wrapped both fists around himself, his head red and full spilling pre cum still a good inch above his immense hands. "You want to see?" He released his left hand started rubbing Britt's thigh, His right hand tight around the base, stroking up and down. "Is that what you want, Princess?" His voice growled out husky and deep.

I couldn't talk. I was mesmerized. It was amazing. I wanted to lick it. I couldn't keep my eyes on Britt as I was so transfixed on Graham, but I could hear her. Her fingers making wet suctions noises every time she plunged inside herself. He was stroking in tandem with her noises. I couldn't take my eyes off the drips escaping and running down his hard on.

"Lose the shirt, Princess. Show me your tits." I was slow to process it, but when he demanded "*Now,*" I all but tore the shirt from my body. I didn't just open it, as I should have, and so it went sailing across the bar. My body shook from the demand. I felt it in my core and in my soul. I was sitting on a table in a bar naked except my little black lace thong. My cream was leaking on the table where we were to have had dinner, and two of the most gorgeous people I know were masturbating, wrapped around each on the bench. Who was I? I couldn't keep my hands from my breasts if I tried. I was lifting and squeezing, pulling on my nipples. The heat rising from Britt and Graham was immense. Every noise and movement sent shockwaves through my body. I was going to come just like this. I could feel the cold table on my hot skin, leaning forward I could rub my clit on the hard surface. This was good, this was relief. Britt shouted her release, wrapping me up in it. I felt my own build. The lightning lashed me and forced my juices from my body. I couldn't take my eyes off that huge erection. I wanted it in me; I want that cum on me.

My orgasm was immediate and intense, white hot power pouring through me. I humped the table my hands on either side of my knee and Britt's leg. I have never screamed during an orgasm, but I couldn't hold it back. I heard Graham grunting, his hips lifting, his cum shooting on Britt's thigh, and my next orgasm exploded in my head. . I couldn't stop the nonsense shouting or my body from pulsing. Graham grunted, Britt moaned and whimpered at her come down, and mine would not stop. My back arched, my knees spread as wide as they will go, and my clit pulsed against the table. I was in heaven or hell and I didn't care.

When my world returned, I realized they were both watching me. The only thing I could think was well I did that. "So, um…." I could feel my blush taking over my body. My body I was naked. Before I could register the cold I felt a tee shirt drop over my head. It was hot and smelled spicy and musky. Grahams! He was bare chested and holding Britt's leg while he wiped her off with a cocktail napkin. His chest is wide and hard tattooed from elbow to elbow, with a thin line of dark hair running from nipple to nipple and down to a still enormous hard on. His pants were still down around his knees, he was taking care of us before he took care of himself. When he helped Britt sit upright, he turned another cocktail napkin on himself and I still couldn't take my eyes off him. He was still hard. I wanted to lick him clean. I wanted to beg him to not put my toy away.

Britt, obviously back to herself, pulled up and said, "Come on, Sweets. Let's get you a drink before you get skittish." Skittish? Me? Did she just see what I did? I felt…what did I feel? Strong, in control, I felt powerful. I let Britt lead me to the bench. Graham pulled the table back, and used the last cocktail napkin dipped in his drink to wipe it off. "Beth, do you have any idea how extremely hot that was? I mean, I knew you were going to be good once we got you here, but damn girl. That deserves a toast!" She slid from the booth to walk to the bar.

"You know she is right, Princess. You are probably the hottest thing I have ever seen. I have never seen a woman so amazing." His hand around the back of the bench rubbed my shoulder and down my arm. Fire raced through my body again. Everywhere he touched was alight with flames. I wondered if my orgasm could do that. Could it recede and then come back?

"Do it again," I commanded when I noted his bewildered look. "Touch me. Oh Graham, please touch me again."

"I didn't, I only…okay, Beth" He pushed the table again and lifted me to it. "You're still orgasming, aren't you? My naughty little Princess…you should have told me. Lift the shirt, let me help." I could feel his hands start at my knees and run up my thighs, grabbing my hips as he pulled me hard to him. He was too tall to rub himself against me. He growled and pushed my shoulders back. I felt the table sliding back to him and he was lifting my hips off the table. I didn't know where I was going, but I knew instinctively that Graham wouldn't let me get lost.

I felt his bare shoulders under my thighs only moments before I felt his hot breath against my soaked panties. Whipping passion raced through my blood. I felt him break the string and lift my panties from me. With a long hot breath, he laid the flat of his tongue to my throbbing clit and I exploded. White light and heat filled my body and warmed it to a temperature only he knew. Lifting his head, he slid two fingers inside. His hands were so big and it was more than I have taken in so long. "Princess, you are so tight and hot and would feel so good around my cock."

His scotch hot voice stroked around my brain and sent me higher. He laid his mouth back to my clit and pulled it into his mouth, lathing every inch of me. I couldn't stop it. I could feel him inside me, winding his way around my soul. The lights exploded. I couldn't hear anything or feel anything except his fingers moving inside me. His hand gripped and pulled at my ass, his tongue scorched heat through my pussy. My body jerked and tightened and I felt it go on forever. I was perfectly content to burn. I don't know how I ended up sitting in his lap, with Britt rubbing my feet and crooning too me. Graham was pushing something wet into my hand. Oh, my drink. Water? My throat hurt.

"Britt, why does my throat hurt?" I really couldn't think of what I had done to my throat. I could identify why my entire lower body was numb. Why my head was cottony and why that large hard thing was poking my hip. But why did my throat hurt?

"Sweets, you screamed for like forever. We were all wondering if Graham broke you. Beth, have you ever had multiple orgasms before?" She didn't stop rubbing my feet, and it felt so good that I laid my head against Graham's shoulder. One of his hands held me right beneath my breast while the other made a fire path up and down my leg.

"I have had several while having sex. Is that what you are asking?" I never lifted my head. He smelled so good, warm and spicy. I was safe and sated.

"No, not one, then you come down, then another. I mean have you ever had one right after another after another? Because, Beth, it is a rare treat and knocks you on your ass for a while. Let's toast!"

Toast, huh? What? "Okay, I can't toast with water" I said handing her my water my head still a little fuzzy.

Handing me a shot glass she yelled at the top of her lungs, "*To the girl I love bestest, her first multiple orgasm and the man that gave it to her!*"

I wanted to crawl under the table. What sounded like thousands of people yelling *Here! Here!* and *Hurrah!* was probably only a handful, but it was a handful of strangers that just witnessed my slip into the extreme.

I felt Graham lean against my ear and whisper, "This is how it will always be, I promise." What the hell was that? Alright then, it's probably time to go. I came, I saw, I came, I must have conquered something. "Um, Britt, what time is it? I have to get home to the boys and I lost my purse."

"Your purse is in my office," Graham answered instead. "I brought it up with me earlier." He glanced at his watch. "It's two am."

"Oh crap. I have to get home." My mommy brain kicked in; football practice starts at six and Peter is going to need carbs for breakfast. I don't have any pancakes made. I started running a million miles an hour.

As I pulled away to exit the booth Graham said, "Are you coming back tomorrow?"

"Tomorrow, no I have to be home with the boys on Saturday nights. They aren't old enough to date so their friends come over to our house. We have early mass the next morning" I was really going to have to confess. How did one confess something like that? Forgive me father, but I let a man eat my pussy until I was unconscious? Oh yeah, I am going to hell. I started to pull Britt to a standing position so she could walk me to my car and then I started to think of all I had drunk and the way I looked. It was quite possible I would get arrested for a DUI and have to go to jail in Graham's t-shirt with no panties. "Um Britt, how much have you had to drink?" I wasn't drunk, I didn't usually drink heavily. I was planning on driving home tonight but I just had that shot. Probably only 2 glasses of Gin all night, but I refused to go to jail with no panties.

"I will drive you home. Britt, go gather her things from our office." Just few more minutes with his scent around me and I would orgasm again.

"In your police car?" I really wanted to know, as my neighbors would get a big kick out of that.

"No, of course not I will take you home in my pickup. I am a plain-clothes detective and don't drive the cruiser anymore. But even if I did, no, I wouldn't do that to you again."

There it was…that stabbing pain again. I could smell the inside of the cruiser, feel the boys curled into me sobbing. No, not now breathe, I am okay.

"Princess, are you still with me?"

He must have seen my retreat. It is visible like a turtle pulling her head in her shell, at least that's what Britt told me it looked like. "No, I mean yes, I am okay." Deep breath, stand up tall, nope that makes the ass hang out again. It's hard to slouch with your shoulders back.

"After you, Princess."

"Why do you call me Princess? I mean, it's better than Ma'am. That just makes me feel old. "

I like that he calls me princess because it make me feel safe. The emotions and thoughts are swirling through my brain again, must be too many orgasms in one night. I shouldn't want to be his princess, but I like the feeling of belonging to someone again. I know he will take care of me and I don't have to be strong all the time any more. What the Hell? No, he is a stranger I just fucked in "The Club". He isn't going to move in and take care of me. I don't even know him.

Rebekkah Rogers

Chapter 4
Graham

Why do I call her Princess? Doesn't she know? She is the most erotic, beautiful woman ever made. She should be treated like a princess. I call her Princess to remind her and all those other losers how precious she is. "Because you are a Princess and it reminds you to demand to be treated like one."

Her ass is amazing; I could tell she was slouching a little to keep the shirt down in the back. She was not a petite lady. Nothing she did was going to hide that ass, and when she walked, I got a little peek of rounded bottom. I wanted to bend her over and feel that skin against my thighs. I had those cheeks in my hands while I was feasting on her sweet pussy. It was soft and firm…it was the hardest thing to not demand her ass in the air when she was screaming. I knew if I shoved into her, it would only make it better for her, but I couldn't do it. I wanted her aware. I wanted her to feel every inch. I wanted her body to want me to pull out and slide into her ass. I want that ass; my cock is yelling at me to just take what we know is ours. Claim it.

Focus. No response from her on the Princess comment…huh. I wonder what is going on in her brain.

Britt met us at the bottom of the stairs and followed us out to my truck. I watch my Princess maneuver into the center trying to keep herself covered, as Britt climbed into passenger side. It was all I could do to not laugh out loud she was never going to cover that ass in only a tee shirt. "Home, James," the little blonde wench demanded.

I slid my hand up her inner thigh; she was wet and hot. The smell of her sweet arousal filled my truck and I wonder how well I could drive with my fingers deep inside her. Opening her legs just slightly, I slid my finger higher up her thigh. She clamped her legs shut and held my hand in her heat.

As I was pulling down the lane, my Princess gasped, "Britt, didn't you make plans with James for tonight?"

"No problem, Sweets. It's you and me tonight. I am going to stay with you if that's okay. I can help with the boys in morning doesn't' J. have baseball?" James? Was Britt seeing James Simmons? He was patrolman on the metro department and he was strange. I let him in because he is cop and I originally thought I was being investigated. Turns out he is just a weird duck, but I have had no problems, so he stays.

"No, P. has football and J. has practice today." They were discussing this like Britt was one of the parents. Maybe that is how they all survived. I knew Britt helped her, but I just didn't realize they were close enough that Britt should know the kids schedule. Why do I care? Sure they are great kids, but they aren't mine. Why am I envious that Britt gets to go home with her? Does Britt sleep in her bed? She said they never, but what if they do? I want to strangle Britt. Maybe that would put me out of the misery of imagining the two of them together. "I promised P. that I would make him pancakes. I should do that before bed so I don't have to do anything but drive him."

I heard my words before I could stop them. "I'll help you." Where did that come from? I can make pancakes, but I have never wanted to make them for woman's kids before. What the hell is wrong with me? I know I can't be part of her fairy tale. "And what is with the letters? Don't your kids have names? Nice names if I remember, right?" The feel of her skin under my hands is torture. I want to lick at her sticky wetness more. I can feel her pressing against my side so I move my hand higher on her thigh I brush her soft damp curls.

"Oh, um well...." She was blushing again, I could still taste her on my tongue and she was nervous again.

"Sure, that would be great. We can bang out some pancakes, have some coffee, and watch the sun come up. Then we'll get the boys off to practice and sleep away the morning." Britt seemed to take delight in everyone else's confusion about the situation.

"I have teenage sons; I don't bring men home. No. I am sorry, but no, I can't. We aren't ready for that yet." She tried to slide away but my grasp held her firm.

"Don't panic, Princess. I offered pancakes, not adoption. I understand. Nothing untoward will happen in your home with your impressionable children present. I promise you pancakes, and coffee. Then I will leave you and your wicked wench to sleep away the morning. Just don't play without me." That would be too much to know Britt got to taste what's mine. I could feel her looking at me, assessing. I don't want to be part of her family. Well, yes I do. I want to spend every day slipping into her tight pussy in the morning, knowing that it is ready and waiting in the evenings. Still, I know that isn't the life she lives. She won't be sitting in bed waiting like a good, little sub. I will have to hunt her down and drag her to bed, making me all the harder and her all the wetter for the play.

"All right, but you can sleep in the guest room no driving home that tired. I don't think it is a bad thing for the boys to know we didn't drive if we drank. That is responsible, right?" She turned to Britt for confirmation, as though she were the partner in parenting.

"You're a good mom, Beth. After the condom talk, they aren't going to want to talk to you in while any way. So don't worry."

"Condom talk?" It hits me; she had to be mother and father to these boys and they were dating age now.

"Yeah, I found out Peter," she emphasized his name for me, "is not having sex, but is very close or so he says, his brother says he is. I don't really want to know. I bought a jumbo size box of condoms and put them in their bathroom. I told them over breakfast the next morning by putting them there, I was not condoning them having sex. I think they are too young. I told them I did however, have realistic expectations and if they were going to do it, I expect them to remember that it is their job to protect not just themselves, but their partner as well. They are fully responsible and I would hold them to that responsibility. I then told them if they need more, they just need to put it on the grocery list, no questions asked. I would buy them and put them in the bathroom. I also said I would answer any questions they have and I promised no speeches, no judgment, and no punishment if they asked. I didn't know what else to do, so I figured the less I said but the more I gave, the better they would respond. They are smart boys, but they are teen boys nonetheless and all that encompasses."

"I think it's a great idea. You offered them respect and an open door, but pushed the responsibility and consequences onto them. As having been a teen boy once and mostly I still am, I think you are spot on and certainly better than most."

I can't stop the flash of my father naked with my girlfriend bent over the kitchen table in our shitty, little trailer. "All women are whores," he had said when I called him out on it. His cock was still buried in her. "Just don't get attached, son. They only want your dick and your wallet." He started to slap her ass. "Tell him...tell him what a whore you are." I'll be damned if she hadn't orgasmed and yelled what a whore she was.

I pictured that every time I tried to be in a committed relationship. I couldn't get close and I needed to remind myself. That fucker was dead, though, and my Princess isn't like those women had been. Well, that fixed the raging hard on that was sucking the blood from my brain. Just think about good old Pops.

Pulling up to her house had to remind her that I had been here before. "Do you want to go in and let me park in the garage so the neighbors don't see the truck?"

"What? Oh, no. I don't care. There are always cars parked out front here. Most of the boys' friends drive. I refuse to be a slave to my neighbors if they are going to be petty and judgmental." Wow…backbone too. She truly had everything. I have to stop licking my lips but she's still there her flavor is still in the small hairs around my mouth. She is sweet inside and out, and back comes the boner.

As we approached the front door, it slammed open. "Mom, where have you been?"

"P. Bear, you don't talk to me like that. I am a grown woman and your mother. Now what is the matter?" Oh shit. This kid was pissed and giving all of us an assessing eye. Yup, saw mom wasn't wearing pants. This is not going to be good.

Backing into the house so we could all follow, he said, "We tried to call you an hour ago. Someone set the alarm off again and the security company wants to talk to you though we gave them the code. I wonder if there is a problem with the system. That creepy cop keeps calling, too."

"What creepy cop?" I tried to keep my cool and I didn't want this kid to realize who I was until things were more settled.

"Some cop that investigated a break-in a while ago keeps sniffing around mom. He's a tool."

"You had a break-in?" I couldn't keep my eyes from hers. She met mine and I read in her what I was feeling. She didn't want me to meet her kids like this.

"Yes, no. It was a rock through the window and it turned out to be a prank by some boys in the park. They were aiming for the girl next door. They were trying to wake her and hit my window instead. Because they threw too hard, it broke. The *tool* as my brilliant son so eloquently put it, became smitten and won't really take no for an answer. He is harmless, but he is kind of a tool."

"Who is it?" I will make him take no for an answer. I can do that with a booted foot to his front teeth.

57

"Nuh-uh, no way. Not saying." Then she eyed her son. They had a complete conversation in seconds and again that envy flared to life.... Oh hell no. I wasn't jealous of her son. That wasn't happening. "Where's your brother?"

"He's asleep on the couch. We watched that creepy dead people movie you love so much. He passed out half way through." He put his arms out and she walked into them he all but picked her up and her shirt rose above that beautiful ass. Obviously, he didn't realize she also had no panties on.... Thank you Peter. She started pulling on the shirt as soon as that cold air hit her ass.

"I need to change, I yucked up all over myself." She started to head up the stairs.

"Nice mom," Peter exclaimed. "I thought you could hold your liquor."

"Har har har, laugh it up, you little monster. Just remember that I am the one that cooks your food."

"I'm not little anymore mom you have to change your attack." He said with a laugh.

"Hi Auntie," the boy who stood in the living room in his boxer briefs said. "Did you drink too much as well? Help yourself to my closet if you want to change." Wow. This family was comfortable with each other.

"Thanks, Baby. Speaking of food, I think we are on pancake detail, Graham. Oh, and because your mom was ever so polite. Graham please meet the ever so lovely and polite Peter Williams. P., meet your mom's new boyfriend, Graham." And at that, that crazy bitch walked out of the room, leaving me and young Peter staring at each other stupidly.

I put my hand out to shake his, remembering where my hands had been that night. Of course I was clean, but I wasn't fit to meet this kid. I had my hands in a random woman's and his mother's pussy, and around my cock stroking a woman he called Auntie. He took my hand, nonetheless, and said, "Nice to see you again Deputy McDell."

I couldn't hold back the choke in my throat. "You remember?" I was dumbfounded.

"On the worst day of our lives, you're the one man who helped us when no one else showed up. None of our friends, none of Dad's partners, no one but you. You drove us to the morgue, you held mom's hand. You stayed all day. Auntie couldn't leave court in the middle of a trial and so you waited for her. We would never forget you." Aw crap. This kid was deep. He was going to kill me. "You are why we haven't killed that stupid cop that keeps trying to piss on her like a dog with a bush." Nice image there. "That and she won't let us. Something about jail and college not being the same place." This kid really is too good.

"Who is the cop? Is he with the sheriff's department?"

"She told me not to say and she threatened me with poison. She can be really frightening when you cross her. So, you really her boyfriend or is Auntie messing with ya? And where are my mom's clothes? Nope, don't answer that last question." He crossed his arms across his chest. He was going to be a huge man when he grew into those shoulders.

"Her clothes are in her car, she was sick not because she drank too much, she really didn't, but when she realized who I was it was like a punch to her gut. She quickly recovered and is fine and if she will have me, yes I would like to be her boyfriend." I had never really been anyone's boyfriend before. I had some short term relationships, but they were usually based on sex and the woman always wanted more than I could give. I would eventually have to end things to protect her feelings before she was too invested and by that time I was usually bored anyway. I have never invested myself enough to want to spend time with a woman for the long haul. But I would like to spend time with Beth, she is funny and I think it will be a good long while before I tire of her sweet innocence and innate sexuality. No, no, no, I can't live in her fairy tale. I have killed people in the line of duty, arrested people, and seen the worst in humanity. No, my Princess deserves better than me. I'll be damned, though, if I am going to let some other weasel patrolman get her. "Alright then, Peter. Don't you have football at like the ass crack of dawn? I believe we came here so she could get up and take you?"

"Yeah, I am heading up now. Night mom." I saw her coming down, still in my shirt but a pair of flowered boxer shorts. My hardness pushed against my zipper. This is what I wanted–her comfortable and casually licking her lips while on her knees.

Her smile was electric and shot through my whole body. Lush lips…they would look fantastic around my cock, and that was not helping. As she reached out for my hand, I walked right into her and kissed her. I hadn't kissed her yet, and I needed to know what she tasted like. She was minty and sweet and just a tang of that something spicy that was all her. As I pushed against her and slid my tongue in, I knew I was going to die right here with her hands clutching at the shirt I had picked up off the floor of the bar. I licked at her mouth, tasting her minty honey breath and feeling her body pushed against mine. Fire raced up my arms where my hands gripped her hips and pulled her closer. She would never be close enough. Her tongue darting into my mouth sent the world spinning and my thoughts racing off. What would her tongue feel like on my body? I could feel her body shifting into me, my cock rubbing her lower belly. Heat seeped though her clothes and into my body, thawing something I didn't know existed. She was tall enough that I didn't lose her when I wrapped around her. I could feel those tits, no bra, hard as rocks poking into my chest, sending pulses of heat into my body. I wanted to sink into her and feel her heat warm me from the inside.

The throat clearing was obvious and ridiculous, but it was not Britt and that made my blood run cold. I have done many things in public, but I have never molested a mother in front of her children. She was panicking. I could feel it in her posture and how quickly she pulled away. She had said *we* aren't ready. She meant she and the boys weren't ready. I looked at the boy standing in front of me thinking he had just walked up the stairs. "J., you're awake? Please head on upstairs, son. I am going to make pancakes for P. tomorrow and we can talk in the morning."

"Um mom, are you forgetting something?" She really didn't want me to meet him, but he was going to push her.

"No, I don't think so. Oh of course. J., this is my friend Graham. Graham, this is my son, Joseph."

Joseph stuck his hand out. She really did a good job with these boys. They stood tall and they protected her, but I had the same flash I had with his brother. My hands were warmed on the heat of his mother's body. This boy, no man, was so much more than I was at his age. I took his hand. "It's a pleasure to meet you Joseph."

Joseph just looked at us, her then me, then her again a huge question in his eyes. "Really? Deputy McDell? That creepy cop wasn't enough, so you brought in this one?" This was not at all how I planned this. His brother did not prepare me for this one. They were so different. "I thought you were meeting someone new?"

"Joseph Marcus Williams, you fix your tongue or I will remove it from your head," and then the plastic spatula flew.

Britt was behind him bending to pick up her instrument of torture, while Joseph rubbed the back of his head. "I will listen to a lot of things from you my babe, but I will not have you deter your mother on this. I thought you wanted this. I thought you were with me. She did meet someone new, not creepy cop." Who was creepy cop? My mind would not stop at the question. "She met someone good and right, someone that deserves her." That bitch looked me dead in the eyes, like she had picked straight from my brain my greatest fear.

I had to fix this. I knew in my bones that if he said no, the answer would be no forever and I would lose my Princess. "Joseph, I am sure it is a lot to take in and you didn't exactly see what your mother or I would have preferred. But we are all adults and we can all respect each other's choices. I will not hurt her. I will not push for more than she has. I will respect her time and space with both of her sons. I only ask that you allow me the chance. I can see how tense she is. She respects your opinion, and if you tell her no, she and I will lose out."

"No, I wouldn't say no. It's not my place, as I am reminded daily." His eyes flashed from me to her then back again. "I am the child and she is the parent. I just don't want you taking advantage of the lonely widow. Fish in your own pond."

She gasped, but I needed to fix this and show him that I respected them both. "Joseph, she came to my pond and I want her." I kept my eyes on him making him see how I felt about her.

"Night mom, I love you." He ran up the stairs at once without saying goodbye.

"Well, that could have gone better." She was so worried, but I thought it went ok. He will come around he just wants to protect her.

"It went better with Peter, but he didn't catch us kissing." I snaked my arm around her waist and pulled her to me. I caught Britt's eye as she nodded and walked out of the room. Against her lips, I said, "He did ask me why you weren't wearing any panties."

I ran my hands down that ass. I had to feel those globes filling my hands. Lifting her to me, I wanted to rub my dick on every inch of her body. I wanted to see her straddling me while I was buried deep inside her. Her hair would hand around us like a curtain keeping the world out. If I kept this up, I was going to cum in my jeans.

"He did not." Her thump to my chest was like a balm. She was ready to play.

I couldn't hold back the chuckle. I liked teasing her, "No Princess, he didn't. He asked where your clothes were, though. He was kinder, although he seems to get angry fast and run out steam quickly as well."

"Yes, he's just the opposite of Joseph who takes forever to work up a lather and then never comes back down."

"They are great men. You have done well." My lips touched hers and I was lost again.

Rebekkah Rogers

Chapter 5
Beth

I could feel his tongue in my mouth on my lips. I could smell myself on his unshaven skin. I could taste my cum on his lips and still I wanted more of him. I felt him sliding his hands around my hips and lifting me to him. I could feel his hard length against me. I had to stop. I couldn't process why but I knew I had to stop. I was not having sex with him in my house. I was not going to have sex with him in my foyer.

Relief swept through me when Britt's voice shouted, "Bitches, why am I the only one making pancakes?"

Pulling away, I recalled the way he had sat on my couch in his uniform. I liked him from the moment he walked into my house. He is tall with dark hair showing his gray, but he is fair with bright blue eyes. I couldn't help but stare. "You want me?"

"Oh, Princess. I would take you right here on the tile floor if I thought it wouldn't get us both killed." Heat streaked through, almost as hot as the disappointment.

"Okay, well, let's make some pancakes." Did he just tell my son he wanted to have sex with me? I must have misread that. Maybe he was just soothing Joseph. I needed to get control of myself. Of course, this isn't forever. That is why I didn't want him meeting the boys. J. saw us kissing. He is going to have no respect for either of us if I don't get a hold on this.

I walk into the room and knew just where to start. "Britt, why did you wake up J.? He would have slept in the chair all night. A nuclear bomb wouldn't have woken him and you know it. You had to have woken him. Why, Britt?"

"Sweets, you needed those boys to see you as a woman. Yes, you're a mom first. I get that, but this was hard on all three of you tonight. P. sat up worrying and working J. into a fervor, so when you came home with a guy, of course J. was going to go off. It would have happened in the morning or a few hours after. You will all be okay with it now."

"That is the most manipulative move yet. I thought you were going to stop managing us." As she handed me two coffee cups from my cupboard, I thought she was a bossy wench.

"I am, when you are all running like a well oiled machine. Now pour hot and steamy for hot and steamy, pretty please." Hot and steamy; shit, she was right. He was steamy. Coffee...she was talking about pouring coffee for Graham.

"Hey, sorry to break it up, ladies, but who is creep cop?" I so didn't want to tell him about the only other date I had ever gone out on. I hadn't even told Britt.

"He is the cop that responded to the break-in not really a break-in call. He has asked me out several times. He gives me the creeps, hence the extremely clever nickname the kids gave him. The boys have been fielding his calls because he doesn't take no for an answer and he starts talking about all the fun we will have and generally being well, being creepy. He doesn't bother the boys except to leave his phone number every time he calls. Cream and sugar?"

"Yes to both. Did you go out with him?" How did I know he was going to ask? No one had actually asked me? They just all assumed I hadn't and let it go. It was the worst date ever.

I was blank faced and trying to come up with the lie, but it wouldn't come out. "Yes, I went out with him once in the beginning, right after the rock." He had looked almost pathetic asking.

"*What*? You never told me about this. Why not? Come on. Spill it."

This bitch is going to be the death of me. I didn't want to talk about the worst date ever with Graham.

"What happened, Princess?" This was humiliating.

I sat at the bar while Britt continued at the skillet. I stared into my coffee while I contemplated how to tell them. "Ok, so the full story if no one judges."

"Princess, come on." His eyes were piercing and I wanted to kiss him so badly.

"Just promise." They were going to think I was some crazy bitch if they heard how I flipped on the poor guy.

"Pinky swear." She sounds so small and sweet when she does that. Britt, though, is anything but sweet.

"Of course, on my honor." He says smoothly.

"Alright, so the rock came through the window at about midnight. It set off alarm and scared all three of us. The boys are in their underwear standing in my bedroom while I am still trying to figure out what my name is. Security company calls and I answered the phone at my bedside and tell them my bedroom window broke. They tell me to lock myself in the farthest bathroom from the broken window and wait for the police. So the boys and I do that. We wait in the bathroom. Luckily, it faces the front of the house so we were able to see when the security guard and police arrived. The security company guy told me to stay in the bathroom and not to leave until the police came in to get us. The security guard unlocked my door and then stood on the drive. He saw us through the window, waved, and yelled to the cops where we were. They were all so fast and efficient. The cops came and told us it was just a rock and not a very big one at that. There were several foot prints outside in my yard. Probably some kids trying to get the boys attention. The boys later heard about it at school and found out they were trying to get the girl next door's attention. So anyway, one of the officers would not stop staring. He was eating me alive with his eyes. It was almost palpable. When it was all wrapped up, he told me he would stay if I needed. I told him no, the security company had boarded up the window while the officers were there. It was all pretty well done. I would sleep in one of the boys' room until I could get the glass out of the carpet. We would be fine."

"A couple of days later, he stopped by to tell me there were no leads on the case and to ask if I would have dinner with him." I wasn't going to tell them it was after Britt had started laying on the sex talk in an effort to remind me I needed to date. I also wasn't going to tell them I kept picturing a hot cop in full uniform standing on my porch telling me exactly what he wanted to do with his stick. "So I said yes. He was nice enough and you had been harping on me about dating." I turned my full attention on Britt as she put more batter on the griddle. "You had been telling me I needed to get out, so I went. He picked me up that night and we went to a local chain restaurant. It was fine. We were having a perfectly good time until he decided to tell me how he felt about me." I could feel my blush start in my chest and move up.

"You guys don't really want to hear this. Just rest assured that it gets weird. He weirded me out and I told him to take me home. He was a little huffy that I couldn't finish the date."

"Slow down, Princess. I want to hear it all." But he really didn't. His tension was radiating off him.

"All right. He told me he thought I was a great mom that I had made such sacrifices and I should be so proud of myself. He told me he had watched the boys and knew they were great kids and wouldn't get into any trouble. I didn't know if I should agree with him or remind him they are teenage boys. Of course they are going to get into trouble. He seemed so focused on how well they behaved. It was a little weird to hear him speak about them like he knew them."

"Was he watching them?"

"I don't know, Graham. He then started telling me how much he respected me and how he thought I would be beautiful

68

with a couple of daughters as well." At Britt's choking laugh, I had to look up from my coffee and see the humor in the situation. "I told him there would be no more children for me. I had twins the first time and that was enough. He became a little belligerent about it and asked if I was sure and why would I make such a big decision when there is so much more living to do. I told him I was positive." Tipping my head to catch Graham's eye, I wanted to know what he thought. "I had to have a hysterectomy after the boys, I can't get pregnant."

Nothing; he didn't react at all. Well, okay then.

"I didn't want to tell him personal stuff, but he was pushing. So I pushed back with the truth. He just rolled his eyes at me and told me we could adopt. Adopt? I asked him. Why would I adopt and what judge would give a single mother of teenage boys a baby. My boys will be in college in two years, they're both planning on going to Notre Dame like their father. In two years I will be child free; this is something I am looking forward too. He just looked baffled like I had kicked his puppy. "But I love you, and I need a family" he says. I didn't know what to do I just stood up and told him to take me home. We hadn't finished our dinners and he was at I love you? I was floored I didn't know what so say. I wanted to kill you Britt."

"It wasn't my fault the guy's a nut job."

"No, it was your fault I was there. All my really stupid ideas come from your brain."

"Not fair. Tonight wasn't a stupid idea." She raises her eyebrows like a bad cartoon villain.

"That remains to be seen. The night ain't over yet." I respond with my best bad villain voice knowing I sound more John Wayne than anything else.

Graham grabs his chest. "Oh Princess, you wound me."

"All right, jackasses. You want the rest of my story or what?" I wait for their heads to bob before I proceed, "He was offended I wouldn't sit back down. I finally got him out of the restaurant and into the car. Before he switches it on, though, he turns to me and says 'I don't know why you're so pissed. I know you want me. If you didn't want me, you wouldn't have answered the door in your underwear.' He started his car and started driving I was clueless. I was in Jeans and a button down blouse. I looked nice, but I was being very conservative. I didn't want him to get the wrong idea off the bat. So I asked him when and he says the night of the break-in. I couldn't figure it out. I sleep in boxers and tees when it's really hot I will sleep in boxers and a cami, but I have boys who often have friends over. I don't walk around naked or even risqué."

"I don't know. Those boxers with my shirt are pretty hot, Princess."

I felt the blush steal up my cheeks.

"Knock it off, Graham, or she will quit telling us." Britt was still waving the spatula. How many pancakes was she making? I guess I hadn't been talking as long I thought I had.

"So I tell him that I don't know what he is talking about. He says, and I quote, 'You were wearing a man's underwear and undershirt. What red blooded male wouldn't take that for an invite?' Then I remembered what I was wearing. I hadn't done laundry in like forever so all my boxers were dirty as were all of my panties. I was doing laundry that night but I had already changed out of my suit into a pair of Marc's old silk boxers and I had a men's white undershirt on." I heard Graham gasping for air and slapped him on the back. "Okay, I concede the shirt probably was more than the cops bargained for, but I am sure it is not the worst any of them have seen. Don't you think if it was really bad one of them would have told me?"

Shaking his head he said, "Damn, Princess. You probably made some wives happy that night. You have great tits and in a wife beater, I bet they could see it all. You are correct Beth, experienced cops have seen much more and wouldn't comment. We are trained to notice everything, but unless it's part of the investigation, you don't take it into account. You must not have been that bad because yes, one of the other officers would have recommended you change."

"Okay, so yeah, I should have put a shirt on. I was worried and the security company told me very clearly to get in the bathroom, don't worry about anything, and stay. Then I was locked in a bathroom with two scared and tired boys for what felt like an eternity. When the cops came to get us, we were all just ready to know we were safe. I wasn't thinking about a perverted cop taking it too far." I bump Graham with my knee because I just wanted to feel him against me again. His hand crept down my back and I stifled the moan that wanted to escape at the fire his touch evoked in me. "So anyway, creepy cop proceeds to tell me how I invited him. To what, I don't know yet, but it was an invite. I couldn't control myself and my inner bitch ripped forth and I started yelling at him about how it is inappropriate for a cop to assume a victim wants him because she was victimized in her pajamas. He says he loves me and just wants us to work this out. I shouldn't have and I knew at the time I shouldn't have, but I told him I would turn him in if he came over again. He hasn't come over but he calls several times a week to apologize. He always tells me how much he wants to be with me. The last time, I told him I was turning him in for stalking. He hasn't called since, well, until tonight."

I felt like a cat, with Graham stroking my back running his hand through my hair. I wonder if he can't keep his hand off of me. I slide closer and conclude, "So, you see, it's nothing out of the ordinary."

"What's his name?" His hand tightens on my hip and tucks me against him.

"Nope, I'm not telling. I am not having you go in and start a problem. He is with the City Police department and you're not. You probably know him, but maybe you don't. I am not taking a chance. So where do you live, by the way?"

"I live above the club now. I had a condo not too far from here, but when we bought the house and started the club, I moved in upstairs. What's creepy cop's name?"

"You have partners?" I wanted to know what possessed a good cop to decide to open a place like that, but I wasn't going to ask. I still wasn't telling him the guy's name, either.

"Um, well yeah. Just the one. Doesn't she know who my partner is, Britt?" Britt whipped around so fast she damned near lost her spatula. I have never seen her so flummoxed. She was stuttering and spluttering. I think she may have sprung a leak.

"Britt? You ok, Sweets?" I rushed around the counter to hand her the glass of water nearest her.

"Yes, I am. Well, you remember I told you I was moving a large chunk of money and investing in a private venture. We talked about risks and you helped me determine how much I should use and how much to hold back." Oh, man. I helped her invest in a sex club. Was that what she was saying? "Well, I knew Graham from some of the other clubs." Has she had sex with him? I didn't think so, but they knew each other and apparently well. "None of them were really what either of us wanted. We were drinking one night and bitching because we couldn't find what we wanted. I had seen this house go on the market, because I had loved it from the start. I wanted to buy it, but it was way too much house for me. I thought about talking you into moving into it with me. I could help with the boys, but they're leaving soon. I really had no reason until Graham mentioned needing a space. I have all this money I inherited, so I figured, why not? I made a cash offer on it the day after talking to you. I brought Graham out to it the day after I closed, along with an architect who could redesign some of the rooms, build on the industrial kitchen, and turn the kitchen into the bar. Our office is not accessible from the front of the house. You have to go through the kitchen and Graham's apartment is right off next door. You can walk through the bathroom to his closet or his private bath and bed. He also has a private entrance in the hall, next to the fire escape. He can come and go and no one would know because it's all very private for him. I share the office space, but I hardly ever work there. Graham does all the books."

"Well, I hire the CPA to do the books."

"He manages the club entirely; he does all the hiring and all the guest requests. I just show up and look pretty. I had to ask him for that pretty little bracelet you wear. In five years, possibly less, he will have paid me back for everything but the real estate. That I plan on holding onto indefinitely. The club will continue to pay rent for ten years after he has paid me back and at that time my shares will decrease from forty-nine percent to five percent. It's a good deal. He is making money hand over fist with it. He has gift."

"Knock it off, Britt," Graham said pulling me back to him. "I want to retire from the force as soon as possible, but I want Britt paid off first. I plan on hiring a manager once I get a good hold on what is going on and have seen all the catastrophes that can come. Then I will retire from the club in another ten years with ninety-five percent of the shares and my Sheriff's department pension. I should be ok." It was weird talking retirements and investments like we didn't just have wildest night of my life. Finally, Britt concedes to the pancake gods and I realize I was starving.

I got up and pulled the maple syrup, the good stuff not the fake crap with the old lady on the bottle the kids like. Mine has trees on the bottle. Yummy! Pulling butter and grapes from the fridge, I moved on to the cupboards. They were looking at me like I was nuts. "What? I am hungry." Then I realized I was shoving grapes in my mouth like a squirrel. "Let's eat."

Graham chuckles but looks guilty. Why would he feel guilty? "I should have found us some food; you burned a lot of calories tonight, didn't you? Come on; let's eat before you starve."

Britt looked almost angry at Graham. "Dumbass, it's your job to take care of your Princess, but I did make her food." What? What was that all about?

"Um guys? What's going on?"

Walking to me with his arms out Graham gestured for me to come to him. His arms around me were tight and corded with muscle. He wasn't a weightlifter, but rather, he was strong and lean, not to mention so damned hot. "Princess, it's my responsibility to take care of you and to make sure your needs are met. You spent so much energy earlier; I should have remembered to feed you again. Britt is angry because I forgot. It's a sure sign I am a bad dominate to you. She worries I won't take care of you. You just fry all my reasoning and I can only think about touching you again. I am sorry, baby. I will do better." Do better, like in the future? A dominate to me? That is actually kind of hot, but so not the point.

I figured it out. "Bitch, is that why you are always taking care of me? You think I need to be handled? What the hell is going on? Why do I feel like a toy being handed down?" I couldn't decide if I was pissed or if I wanted to crawl up in his lap and let him stroke me more.

"Now stop it, Beth. You know I love you. You are my best friend. You deserve, not need, but deserve to have someone take care of you. You're incredibly sexy when you submit and you like it. You're just afraid to take it." What was she talking about, submit? When had I ever submitted to her? Walking to the table, I sat and started dishing up food.

"What? Britt, you and I have never had sex, well unless you count tonight. Does tonight count? When have you ever seen me submit?" Did I have sex with Britt tonight? I saw her come twice; maybe that counts. They both sat and started dishing as well.

"No, we didn't have sex tonight. Maybe Graham and I did." Wow that was like a punch to the gut. "I guess when a guy's cum shoot so hard it reaches your pussy, its sex."

"Britt, knock it off. You're avoiding her questions." *Okay; eat, think, and breathe.* Graham was very attentive. He handed me things and made sure I had what I needed. Was he going to cut up my food as well? I guess not, his left hand rubbed high on my thigh while his right hand cut his food.

"Yes, Beth. I have been pushing you and dominating you in your own home for just over three years now. It started just before Marc died." I waited for the punch in the gut at the words. It didn't come. "I would come over help with the kids, talk dirty to you and your hubby, and send you up to get some. I knew you guys were so busy and you needed more. I could see you needed more from him, but you didn't know what it was you needed. So I would plant ideas in his head by teasing you. Then he would satisfy you. I could see you enjoying it. We talked about it." She was right; Marc had started experimenting more towards the end, and he always liked to talk dirty to me. Now that I think about it, he sounded a great deal like Britt. "Then when he was gone...."

"You were the glue that kept me from falling apart, I know. You slept in my bed, dressed me, fed me...."

"I held your hair while you vomited and washed your hair while you cried. I love you so much and it was the least I could do. You gave me a family to be part of; you never questioned why I wanted to be here or why I wanted to sit on your couch watching the boys while you and Marc had sex upstairs."

"You did that, Britt? That must have been hard." What was Graham talking about? She would push us up the stairs for some time alone while she taught the boys how to play video games. I thought it was because she wanted to corrupt the boys without us watching.

"Yeah, I did, but it wasn't hard. I didn't want Marc; he only ever had eyes for her. She didn't want me; she only saw him. She would hear me and I could see the thought intrigued her, but she only wanted him. Graham, she is a one man woman. She may play and she may look, but she won't share and she won't want to be shared."

"I know, Britt." Of course I am, I can't do... well maybe I could. Today, watching him rub Britt's leg was pretty hot, but my stomach ached at the thought of him actually touching her. Yeah, she was right. I don't share well.

"Britt, did you want me?" Was that what this was about?

"Princess, it wasn't about Britt wanting you. That's not the point. Of course, she wanted you. Who in their right mind wouldn't? Britt staked a claim on you a long time ago. That night when I called her, do you remember the first thing she did when she came in."

No, I don't remember. How could I think of that, I barely remember getting dressed that day? There are only two very vivid memories of that day and I am sure he doesn't want to know that he and my husband's body are my only solid memories after my completely innocuous conversation with Marc that day. The call that ended up being the last time I ever spoke with him, at least I did tell him I loved him. Oh no, I can feel the tears threaten as my throat tightens. *Breathe in, breathe out*, wow it works. Look at me calm and cool.

"She called for you; put her arms around you kissed your tears and turned you from me. You couldn't have seen me or come to me if you tried. You were Britt's. I left as soon as I realized you were hers. I knew her from work and from the clubs, I knew what she was. I thought she was your dominate. A couple of days later, she told me about your relationship. That was the night we decided we needed a new club."

"Have you two had sex before?" I had to know, I had to be prepared.

"No, we are business partners and friends. Nothing else." His answer was fast and decisive. All right then, I recalled that he wanted monogamy and that was not Britt.

"So, Sweets. When you ask if you are a toy being passed off, yes, I would imagine that is what it feels like. But I have to be specific and clear because I so strongly staked my claim before. Graham and I need to know where we stand. As much as I love you, I love him. I want you happy, but I want him happy too."

"Hey Britt, did you stage this whole meeting with Graham tonight?" His hands rub higher on my thigh and sends little licks of flame straight to my core. My boxers weren't helping me at all here.

"Yes and no. I have wanted you two to meet for a while. I completely forgot that he was the one from that night, because I just knew you would be great for him. But no, when we showed up, I walked you through the house with my arm around your waist. I was touching you and blocking you from anyone else thinking of trying you that night. When I introduced you to Graham, I told him you were "my" guest. Not a guest, but mine. The gestures are subtle but clear. It wasn't until dinner and I saw the light in your eyes that I knew you would work for him. I knew he was what you needed and I could loosen my grip. I kissed your hand and gave it to him, in essence passing you off."

"You got all of that," turning fully to Graham his hand slipping between my thighs, "from those simple, innocuous things?" I could feel my breath catch and his hand rub over my clit lightly.

"Yes Princess, she was very clear. She is not giving you away, but she has told me she will share you. She still plans on being part of your life and family. I get the feeling that she is the other parent to the kids and will remain here and if I want you." He leaned right into my ear. "Oh, and trust me, princess. I want all of you." He laid a kiss on my neck and sat up still stroking me "I have to accept her as part of our lives. Not necessarily our bed, but lives fully." How can he think when my body is pulsing, his hand rubbing me gently?

His hot syrup sweet breath had my head fogging. "Well yeah, she's my girl. She stays." Graham just nodded and pulled back just to my thigh, just enough to slow my heart. He turned to finish eating. This was the weirdest night ever.

Rebekkah Rogers

Chapter 6
Beth

It wasn't much longer before P. came down the stairs, dragging his ass and football gear behind him. "Mom, I can't do it. I am so tired."

"Sit, eat, and drink some juice." I handed him my glass. "You'll feel better in few minutes, P. I will take you and drop you off. Please ask one of the guys to bring you home. I am going to get some sleep. If you can't get a ride call, but please try."

"All right, mom." That's my boy. I can get anything I want when he is tired, as he just submits and goes. His twin is not like that, though. Peter and I both stood at the same time.

I turned to ask Britt to show Graham to the guest room. As much as I want him in my room, I couldn't. He was standing, as well. "Let me take him so you can get some sleep."

What? No, he can't take the kid. "No, I really can do it. It is only a few blocks. I just don't like him walking alone so early.

"Princess," at that, P.'s eyes snapped to him and his shoulders went back. He was alert now. "I am used to working nights. I am going to drop him off and head home. You and sleeping beauty there get some rest. I am on shift tonight again, so I planned to sleep most of the day anyway. I will call you tomorrow, or rather, tonight. Give me your number."

While I searched my purse for my business card, I looked P. in the eyes. He seemed to have cooled considerably. "P., is it alright if Graham drives you?"

"Sure, mom. I have to get going though." I glanced at the clock; shit. He was going to be late.

I handed my card to Graham and said, "My cell's on the bottom." I turned to P. "Call me if you can't get a ride." I wanted to kiss Graham goodbye, lay him down, and ride him. I opened the door, though and stepped back to let them through. P. kissed my cheek and walked out.

"Store your gear in the back. I will be just a sec." Then he kissed me, deep and hard. My body arched into him and fire shot through me. Then he was gone. He was walking out the door before I had time to process the kiss. "I will call you, so be prepared." I stood there and watched them pull away. I was never going to be able to sleep.

Well, I was wrong. Britt and I ended up sleeping the better part of the day. She got up and headed home; I ran errands, groceries, movies. Graham called at nine we talked for almost an hour. Apparently, he was on a stake out watching for some guy to arrive.

He called at the same time every day for the next two weeks. We weren't able to see each other again until tonight, Friday night, and that was only for an hour. I bartered with the boys on chauffeuring them to their school dance. It turns out that they planned to take the young ladies to a nice seafood restaurant; however, J.'s date was allergic to shellfish. I took them to the only place I could think of that would be able to get them in without reservations and a two hour wait, which was the Italian restaurant by Britt's office. I was walking into the bar when Graham called. I realized I was only blocks from his house "The Club". I still didn't know what to think about him living in a sex club. I told him where I was and he was there in ten minutes.

We were able to have drinks, me an iced tea, him a scotch, while we waited for the boys to finish their dates. We always talked about things like work, the kids, my house, his house…just generally sharing our days. We were starting to share insights and feelings and I would often wonder if he ever got bored with my rather routine life. It was so different from his. He walked me to my car while the boys were still paying and gave me a scorching kiss that I would feel all night. He told me to call him when the boys were safely in the dance.

I dropped the kids off, and told them to call when they were ready to leave. I was home and dialing him minutes later.

"Take off your clothes," he commanded. There was no *hi* or *how are you*…just that dark voice in my ear. "Are you naked yet, Princess?"

"Um no, I am walking in the house now." I wanted to take my clothes off.

"Go to your room, keep the lights off, and strip naked." Hell yeah! My whole body was aching with want and need.

"I'm walking up the stairs now." It was the longest flight of stairs in my life.

"Have you got a favorite toy, my naughty little princess?" I loved when he called me that.

"I've got you, don't I?" I turned the corner into my room. I was dropping clothes as I went. My brain working only on making sure I didn't drop my phone.

"Pull out the biggest dildo you have princess, and rub it across your nipples." I really only have my rabbit, which of course, was a gift from Britt. My body is hot and I can feel sweat starting to run down my back.

I pull it out, turn it on, and start rubbing my nipples. They are so hard and so sensitive that I can feel it like a direct line to my pussy. I have never used it on my nipples before. "Let me hear you…does it feel good?"

"Yes, oh God, yes, it feels good."

"Are you wet yet? Close your eyes, can you feel me touching you to find out?" I could feel myself creaming getting hotter by the second. I have masturbated every day sometimes twice a day just thinking about him masturbating in the bar.

"Push that vibrator deep inside yourself with one hard thrust." I slide it through my cream and can feel myself leaking as his words wrap around my body like a physical hold.

"Oh. Yeah, oh Graham" It was so much harder and deeper than I had ever done before.

"Pull it out. Is it dripping?" Empty, I want it in me. I want it to be that hardness.

"Yes," I answered breathlessly.

"Yeah good, lick that cream and tell me if you taste as good as I remember. Because damn, Princess. I miss the taste of that dripping pussy." His words send little shivers through my body. My hips lifted as if his words could fill me.

I ran my tongue over my vibrator, which is not something I had done before, but I know what I taste like. "Mmm, I am sweet and kind of spicy, Graham." I wanted his tongue to taste me.

"Come on, Princess. Let me hear you fuck that thing. I want you to shove it in hard enough I can hear your wet pussy. Scream for me baby. Harder...leave it in there. Rub that clit and let me hear you. Come now."

His demand was enough. One hard tap and I was coming, screaming, panting, and picturing him pleasuring himself. His hips would raise and his come would leak down his hand.

One thought filled my mind—not my taste, but his. "Graham, I want you in my mouth."

"Princess, tell me how I taste." Now he was grunting and groaning.

"You're salty and hot running down my throat. You're deep in my throat as I swallow the whole head with my hand tight around the base. I want to feel you pushing inside my mouth." The little rabbit is doing its job and I am swamped with heat and light. Once again, I am coming. Our combined groan drawing out the white hot heat ripping through my body.

"Graham," I finally pant out.

"Yeah, baby I'm here." That dark voice, smooth as scotch and filled with heat, scraped across my senses.

"I want you inside me." I miss him. Not just the sex, but I miss the contact of his body against mine. I do not know how I became so attached to him, but I am.

"I know. When I had my fingers in that juicy little body, you were so tight and unbearably hot. It keeps me awake at night thinking how good that would feel on my cock. I want to see you riding me, your head back, you tits bouncing." He starts growling deep in his throat. "Oh yeah, you slamming up and down, so tight and wet with your nipple in my mouth as you scream my name. *Fuck.*" I know he is coming hard, as he is grunting and panting now.

When he's finally quiet for a second I ask "Graham?" I am going to tell him because it is eating me alive.

"Yeah baby?" His pant reminds me that we weren't just pouring our hearts out.

I know I am falling for him, but I haven't figured out how it works yet. I can't say it. "I need to sleep now." *Chicken shit.*

"Goodnight, my sweet princess." The fact that I belong to him so completely scares me.

Rebekkah Rogers

Chapter 7
Graham

She kills me. She is so hot, I haven't jerked off this much since I was in high school. Just the thought of her taking me deep in her throat has me coming in my hand like the little juvenile delinquent I was. I haven't been able to jack off twice in one setting for years, but just the thought of her tits in my mouth make me want to come again. It was suppose to be about her, but I have no control with her. I can see that auburn hair spread out and those tits bouncing as she's shoving that vibrator in herself. Her back is going to arch, as she does that when she comes. Her breasts point to heaven and she would be pinching and pulling on her nipples. She likes that whip of pain. I need inside her. I need to mark her; I need to know she is mine. I need her to know she's mine. I feel like I have a one track mind and can't get her out of my head.

I have resolved myself to this slow, painful death. I want her, all of her. I know I shouldn't and it will be a sham, but I can't give her up. Every night, I call her and we talk about the dumbest shit, all the while my mind is running around doing her ass while she bends over the tailgate of my truck. I open her up on my bar and feasting on her like a full course meal. In reality, though, we talk politics and smart stuff. She is brilliant, kind and generous, but mostly all that just makes me want to do is fuck her.

I haven't seen her in two weeks but for the short time tonight. It was brutal sitting there drinking with her, her in her jeans and fitted tank top. Her nipples were hard the whole time. I wanted to pull her from the table, strip her there and take those nipples in my teeth. She would be sweet with some musky spice. I wanted to feast on that whole body, just licking her from one end to the next. I know her cream would run when I started on those nipples. I want her thighs soaked before I open her up and lick them clean. There was so much we haven't done. I have never been this involved with someone and have it not revolve around sex.

I haven't seen Britt recently, either. She sometimes goes a couple of days, but not normally this long. Beth said she spoke with her this morning, so I am not really worried, but I want to retire from the force now. I want; no, I *need* time to make Beth mine. I dial Britt, but her abrupt "What" puts me on edge.

"Hey Darlin', I haven't seen you in a while. Is everything okay?"

"Now I know damned well that you talked to Beth today. She told you I am alive. You are not worried about me, so what could you possibly want?" Wow, who was this bitch? Sure, Britt is tough sometimes, but not like this.

"Brittany, you know full good and well, I worry about you. You are my partner, but you are my friend first. Beth said you were working hard and I hadn't seen you in a while. I want you in my office in one hour with an explanation." She loved to be dominated. I have seen her come just by having someone push her buttons hard enough. Can't be rough with our Britt, but firm will get her coming every time.

"I'm on my way, Sir," and she hung up. That's what I am talking about. I need to get my naughty princess to call me Sir. She is the only one I have ever had that called me Graham. In the club, all the women except Britt call me Sir. I have never topped Britt; she is more than I ever wanted. She is gorgeous, but I don't share well. Like Britt, I am turned on by showing my goodies around. My goodies are my subs' beautiful bodies. I would love to strip Beth bare and stand her on the bar so I could lick her while everyone fantasizes about what they will never have, because no one touches what's mine. Britt would never be happy with a dominate that didn't let her dominate a little herself. She needs a couple that will let her be in the middle of them. She puts on a good show, though. We had a couple here that she hit it off really well with.

That was the most I saw of her. She was here every night for months until they moved away for his job. But damn, that was hot to watch. Every night in our lounge, he would pound on Britt, her pussy, her ass, her mouth, while her hands were all for his wife. I don't know that he ever touched his wife. Maybe another image will help control my cock. The scenes in the bar rarely turn me on any more so I let the images run…Britt with that gold chain around her waist…him lifting her by it while her legs are locked around his waist…him not moving but pulling her and pushing her by her chain...his wife straddling her face as she watched her husband's cock slide into Britt. For as long as I could recall, Britt has been shaved bare. Another image of Britt on her knees in the sixty-nine position while he pounds in her ass and the wife licks Britt's dripping juices comes to mind. That one was hot. He came all over his wife's face and Britt rubbed her soaking self on the woman's face while pulling her clit ring with her teeth. You could hear the woman's screams throughout the whole house. And now I am hard again. I know nothing will stop the blood coursing so hot until I sink into Beth.

The pounding on the door reminds me of my mission; Britt, right. "Come in darlin'."

"I ain't your fucking darlin' but I'm here, so get to the point." Damn; what was her problem?

"Brittany, take a seat and tell me what is going on now." Something is really wrong with her. She follows me as I walk to the couch and plops down. Now I see why Beth says she behaves like a child. "Tell me." Her hands are freezing. It's like a thousand degrees outside, so how could she be cold? "You're avoiding me and Beth. She says she has talked to you, but you seem distracted and anxious. She thought it was a case, but in the worst of the cases, you come here. You don't go to her for relief from the bad shit; you come here to let that out. What happened?"

In a shaky voice I hardly recognize, she starts, "Ok, so I lost a case. It was terrible. The father was extremely verbally abusive and controlling. He's a real jackass." I knew exactly which case she was talking about. Our paths crossed on the case, as I investigated the allegations. "But the Sheriff's department," she says very pointedly, "never found any traces of physical abuse. So I lost and his wife has to see him every other weekend and every other holiday. He is now suing her for full custody because she is slandering him to the kids."

"Britt, darlin', this is nothing new for you. Is it building up? Maybe it's time to take a break for a while."

"No it's not really the case. The case sucks, but the father started calling and leaving obscene voicemails. At least I think it's the father. See, that's the problem. I can't prove it's him, so the sheriff's department can't stop it. He calls my office, telling me I'm a whore and I deserve to die. He tells me all about the love I stole from him. But the worst part, Graham, is that he mentioned you. He said he knows I'm "fucking that cop" and we stole his love and we will pay for it. He said he knows about our lives and he will ruin us. I was trying to stay away from you to shield us from this fall out. I didn't recognize the father from "The Club". I can't see how he would know. We have only had the one case where I did know the mother from the club and I didn't take the case. I actually keep a client list in my office to make sure I don't miss someone by mistake. I'm freaked and I'm worried about bringing my mess to Beth's door. I have to protect her boys. I can't bring anyone here. I don't want you to lose your pension and have to face the backlash. I don't know what to do."

I know she protects us and I have turned down clients that I knew were facing Britt in court, though she would never tell me. I always do a full background check.

I need to get her something to slow the rise of panic. I walk slowly to my desk to absorb what she told me. She's right; we have to protect the boys. Beth finally told me why they are called letters...it's cute. "You're right. The alphabet boys are first, your safety and Beth's safety are the next priority. My reputation and the club don't really factor in. I turned in my retirement docs today. I have twenty years in. I'm vested, so they can't take it away now. My retirement date is thirty days from yesterday."

Her head lifts to me and she sees *it*.

"You love her!" What? No, I can't love her. She's a princess.

"No, Britt. I just want to be done working two full time jobs." I am so full of shit. I think this pounding tightness in my chest may be love, but how would I know? I picked up the phone and called for tea for Britt.

"Graham," she said as she rose and moved toward me. "It's ok to love her. She is awesome, but she is just a woman. She won't hurt you, but she will mess up. She can be a huge bitch when she wants and she has a temper like, well, a little princess. She has always been doted on and she kind of expects it. Marc taught those boys, and rightfully so, to treat her like she is spun glass. She's a prima donna. The good thing is that she knows it and can laugh about it." She ran her cold hands up my arms winding them around my neck.

"It sounds like you are trying to talk me out of her." She was shivering. I pulled her into my chest and she was so tiny that I had to bend down to kiss her little head.

"No, I want you to have her. I want you for her. You would treat her like the delicate flower she is outside of the bedroom, but you understand even flowers need to be cut down now and then."

What is she talking about? "Cut her down?"

"You know...fuck her until she can't hold herself up."

I got it, and the visual that went with it. Soon, I think I am going to have to have a full feature length conversation with my cock. I'm holding Britt and still get hard thinking about Beth. Yeah, I got it bad for her.

Britt must have felt my hard-on because she rubbed her body against me and then backed up. "You are so whipped," she said on a chuckle. Well, let her laugh at me. Maybe that will help her. "You get hard just thinking about maybe possibly having sex with her."

I pull Britt back and rub my hard on against her stomach in a tease. "How do you know it wasn't for you?"

She was giggling like a little girl now, "You have never gotten hard for me."

"That's not true. I have seen you do some incredible things." I had jerked off with her slung over my lap. That's probably the most intimate she and I have ever been. "I jerked off watching you double team those guys a couple months ago. That was really hot."

"Nope, not the same thing." She pushed her body into me again, I was losing my hard-on, and she knew it. "Okay big guy, picture this. I'm straddling a guy, his hard on shoved deep in me. Another man is behind me in my ass and standing over us is a wet pussy dripping on my tongue, you with me?" She rubs her belly against my only semi hard dick.

"Pretty hot. I am with you." It was a hot visual, but not what I want.

"No, you're not. You're losing it even with me rubbing against you and telling you my fantasies. Now picture this: pretty long auburn hair hanging down a long narrow back, a nice high round ass, slightly wide hips, and full legs. She bends over and you see her hand coming between her legs. See you're so hard, you're going to poke through my shirt." Her laugh is soothing and reassuring.

"Son of bitch Britt, don't stop." I can't help but rub up against her and laugh. I think I have lost my ever loving mind. She pulls away as I move her. "Okay, you're a bitch. But your point is taken." Just then a knock at the door announces the arrival of her tea. "Come in. Please, leave it on the coffee table."

"Thanks." Britt bounds back to the coffee table like she didn't just nearly make me shoot my load on her stomach. What a bitch. I wonder if she has any idea how many times I have plotted her death.

"Okay, tell me more about the calls," I reply as I make her tea. She likes it super sweet, unlike the raving lunatic in blonde curls that is actually going to drink it. "Let's get a game plan."

"There's not much more to say. He calls several times a day, but doesn't say much. Not enough the cops can get a trace and not enough for me to identify the voice, though it is familiar. That's why I think it's the father. But he is smart. He has figured out all the ways the cops have of tracing the number. It's a disposable phone sold at any major retailer. He only talks for about thirty seconds and then nothing. It is starting to creep me out. I have a good security system. I live in a secure building on top of that. I should be okay at home. My office is across the street from the county court house and a block away from the metro police station. The metro cops pushed it to the Sheriff's department because they think it s a family matter gotten out of hand. The Sheriff's department is doing everything they can, but that is squat...."

Why hadn't I heard about this? I was in the station this morning. I should have heard something.

"All right, so let's work on security first. You're right about your building and the security company, so you should be safe at home. Just don't forget to turn it on and make sure you tell your building security about the problems."

"Done."

"Beth has a good home security system. I will be around more once the retirement paperwork gets processed, and you're right– if you keep your distance, she should be fine. The caller didn't mention her at all right?"

"Right, just me, the cop, and his love I took. The sheriff's deputy was pretty pissed that I wouldn't tell him about *The Cop* the caller referred to. I told them I wasn't seeing a cop and that I had several friends who were cops which is true. I often have lunch with members of the force and then with both you and James here. Hell, I have lunch with Luke, the County Sheriff every week. It is in my political best interest to be good to the cops."

"I know and feel free to use my name. We are friends. I am seeing your best friend, so it's only natural for us be closer now. And, hear me and hear me good—I have always counted you as a friend, and there is nothing wrong with that friendship."

"Right, umm, ok, I'll do that. He was kind of pissed and really wanted more information than I was willing to give." I have to get to the bottom of this. How had I not heard about it already?

"So, I will go in this evening and see if I can find anything out. I want you to go down to the bar and find some fun. Sleep here tonight, as no one can find you here. I'll pull out the couch here in the office for myself. You sleep in my room. Nobody knows it's there, so you should be safe enough.

"Thanks, Graham." I could see the stress falling from her shoulders. "Go get your girl. I could hear her frustration that you weren't there." In the worst Scottish brogue I had heard to date, she added, "Give the lass a right good pounding!" and walked out of my office.

"Hey, I'm Irish, not Scottish, you crazy wench," I yelled in my grandfather's burr. She was right, not about the brogue that just hurt, but about the pounding. My girl needed it. I could hear it in her voice when we spoke. I could see it in her fingers as she rubbed her glass in bar this evening. This cock and I are going to go the rounds.

Splashing water on my face to try and get my teenage-like hormones in control, I plotted the best way to insert myself into Britt's investigation without stepping on toes.

Chapter 8
Britt

Graham was right. I needed a distraction. I wasn't exactly dressed for entertainment. Maybe I will pull a page from Beth's book and run around in Graham's shirt later. I didn't mean to let him know how scared I was, but this was the first time I was really frightened. I didn't tell him that my caller told me he planned on ruining "my cop" so no one would touch him. There is nothing anyone could do to Graham that Beth wouldn't overlook, because I think she is falling in love with him. Besides, he knows how to take care of himself.

Damn. There was a packed crowd tonight. At seeing some of my guys waving me over, I feel better already. I always feel a sense of belonging here. It's like coming home for me. The guys get me. I had been at the office when Graham had called with his demand that had made me cream my panties and come running. It wasn't until I was half way here that I realized I would never get to have sex with him. He was Beth's and I know beyond all reasoning she would never share him. He and I have been friends for years, always circling each other sexually but never actually getting there. Now I would never know. I have heard he is far and away the best, but he's always so discerning that not many can tell the tale.

I fit between James and Danny and feel Danny's hand move across my ass. Then he asks, "How's my girl?"

"Horny. How're my guys?" James just grunts low in his throat and turns to look down at me. He is not the most handsome, but he is a good looking guy. Mostly, though, the guy goes down like a pro. He could go on a circuit and make millions at it he is so good. Someone taught that boy well. He keeps this crazy blank face all the time though. He's a cop. Maybe my crazy caller is talking about James. *Deep breath.* I'm not going to worry. He can take care of himself. He is huge and strong. He grabs my shoulders and turns me to face him. I am still in my business suit and he is wrinkling the jacket. I should have left it in the office. Obviously, Danny empathizes and starts pulling it from around my neck and down my shoulders. His touch never sends sparks, but always sends waves of comfort to me. He is good and kind and warm. James lifts his hands for Danny to remove my jacket and then settles them back down on my now bare, save for the spaghetti straps from my camisole, shoulder. I have hardly any tits to speak of, so I don't wear a bra. I just pull a jacket over my camisole because its cooler and I like the feel of silk on my nipples. It makes me feel kind of naked and sexy all day. James inspires the kind of lust that they tell little girls to run from. He emanates bad boy from his motorcycle boots and leather pants to his blank stare and hard calloused hands.

I feel the zipper of my skirt slide down and Danny's hands slip in and rub my bare ass. James is holding me still in his vise like grip. Our gazes lock, but he's watching my reaction to Danny's hands and never gives away his own thoughts. Danny's hands warm my shivering body. My skirt pools around my ankles and Danny lifts my legs one at time taking off my skirt. The lust is building in me and I can feel Danny getting hotter. I have walked around this club naked for years, but today I feel eyes on me. Someone knows who I am. Danny's hands are on my ass, kneading it hard and scraping his jean-clad hardness against me. The rough denim on my skin has my head spinning. The hard hands on my shoulders start to run down my arms. Lifting my arms around James' neck and pulling me to him. I have always received a level of comfort from this play.

The slap on my ass sends a stinging fire straight to my pussy. Again and again, Danny administers a brutal punishing slap. Tears are running down my face, I am leaking. "I'm sorry." I know I am being punished, I need this. I feel safe with Danny taking care of me. A slap comes, and then the warm skin soothed by his hand, followed by another. James teeth in the side of my neck remind me to wait to talk. Again, and again, and again still…oh I know what he wants. I know what I need. "Seven sir, eight."

I can't count anymore because James's fingers are slipping down my belly and his mouth is moving from my neck to my breast. He takes my nipple in his teeth through my silk shirt while Danny is still delivering the punishment. I feel my body bowing forward my ass rising to his hand. I have no control over my body. It belongs to Danny. The fire from each touch is like an iron to my core. "Nine sir, ten sir." The heat is whipping through my body. I'm a ball of nerves lighting at every touch. I can feel my honey running down my legs. James's finger slide over my bared hot skin and flick at my engorged clit even as he and pushes deep inside me and Danny administers more strikes. "Eleven sir."

"Don't come." How was I not going to come with his fingers deep in my pussy his palm flat against my clit, his mouth pulling on my nipple? His other hand was the only thing keeping me upright. The fire, the heat, and the lightning seared my brain.

"One last one pet, just for you." Danny says as James pulls my head down. His hand came up and caught my pussy and ass all in one shot. "Now, come now."

He didn't have to tell me twice. I was already there my head back I could hear the panting and whimpering and Danny's pants unzipping. One of his hands was in my hair and fingers from his other shoved into my throbbing pussy and pulled out my juices. Pushing my head down, my ass went up to meet the big hard on that I knew would feel so good. This was the same scene Graham had told me he jerked off to when he watched it. I wanted to see who else was enjoying themselves. I know what this looks like and I love the eyes on me. I turned to look and felt him push inside me as he pulled my hips back. I am so full of him and I know this is only the beginning. Danny is huge and relentless. James wraps himself around us and pushes Danny onto a bar stool. I'm impaled on that hardness and I can feel him throbbing inside. His body is still but his cock is jumping and making me leak down to him. My head spins at the force and security he provides me. Danny is always so quiet. His hands and expectations lead me, not his words. He told me once that he can talk dirty, but he just doesn't get off listening to himself. I want to hear him and know that I am safe. His hands came around me one on my nipple, and one holding my lower belly back against him. "Just like that my pretty little pet, so tight." I grip him, tightening sending shocks through my body.

James leans over putting his mouth right by my ear "You're a dirty little whore, aren't you?"

What? He knows I don't like that. I may joke about it, but when I am submitting, I need to be petted and loved. I do this because I need to be secured. I know myself and I learned early on that I may not get any attention or affection with my cold reserved family. But with a good strong dominate I can feel loved and touched. I need this because I need to know I am okay and for just a little while someone else will take care of me. "Please James, don't."

"My pretty pet, you know how much you mean to me." Then he pushed against me and pushed his full length into me. My head swings back against Danny's chest, but James pushes in farther and farther. "I'm in. Jesus Britt, I haven't figured out how you stay so tight." His words don't comfort me; instead, they almost feel like a sneer. He isn't usually this way. He has all the words Danny never uses, the words that make my skin prickle and my head swim.

"Like a damn fist on my cock, sweet pet," Danny breathes into my ear and lays his hand on my clit. James grabs my hips and lifts me, almost pulling me off Danny, and then he slams me back down, using his hips to thrust up which pushed Danny almost out and him in, pulling back when I slip onto Danny again. I can feel myself dripping, sweat, tears and honey. All the while, Danny pulls on my clit with small pinches and hard slow strokes. White noise takes over and my head is full of grunts and groans and panting. Both men growling out words, nonsense strings of shits and fucks and damn so good pets. I feel my orgasm coiling in me, deep in the recesses of my brain.

"Harder, now," I cry out. Danny pinches my clit and growls bad pet, and James slams home and my body short circuits electricity running from my core to my nipples rubbing James's chest hair. From my stuffed, full ass to my clit, I am coming and screaming and bucking against them. Nothing can contain the explosion of heat and the sensation of peace as I feel both men pull out of me together. One releases on my ass and the other finishes on stomach. Both men sit down on the stools behind them. James pushes me into Danny's arms, being held like this makes me feel the security and safety I haven't felt in weeks. Graham was right; I needed this. Apparently, Steve the pretty little bartender tonight had set out a wet bar towel for him to clean me.

As Danny wipes me, he tells me in a somber voice that does me in every time, "Bad pet. You came without permission. You made both James and I lose control because you came without us. You know you will only get more of the same if you continue." It's a game we play. He doesn't want a permanent sub, and I'm not sure he is strong enough for me permanently. James is, maybe, but he is so distant I can't get in to find out what he wants. He is usually great with me though, so I am not complaining.

"Hey Steve, hand me a towel, would you? A long neck beer as well, please." Yes, this is James' favorite game. "Danny, our little pet is going to put on a show for the folks that missed out on our fun. Please invite them closer. My fuzzy brain perks up, and my stomach warms.

"Ladies and Gentleman," I hear Danny say as James slams his beer. "Our beautiful little pet would like to invite you to pull your chairs up closer for a show of epic proportions." I can feel my skin prickling and my belly tightening. This is a lot for one night, and I am turned on at the thought of all of them watching me. I feel James lift me onto the bar, Danny lifting my shirt off of me. I look James in the eyes, blank nothing. Danny is full of radiating lust and heat he fuels my lust and fire shoots through my body. People are starting to walk over. I catch some eyes, people I know, some I don't. My body is coiling and getting hot. I can feel my skin prickling at the thought of all those eyes on me. My legs are lifted so my feet are on the lip of the bar. James pulls my legs apart to bare me to the room. I can feel my whole body wanting this.

James looks me in the eyes. "Okay, lay back now and show the folks your pretty little clit." I reach between my legs, my bare lips already wide open and I run my hand along my seam, pulling dripping honey onto my clit. My head is not quite hanging off the bar, it's a good thing I'm short. The air conditioned air mixing with my hot honey sends me spiraling fast. "Come on pet the little pussy that was naughty and came without permission. Give it a good spank for me." I slap my clit and fire roars through my body. "Again, pet. It was very naughty. Sir, how many does she need?"

"Twelve and she needs to count them." Danny knows he is killing me. "Do it pet, now?"

Another slap following by more "two sir, three sir, four oh yes sir, five." There is no way I can get to twelve and Danny damn well knows it. My body is on fire, my clit is so swollen that I feel it throbbing all the way to my hair. My orgasm is coiled in my belly growing and ready to take me over.

"Pet, what do you say?" Danny demands and his words spiral through my body and wrap me in more heat, safety and warmth.

"Sir, six sir." I can barely breathe the words.

"That's enough for now," James says gravely. "We'll get back to that." Apparently, it is affecting him as well. I also hear the slap of skin on skin; someone is jacking off. That just makes it hotter. I want to see it, but I know I can't lift up; the punishment would be too great. My skin is on fire and I can feel myself leaking on my ass. I feel the cold rub against my hot opening. "We are going to bottle those sweet cunt juices." The fire is taking over my body as the cold slowly invades me. I feel the flare of the bottle against my lips. Only the neck is pushed in and I feel myself tightening on it. My throbbing walls want something, anything, in me. I feel my body involuntarily trying to pull it in. It is cold, but it does not cool my body.

"Look at our beautiful little pet. She is always so responsive and willing. Anyone want to come up and kiss that swollen clit and see if we can fill my man's beer back up?" Heat shoots through me as Danny's words work through my fog filled brain.

"Fuck, oh fuck." I moan as I feel the bottle twist and hear Danny announcing to twist, not push. I feel hot lips pull on my clit. My back arches from the rising electricity and the lips are gone. Then there is cold against it with a hot tongue. I am lost to feeling the rise and fall over and over again. No one person stayed long enough to get me all hot there. Finally, I know whose mouth is on me. He knows what I like. With the bottle twisting and plunging in and out, his fingers slide around and slip into my honey-soaked ass. I can't feel anything but him licking at me like I am his favorite treat. Finally, he doesn't pull back, the crest is right there.

"Come for him pet and make it good." I fall and wave after wave rack my body. My back arches and my hips rise to his mouth. I feel the bottle now warmed from my skin being pulled from me as I am lifted like a rag doll and handed to Danny to hold my thighs open around James's hips. My head rests on Danny's shoulder and I feel the hot stream of come as it splashes my pussy. James is grunting his release. It's so hot against my skin, but I can only feel the hum of my body and feel of hands and hot sperm. Danny hands me back to James, who holds me over his knees while Danny finds his release against my ass. I feel his skin as he rubs his himself in his cum, using it to spread it over my ass, against my hole, it's so hot, I feel my own cream running down my leg mixing with James's cum and Danny's cock mixing it all up. I know I can't stand up, but I know I don't have to right now.

I can hear James asking the bartender for a room upstairs. I can only form thoughts and images, not words, and then I can say, "Office. Take me to the office." Since none of the guests know how to get to the office, the bartender has to show James the way.

I hear James muttering what a nice set up it is. All I can think about is Graham works damn hard and deserves it and he must love me because the bed is already pulled out and made. James tucks me tight without cleaning me up. My head hits the pillow and I am asleep.

I feel the bed dip…Graham. He forgot that I don't sleep in his room. "Graham, go away. I'm sleeping here." Didn't he see me? "I had a rough night, so leave me alone." The sleepy fog in my brain clearing out when I feel him slide closer to me. "What the hell Graham? Get off me." His hands sliding up my body are rough and calloused pushing my hands over my head. I know he won't hurt me, but what is he doing?

"Hang on. I have to do just this one little thing." It was such a quiet whisper, but I couldn't tell what he was doing.

"I'm awake now. What are you doing?" I hear the click at the same time I feel the cold metal press on my wrist fast and efficient. What is he doing? "No, I don't want this. No, Graham. No!" He is so much stronger than me and he pulls my other wrist up and click. I am swamped in fear. I know Graham would never hurt me, but neither would he do this. As he straddles my waist, I feel that he is completely naked. He is grinding into me, his balls on my hip bone. "No, Graham. What are you doing? Don't do this, please." I feel my hot tears slide down my face.

A quiet growl in my ear says, "You dirty little whore. I told you to leave her alone." Graham was the caller? The panic came in waves I started to scream, but I knew, I knew unless someone was right outside the door they would never hear me. I'm the one that made sure the room was sound proof. The whole side of the house was soundproofed. I had to get out of this, bucking and screaming. "You stupid bitch, shut up!" He starts to hit my face and head with his fist. The pain exploded in my skull and I could feel the blackness swamping me.

"Brittany darlin', wake up. The ambulance is on the way. Britt, can you hear me? Oh Britt. Baby, wake up."

"No Graham don't, no please don't. Don't do this. Don't touch me." The pain is throbbing and I can't see. I have to move to get out of here. My wrists are free, so I pull myself to the top of the bed.

"No baby. Don't move. You'll hurt yourself."

"Don't you touch me again." If I am free I can run, so I start to stand but he's right. I can't feel my arms and hot stuff runs down my face. Oh, god. What is it? *Get it off me*! I start rubbing at my face with my arm. Ouch, that hurt.

"No, Brittany. I am not touching you. No one will touch you. The ambulance will be right here for you. I am calling Beth to meet you at the hospital."

Beth, my beautiful Beth. "No, you stay away from her. You stay away from my boys! I will kill you for this, Graham. I will."

"Britt, baby. I can hear the ambulance. Don't move; I am going to go get them." Move? Where was I going to go? I had to get up and leave. I can't do this. He's a cop; why would he call an ambulance? Maybe if I try now, I can stand up, but as I pull myself up, I feel the lights twinkling in my head and darkness takes me.

"Ms. Morressey, can you hear me?"

"Huh, yeah I can, but it is too bright to see you." A dark smoker's voice, I should know him. "Who are you?" Then the face walks into my vision. It is Sheriff Carver.

"Luke, it was Graham."

Chapter 9
Beth

"Britt what are you saying? Are you saying Graham raped and beat you?" Why would she say that?

"Sweets, why are you here? What's wrong with me?" Oh dear lord let me be able to fix what is going to be broken in her when I tell her.

"Britt, we need to talk to you about the assault." Said the Sheriff

"I told you that it was Graham. Why won't you listen?"

"I understand you think Deputy McDell was the offender. Can you tell me why you think that? Please, Britt. You have seen this before, so you know I have to have your statement." The big hulking sheriff, who is apparently Graham's boss, turns to him with death in his eyes. "Leave, McDell."

"Sir, I will be right outside." Graham lets go of my hand and walks away. My heart hurts.

With softer eyes and tone, he continues, "Now tell me, Britt, why you think McDell did this. Let me hear the whole story from the beginning."

"He is the only one that knows how to get into the office, except for a few of the staff members. The office is off the kitchen but the door is hidden and only Graham knows I was sleeping there."

"Britt, why were sleeping in his office?" I could feel the Sheriff's eyes on me.

She sounded like she was talking through cotton, "I was getting calls from a crazy guy who told me to stay away from his love and other crazy stuff. He threatened Graham. I didn't know how he knew we're friends but he told me he knew that I was sleeping with him and he was going to make Graham pay for me ruining his love."

Of course, the sheriff asks the stupid questions, the ones I don't need the answers to. No, she is not having sex with Graham. They have been friends forever…blah blah blah. "Britt, what happened today?" Why wasn't the Sheriff keeping her on point she has rambling about investments and buildings.

"I got a scary call and then I got another from Graham right after. He told me you were worried about me and he said that he could hear something was wrong by my voice. He told me that I needed to make an appearance so he could make sure I was okay. I was so shaken by the call and he genuinely sounded concerned so I went to the club. I met him in his office. He made me tea and I told him about the calls and how scared I was. We talked about keeping you and the boys safe. He told me he was going into the station right away, anyway, and would check into it and see if he could help. He told me after he got off duty that he was going to your house and then he would be back. He told me to stay in his bed and he would sleep in the office. He said I was safe there."

"You should have been the club has great security. You made sure of that."

"Yeah, that and I made sure his office is soundproof. The girl he was dating when we built the office was a screamer and use to drive me nuts." Oh, gross. I so didn't want to hear that.

She seemed so calm and I was falling apart inside "Tell me what happened Sweets to make you think Graham did this." I can only think please don't let it be Graham. I don't think I can deal with this.

"So I went to the bar, played a little–okay, well a lot– and then made my way to the office. The couch was already made up and I didn't want to sleep in his bed. That is his space, not ours. I was trying to respect him. I woke up to him leaning over me telling me he was fixing it and to just hold on. Then I was handcuffed so fast, it took me a minute to figure out what happened. He straddled my hips and started yelling at me about how I am such a dirty little whore. He also told me to leave you alone."

"Me? He used my name?" Wasn't the Sheriff going to do anything?

"No. He said 'I told you to leave her alone.' When I started fighting and screaming, he hit me so hard that I blacked out. I woke up to him shaking me telling me that he called the ambulance, but I should lay still. He wouldn't let me get up until he heard them downstairs. Then he left and I tried to stand up and blacked out again."

"Britt, this club, it's a sex club right?" At her slight nod, the sheriff looked like he swallowed a fish whole. "Graham told me you and he own it together, is that right?" Another small nod from Britt "Do you bring men to the office for sex?"

"No I have never had sex in the office, Graham's apartment, or any other room other than the designated areas for the guests. I try to respect it because it really is Graham's club. I'm just an investor."

"Do you ordinarily sleep there?"

"That does happen. I never sleep in Graham's bed, but I do sleep in the office on semi regular basis, maybe once a month."

"Are these planned in advance? Or spur of the moment?" What is he getting at?

"Usually, if I drink too much or play too hard, I never planned it was more…like a conscious thought, I can do this and just sleep here."

The questions went on and on, stuff we all knew. They were friends, he has never threatened her, and in fact quite the opposite he is very protective of her. I could see she was at her limit.

"Listen sheriff, I know you have lots more to ask her. I know she says Graham did it. I want you to please leave. You can ask her more later. Go investigate it and please prove he didn't do it. It will kill her to think he did this to her. Sweets, I have just one more question. How did you get to the office?"

"James carried me. The bartender let him in and he locked up when he left me."

"What is James's last name so I can make sure you were safe and locked up when he left?" Finally, the sheriff asks an intelligent question.

"It's Officer James Simmons. He's a patrolman with Phoenix metro."

No, that can't be…that can't be right.

"Britt, are you sure of his name?"

"Yes, of course."

"Britt, creepy cop is Officer James Simmons, and he's a patrolman with the city."

"What's a creepy cop?" the sheriff asked.

"He's my personal fan that while creepy, I was recently informed by his captain is not illegal or even necessarily wrong." I proceed to tell the sheriff all my sorted details. "How many officers could have the same name?"

"We are a large city. It's a fairly common name, but the same name and position, not likely. Brittany, I am going to let you get cleaned up and settled down. I will be back in the morning to get your full statement with an accounting of all the activities and participants of the night."

"All right."

Graham stepped inside the room as the Sheriff walked out. I could feel Britt tense where I was holding her hand. I tried to school my face into a mask of understanding. He couldn't have done these things, but I wasn't letting him upset her either.

"Brittany, I did not do this to you. I would never hurt you. You are one of the few people I really love and you know if you search your heart I am not the kind of man that does this.

But I promise I will find out who did it and I will kill him. You call me if you need me, please." Turning his steely eyes on me, he adds, "Beth, I am going to call you to find out how she is. Don't think for a second that you can block me or lock me out. I love you both."

Like that, he was gone. Did he just tell me he loved me? My life is truly screwed up. *This is so not about me. Focus.*

"Britt, you have to know what happened to you. I am going to read you the doctor's notes. He was in here just a little while ago and left me a list. Starting at the top and working our way down: he cut your hair, you have a severe concussion and you have a hairline fracture of the skull. You have massive bruising and swelling over most of your face, neck, breasts and chest. Your cheekbone was broke, but not dislocated and should heal fine. Your hair will grow back and your face will heal nicely." She kept running her hands over the areas I was talking about with tears running down her face.

"Hey, if we get it all out, we can fix what's broken and move on. You have cuts on your stomach, most likely from the broken beer bottle they found in the bed with you." Oh how do I say this? "Britt you were raped, repeatedly and brutally. Your rape kit showed massive trauma and the doctor removed shards of glass from your entire body." Nope, I can't tell her that right now. I scan the page again but I know this shit by heart. Every word on it is indelibly imprinted on my brain. "Your inner thighs and legs are cut up and bruised as well. "You have several stitches in multiple places around your body, but you will heal and most of the damage while awful was not permanent or life threatening. The doctor is watching for internal bleeding from the obvious repeated blows to your body and you lost a significant amount of blood." The pounding stone in my belly is back. "If Graham had been just a little later getting you to the hospital, you would have bled to death." At this try as I might I can't keep the tears at bay. I will not cry. I have to take care of her. She is so strong and he broke her. I didn't think she was breakable.

Like she can read my mind, she says "Like a willow tree, Hun. I don't break."

"Knock it off, Britt. You are not taking care of me. The tears are there, they aren't going anywhere because I can't stop them. But I am not crying for you. No pity, only strength and love. Right! We are strong, we are capable, and this will not kill us!"

"Aw Sweets, you can't dominate me. But I will submit, I think you need it." Her voice is reedy and thick with tears. However, the fear in her eyes is what scares me the most.

"You're a bat shit, crazy bitch. You are going to be in the hospital for a few days. I will be here with you and when you get out, you are moving in with us. They're already packing your lacy under things."

"No, Beth. I have to go home." Was she crazy? Did she just hear what I told her?

"Okay, I will have them pack my lacy under things and I will move to your little tiny condo with my two giant, smelly boys. But you won't be able to take care of yourself; you are going to need help. This is not loan repayment; this is the girl I love bestest needing me. Where would you be Britt, if it were me?"

"All right, Beth. Sometimes you're such a bitch. Now I'm tired. Leave me alone."

I reached over and turned off all the lights plunging the room into darkness. As I was turning away to find my chair and e-reader, I realized she was panting. Oh god, Britt. I flip on the light over the bed and see her eyes wide and panicked. "Hush, hush, I'm here," as I stroked her head and tried to figure out how to bring her out of her shock. "Britt, tell me what you see." Meanwhile, I push the nurses' call button.

"He smells like cheap beer. Graham hardly ever drinks beer. Why is he doing this?"

"Is he tall? Let's look at him." This use to work with the boys when they would have bad dreams, we would give the monsters faces then we could slay them. "Let's make him real so I can slay him for you."

"He's tall, big and very strong. I am surprised that Graham is so strong. He keeps talking quiet and whispering until he is shouting. I thought it was the father in my case, not my best friend. How can he do this?" I can hear, not the fear, but the absolute broken heart at knowing she was betrayed so badly.

"Yes how can I help you?" The nurse's voice breaking up the quiet almost gives me heart palpitations.

"We need something to relax her. She is panicking and scared."

"I'll be right in." Her description does sound like Graham. What if she is right and it is Graham? How will we untangle her life from him? He will go to jail, if I don't kill him first.

"Britt, baby, you are going to be okay. You don't have to see him again."

"Beth promise me he won't go near the boys. I don't want him around. Promise me." There is so much fear in her voice and I will promise her anything to soothe it away. I'm looking for places on her face, head, or neck to stroke just to get her to sleep. The nurse injects something in the IV.

"You let me know if she needs anything else. This should help her sleep."

"When can she shower? I want to get her cleaned up as soon as possible." She has cum in her hair and she is covered in blood and filth that I can't even think about. I can feel it as I run my hands down her.

"The rape kit is done. She can shower as soon as she wakes up, but not by herself."

As I sit by her bed humming the nursery rhymes my babies always loved, as it's the only thing that comes to my mind in stress, I try to put together the events of last night. I called Graham when I went to pick up the boys. At about one o'clock, he said he was at the station looking into a case. He said he was going to do some work and head home around three o'clock. He said he would be at my house by nine to take me to breakfast. We were going to spend the day together. He called me about three-thirty and told me he was on his way to the hospital. I am sure his boss would know or could find out when he left the station. It had to have taken some time to inflict the kind of damage done to Britt. I wonder if the cops would know how to find that information. Maybe Graham would know...no, I can't ask him. If he did this, he might lie and I just can't be sure.

A quiet knock on the door wakes me. "Mom, I brought her some clean clothes and stuff."

"J., how did you get here?" My sleep addled brain hardly processes where I am.

"Graham called me and told me that Auntie need clean clothes, soap and all her good smelly things. He told us she was hurt. Mom, what happened to her?"

"Graham called you, at home?" Why was he calling my house? "Yup. He called me and told me to be ready he was going to bring me to the hospital so I could drop off her stuff. He's waiting in the hall to take me home."

I don't want him around my kids. I promised her. If he did this, what else could he do?

"J. thank you for bringing her stuff. She was brutalized. I don't want you to worry or even look too closely at her, as she wouldn't want that. But sit here and if she wakes up, come get me." I pointed him into a chair as far from her as possible. I didn't want him to see her like that, but mostly I knew she wouldn't want it; I worried too that if she saw another hulking male when she woke up it would scare her. "J., is P. at home still? He didn't come, did he?"

"Nah. He didn't wake up to the phone. I figured he has late practice today so I left him a note and let him sleep in for once." Walking through the door, I saw Graham in a plastic hospital chair outside her door. He looked awful. His slightly wavy hair looked like he had been running his hands through if for hours. His eyes were red and swollen. Had he been crying? He was on his feet the minute the door clicked closed behind me. The lust punched through me–he still looked incredible. How could I want him if he did this to her? "How is she? Fuck, Beth. I can't even think about what happened to her in my house." Is he serious? He did it, he planned it, and of course it happened in his house?

"Graham, go home. You have no business being here. Stay away from my kids. That is overstepping the line."

If it was possible, he paled even more and his hand went to pull at his hair. It's a wonder the man wasn't bald. "Beth, you can't think I did this to her. I love her; I was looking into her investigation. I was on the phone with you when it happened."

"Graham, we spoke for two minutes. That's it. I hardly know you and she is adamant it was you. She knows you and she loved you, she wouldn't make a mistake like that. I have to take care of her. My priority has to be her and the kids. I don't have room to trust, and I can't take your word for it. Please, go home now."

"All right Beth. If that is what you want." I could see the hurt and pain; he wasn't even trying to mask it. It was tearing out my soul. "Call me when you figure out how wrong you are." With his back to me he raised his hand with a wave and walked away. My heart felt like it was in a vise. The sweeping pain caused me to fall to my knees. I was watching him walk away and I knew he wouldn't come back. He couldn't come back. He had told me about trust, about real trust that meant opening yourself up to someone so completely. I had trusted my husband that way. I knew how it felt. Graham had told me he never felt that way, but I saw it. I recognized the look of the crack when that trust is broken. He had trusted me and I did not in return. *I can't do this*. After standing and dusting my knees off, I walked back into her room.

I can't stop the tears, but I can work through them. "J., please take my car keys and go home." I know he's underage, but the kid has been stealing my car for two years now. I know he can drive. I finally took him out driving to make sure he at least knew how to do it and didn't kill himself. "Take P. to practice and have him get a ride home. After you drop him off, bring me a change of clothes." I started rifling through the bag he brought me, "and my cell phone charger. I will be staying here until she is released. Then she's coming home with us. Go to her apartment pick up some of her clothes." I started writing him a list. "Grab the shampoo and face cream out of her shower, she is going to want her things. Mine will work for now, but she is going to need her stuff soon." Tearing the paper off, I saw my son, too young to drive standing like a grown man. Digging in my purse, I handed him my credit card. "Stop on the way to practice, get P. pancakes and get yourself something. Stop and pick both Britt and I iced coffees and drop them off here before you head to her house. Once you are done at her house, go home get a nap and give me call when you wake up." He kept nodding I knew he wouldn't forget the kid had a mind like a steel trap. He probably didn't need the list I wrote him, but it made me feel better to be doing something for her.

"Beth, Beth what's going on?" I pushed J. out the door and headed to Britt, taking her hand.

"J. brought you some clothes, feel up to a shower? We are going to get you cleaned up and that will help you feel so much better." I hope it does.

She nodded and then moaned, "It hurts to nod."

I feel a smile spread across my face. "I'll bet it does; your head is broken, and here I thought nothing could get through your thick skull." Her lips turned up; she was going to be fine. "Okay, give me just a sec. I am going to take the stuff in the bathroom and get it set up." I pushed the nurses call button. "When she comes on, tell her you're taking a shower and I'm helping. We don't need anything, but they wanted me to tell them. Oh and also, ask them if they will come change your bedding while you are in the shower." She nodded again, moaned and closed her eyes.

I didn't want her to see herself yet. She was black and blue all over, and I could hear her talking to the nurse. I hung a towel over the mirror and started the shower before I put out the bath product and her clean clothes. I couldn't keep my thoughts from running to Graham. For weeks now, he has been all I can think of, but now it hurts to think of him. He and the look on his face that was going to haunt me forever, just hurt. It's a forever I wouldn't get to spend with him. Did he do this to her? I only knew him for two weeks, but she knew him for years. She gave him millions of dollars and trusted him to not betray her.

I hope she doesn't lose clients because of this, but I knew she couldn't work now. My mind keeps running a million miles an hour. Graham, Britt, Graham, Britt...I can't slow it down. Britt has a partner at the law firm he would pick up her caseload I didn't need to worry there. I would call him in the morning. She couldn't get fired, as it was her practice, but she could lose her client base. That would be the worst for her, because she loves what she does. Okay, now that the water is hot, I return to Britt and see a nurse helping her to sit up. "You will change her bedding, right?"

"Of course, while she is in the shower. Are you going to be able to help her? Would you like some scrubs to change into when you are done?"

"Thank you, but no. I will just take them off and put them back on when we are done."

"You're getting in the shower with her naked?"

"I'm not a hospital professional, I'm her-"

"Leave her alone. I've seen her goods before. They're great and it will make me feel better."

Leave it to Britt to make everyone just as comfortable as possible. The nurse is choking on her own thoughts. I slide my arm around Britt's tiny waist, "okay, on the count of three we are going up, you ready. One, two, big deep breath, and up we go." I feel her whole body shutter in pain and she is trying to stifle a deep moan. "Let it out, Britt. It will help to release the pain. Remember, your words, not mine."

"Fuck, fuck, fuck on a stick, it hurts." The nurse can't take her eyes off us. We are just standing, me holding most of Britt's weight.

"I know it hurts, but pain is good. We like pain because it reminds us that we aren't dead." I'm making it up as I go. I remember being told that once in a yoga class, the instructor almost got her ass kicked that day. "First step is just like a chorus line. Sweets, start on your left and step."

She was moving and we were in the shower before we knew what hit us. I sat her on the stool under the spray still in her hospital gown while I stripped and stepped in with her. Standing behind her, I washed her hair, just gently rubbing her scalp, she had only small stitches here and there and the doctor said as long we didn't rub the stitches she could wash her hair normally. Running shampooed hands down her neck and shoulders, I tried my best to be gentle but I could hear her winces and hisses when I would hit the bite marks. I needed to get every trace of him off of her, though. J. had been good; he had packed the baby soap I had in my travel bag for when I was sunburned and blistered. I removed the hospital gown fully and started on her front. Her breasts were full of bruises and bite marks and little stitches where the doctor repaired the bigger bites and slashes. He had a plastic surgeon do the repairs and they told me she should have little scarring. I ran my hands over her body like she was a child. The whole time I was talking, I have no idea about what…football, the house, maybe I was singing again. I just needed her clean. It was time to have her stand and I knew this was going to hurt her. I moved the stool out of the shower put her hands on the wall and had her spread her legs for me.

Britt true to form says, "Oh, baby, while you're down there, please make it good." I just bite my lip; I know this isn't going to be good.

"Honey you ain't ever had anything like me before," and I start rubbing her inner thighs. The pain almost makes her knees buckle. "Hang on Britt. It's only going to be bad for a minute." I slide my hand up and start laying the suds against her lips and she cries out, they are all sliced up, little nicks here and there. The doctor told me to keep it clean; I think he wanted her as clean as I did. He told me to use soap once and then just keep it rinsed. My response to him was to tell him I had giant twins vaginally. I know all about tearing and stitches. There were lots of other things the doctor told me that she is just not ready for. I swipe my hand up to her anus and I know it is just as bad, but this time, I am holding her with one arm high around her waist and one hand swiping across her body as quickly, efficiently, and softly as I can. The sprayer on her soft tissues makes her cry out but we are done.

With my hands around her waist and our foreheads against the wall of the shower, I hold her while she sobs. My tears are running, but I will not give in. I will be strong for her. I see the nurse out of the corner of my eye watching us. She probably came at the sound of her calling out. I realize that I am rocking her and singing my kid's stupid nursery songs again. It's all I know, but it seems to calm her so I don't stop until the sobs stop racking her body and she is no longer shaking. I am holding her up fully, though, and I know I can't carry her out. "Britt honey, are you ready to get dress and rest a minute? Let's get you out of this bathroom. I will rub you down with that honey scented cream you like and you can sleep for a few hours."

"Beth, I have wanted your honey cream for years."

I hear myself chuckle.

"Yup, you're going to survive Britt. If you get through this, I will rub that honey cream on your face until you don't know your own name." The gasp draws my attention but it's not

115

Britt's and I don't care about the nurse. "Now lean your head back on my shoulders. Let's get your weight on your feet."

"You promise, baby, anything?" I'll do anything to take away her pain right now. I have always known Britt uses sex to form attachments. We have talked about it before and even she recognizes that she had a terrible childhood full of privilege and wealth. But she was never shown true affection or attention. A series of nannies and boarding schools and irregular if nonexistent visits from her parents was her idea of normal until she was an adult. When her parents died in a car accident her grandfather didn't even bring her home for the funeral. She learned she can get the affection and closeness through sex that she doesn't really form any other way. "Whatever you need Britt," She stands up, naked and dripping, and we leave the shower. I wrap a towel around my body and then start drying her. I slide a giant football shirt and pair of P.'s boxer briefs on her. J. really does know how to take care of her. The soft cotton of the worn briefs shouldn't hurt her too badly and luckily they are long enough, they don't rest on the cuts on her thighs. She has shared these same clothes with my son for years. I don't think these boxers even fit him anymore. But he keeps them, she wears them and I wash them.

"My jammies, thank you," I start rubbing cream on her feet and legs one at a time, lifting her shirt to get her belly and breasts. She lifts her chin like a puppy getting a belly rub and arches into my hands. At least she hasn't lost her spark. I work my way around to her back, laying kisses on the unbroken skin. I know I won't hurt her here.

Standing in front of her, I kiss her on the lips. Its small kiss full of all the love I have for her. "You're a survivor and I will always be here to watch you shine." It's something she use to tell me after Marc died. She would tell me eventually my shine would come back. Taking her hands, I pull her back to the bed one step at a time. Once she is settled in bed, I walk back to the bathroom and drop my towel with her dirty sheets.

As I walk away, I hear her say "nice ass" so I give it a little slap for her benefit. The minute I am in the bathroom alone, the tears begin again. Did he really do this; it's the only thing my brain can process. Someone sliced her up. She will never have children–not that she wanted to–but he damaged her so badly she can no longer carry children. I don't know how I am going to tell her. I can't see Graham wielding a beer bottle, but then who would? Only a crazy person does that. I know full good and well, you can't see crazy. The thought she could have died sends a cold shock through my body. If I had lost her, I don't know how I would survive that. She is my whole world.

Rebekkah Rogers

Chapter 10
Graham

How can she think I would do this? I would never hurt Britt. I have never touched her other than the mocking tease here and there.

"McDell–my office now!"

He better have some leads and a damn good idea who did this. The public is going to have a field day with this and the shit is going to rain.

The Sheriff's voice is booming when I open his door. "The most prominent, well respected child advocate attorney in the state is raped and beat in a sex club owned by a lead investigator for the Maricopa County Sheriff's Department. The Attorney is loudly pointing her finger at said investigator as her attacker." That's my headline, jackass. "I need your badge and gun. Obviously, you can't work the case."

He thinks I did it. I have worked under him for eight years and was his partner for three. He taught me everything I know about investigations and police work. I have been with this department for twenty years. "Your loyalty is a cool breeze, jackass. You know I didn't do this. Yes, I own the club that Britt and I built. I have never hurt a woman. I have never even had a perp complain. I don't get angry and you damned well know it. You promoted me because I don't have that rage or need for power. Rape and whatever else he did to her is a power play and nothing more. You can have my gun; my badge is yours the end of the month, anyway." Handing him my gun is like cutting

119

off my arm, but the badge? He can shove up his ass. "But no way did I do this."

"We are waiting on the rape kit and DNA testing. I want you tested. Have you had sex with her?"

"NO! Never, well not sex no, but oh hell." Yeah…this is going to go over so well. "So her best friend came to the club about two weeks ago. We all played a little. No penetration for either of them. Touching, talking, but I jacked off on Britt's leg. If you ask the staff, they will tell you that's the farthest I have ever gone. That night was one of my most active nights since we started the club. I am very particular and I have always respected my badge, so I never did anything that could be leaked to jeopardize it. Look Luke, we have been friends for years and you know me better than anyone out there. This club is just business, a way to retire. Britt is a business partner." Sitting in Luke's office without permission is like taking his right nut without permission, but I'm doing it anyway.

"Shit, Graham. Cops retire and do security, not pimp."

"I AM NOT A PIMP." *Deep breath.* I can't kill him. I can't kill him. He is just worried about his reelection and probably Britt, since he always treated her like a treasured daughter. "I do not hire women to fill my club. I hire staff to clean, tend bar, cook, and serve food, nothing else. The women that frequent the club are usually brought in by a partner. They like it, so they get their own membership, or…."

"Or what Graham are any of them forced?"

It's like a punch to my gut. Did he think that I would force women to have sex? "Screw you. I was going to say or they decide they don't like it and leave never to come back. They do have to sign a non disclosure form before they can get through the doors, though."

"Why do you have them sign the non disclosure form?"

What a stupid question. "Umm, well, my partner is—how did you say it?—one of the most respected *attorneys* in the state. She is all about the paperwork. Both she and I have outside lives to protect, as do most of our clients, if not careers, family, and friends. They wouldn't want their sex lives leaked."

"Who else do you have in that club of yours?" Was he serious?

I shake my head like he's a child. "Nuh-uh. Not without a warrant. Britt will get her memory and she will remember it wasn't me. She will skin me alive if she found out I gave up her club without a fight. You want that information, you ask her. I love her. She's a bright shiny spot in a shitty world. Please, get a warrant. I won't fight it and I will happily turn over *everything* to you. It shouldn't be too hard for you to get one to search my office for evidence in the rape. That client list may just be in plain sight on my desk if you happen to look in the yellow folder in my bottom drawer. Now, can you please question the staff about who she was with? I think I know, but if I'm right, you aren't going to like it anymore than your current suspect."

"Are you seeing that pretty brunette?" Brunette? She was so much more. Her hair was auburn with streaks of red and chocolate running through it. Her words run through my head on a constant loop. She would never trust me again. She didn't want me around. Her face was so full of fear and pain and I wanted to kiss her and take it all away, but she wouldn't even let me close enough to shake her hand.

"Well, until last night, I thought I was." Keeping the rage in check was never the hardest part of this job. I just didn't care enough to get mad, but I was finally starting to feel my limbs when I would talk to Beth. I could feel my whole body getting warm and my soul lightening. She doesn't want me. She thinks I'm capable of tearing a small woman to shreds.

I must not have schooled my face as well as I wanted to. "You were falling for her? Did she kick you out of the hospital or yell at you?"

"She told me she didn't really know me; I need a drink. What do you have stashed in that drawer?"

Pulling a bottle of scotch from his drawer, he sucked his coffee cup dry and dumped another cup that had pens in it. "Jesus, you don't do half way. This is a $500 bottle of scotch are you still on a sheriff's salary?"

"You remember that pretty little girl we found in her mother's boyfriend's basement?" He opened the bottle and poured it into the cups that weren't worthy of the high end scotch. "Your partner bought me this as a thank you for all my devoted hours."

"I remember that. She was the dad's attorney and the little girl's dad was worried sick. His little girl was missing, wasn't it a routine custody battle gone seriously wrong. We looked for her for days. We even searched the house and didn't find her. I wasn't on that case. I had that murder suicide out on the reservation I was working with the tribe at the time. What happened to the girl?" That was an ugly month and partly the reason that retirement looked so seductive.

"Finally, I asked dad if he knew any of mom's friends. He mentioned a guy she had been seeing while they were married. She had stashed her daughter with this drug addled waste of space. He forgot to feed her and kept her locked in her room.

"She bought the department lunch, I remember." That was the month that Britt was in the club day and night. That case tore her up. I had talked to her every day. How could she think I would hurt her now?

"She and I sat up all night in her office talking about options and solutions this is what she has in her office. I commented and she brought me one the next day. She's a good girl; she doesn't deserve what happened to her." He just kept shaking his head.

I know my grimace was fierce. "No one deserves that. You know I didn't do this. You know I was here until just a little after three. I couldn't possibly have had the time to do that." The disgust was evident even to my own ears.

"I know you didn't do it. I have surveillance tapes that put you here from eleven o'clock, to ten after three. You couldn't have made it to the club, gotten up there, and had time to do that damage. Your call for the ambulance was at three-twenty-six. Your call to Beth was at three-thirty. I checked her cell phone before I left. Tell me: why does she think it's you?"

That's the million dollar question.

"How would I know? Maybe because she woke up to me trying to keep her still for the ambulance, maybe he told her it was me, maybe he looks like or is built like me, maybe I was safe for her so she deluded herself into thinking it was me when she came around?"

"That is a whole lot of maybes Graham."

"I know, but I don't really know the answer."

"Tell me about her. I guess I don't know her as well as I thought I did."

Tell him about her? No way. She needs to be protected. I would never let my guard down again, and no one would hurt her. "Eventually, she is going to remember that it wasn't me and she is going to castrate me for talking to you. You know that, right? She doesn't need that."

"Yeah, I know, but let's try it anyway." He knows me too well. "This will help us protect her from it happening a second time."

That's the rub: revealing all of Britt's secrets may keep her safer.

I took another long pull of Scotch. Britt always did have good taste. "Britt is very heavy into kink. She couldn't find a club that let her do what she wanted without it being seedy and having a criminal element or prostitution involved. Britt only has sex in public. She has to have an audience to really enjoy it. Or so she says; I have my own thoughts on that. Anyway, Britt wanted someplace she could be safe. I have other proclivities that made me also want somewhere to play that allowed me to be as selective as I desired. I don't want people asking questions. I barely tolerated Britt's questions. I am very selective and will go a very long time between partners until I find what I like. She and I were having beers at a very shady club and discussing what we wanted.

"I thought she was just dreaming. I know I was. A couple of weeks later, she asked me to meet her at a house. I was on duty it was the middle of the day. I honestly thought it was a work call. She was all professional, you know? 'Deputy McDell, I would like your professional opinion, could you please meet me?' I showed up and she had bought the house and wanted me to run her club. She had the business license, the building permits…the whole thing. She said she would do it without me, but we had the same wants and she needed a protector. So, I have been there ever since. If anything happens to her, of which nothing ever has before, the staff knows to call me. When she overdoes it in the club, I collect her and tuck her in for the night, but that is really rare. If I'm on duty, the bartenders have a key to my office and they double as bouncers or sometimes refs if the play gets out of hand or if someone is going too extreme. We run a safe club. Britt is never alone and never unguarded. None of the submissives in the club are ever left without eyes on them. We have security dressed in plain clothes, though most of the guests know them by name."

"Do you have cameras and a security system?"

"We are open twenty-four hours, and we have a security system on all the doors and gates. There is only one way in and out for everyone but Britt, I and the staff. The front gate is manned and you have to present your bracelet that only I hand out."

"Not Britt?"

"No, she could, she just doesn't want to. You also have to be on the list. Once you are in the gate, the grounds and surrounding area are all on video as well as security does a continuous sweep. Only the valets are allowed in the parking lot. There are gates that block the front of the house from the back on both sides of the house. The valets pull the cars around the back and bring them out the front. There is no access to the guests." I don't know why I have to tell him all of this; he has been in the club.

"So what about the staff they all come in the front?"

"Yes, everyone comes through the front gate. They can pull their cars around to the back and enter in through the kitchen. There is only one way in that way. The staff locker rooms and break room are off the kitchen. My office is over that space, so it is very quiet. The house as it was originally built is all guest space. The kitchen and staff area as well as my apartment and office were built on secondary. My office is a hidden door in the kitchen, most of the staff probably knows it's there, but never venture up there. Up the stairs is a small kind of cramped hallway with three doors. The closest is my office, from my office you can walk through the bathroom to my closet to my bathroom to my bedroom. My one bedroom apartment opens to the same hallway right next to the fire escape door. The fire escape is how the paramedics got to Britt last night. I park my truck right out the door there and I can leave out the rear of the parking lot, only a few know there is a fire alley back there. It is gated off and security mans it, but that is how I get in and out. I don't feel like I am living under a microscope that way. Though I know security keeps a log of my comings and goings, they are under very strict instructions that only Britt, I, and a search warrant can release those records."

"Can I have them?"

"I imagine you will want to include that in your warrant. Don't forget to include all the books as well as all the other records; you will see everything is above board." He was going to go over my club with a fine toothed comb to make sure his precious ass was protected.

"Tell me about the sex".

"Oh, come on. You can rent a video that teaches you all about that." I was not going to make this easy.

"No, jackass, I mean about Britt, tell me about what she was doing that night."

"Get a warrant. I won't have her sexuality used against her in a rape trial." I have seen that happen too often to count.

"Where did the bottle come from?"

"My guess would be the bar?" Stupid questions

"Do you keep a record of who orders what?"

"It's a bar. We keep a record of the amount of alcohol sold so we can restock. The medical records are gathered for our patrons and tell us how much a person drinks and we don't allow drunkenness on site, but no, we don't keep track. I would guess the bartenders could tell you what the regulars drink, though." Was he serious, keeping track of who drank a beer every night?

"What about the private rooms. How do you get one of those?"

"Marabell is our head of security, hostess, and mother hen." She had to be having a hissy fit in her office right about now. I'm kind of glad to not have to be there with her. She is so passionate when she gets angry it is like watching a tornado consume everything in its path.

"Marabell? You have a woman as your head of security?"

"Remember Deputy Munoz? She left because her kids needed her at home and she was getting crap hours. She was tough but didn't have the patience for police work."

"You hired Marabell Munoz? She *was* a tough bitch."

"She still is and that is exactly what we need. She doesn't let anyone get away with anything. She has the memory of an elephant, three strikes and the patron loses theirs privileges for the year, they can reapply again next year. She also monitors and keeps track of the private rooms. She is like a pit bull; you would think her name was on the club."

"So there are cameras everywhere but your office and apartment?" If he keeps pouring more scotch and topping off his glass I am going to have to carry him home.

"Yes, there are cameras in the kitchen that show everyone that goes into my door. I already called Marabell; she is getting them together for you. She will only show you the door to my office. The rest you need to include in your warrant. You will probably need a warrant just for the videos. Marabell will hold on to those like a dog with a bone. She takes her job very seriously." Draining the last of the scotch and standing to leave, I add, "I am going to go home to look at the videos. If I see anything I promise you, I will send it over. I vowed to protect her and I let her down. Please let me know how she's doing and when you get the results of the rape kit, as I would like to know how many guys left there DNA on her. She had his cum on her face; there was no way that she wouldn't have cleaned that up if it wasn't him."

"You let me know what you find out. I want to know everyone she talked to all night. I want names and addresses so I can get the DNA testing warrants…yours, too."

"I did that first thing. It was fun to jack off with the forensics team watching me." Yeah, that was a laugh. "They took blood, semen, spit, and my soul. Please, have them tested."

It didn't matter that I left my soul on the forensics team's floor, well their bathroom floor really. There was no need for it anymore anyway. The bone cold is nothing new. The marrow freezing is reassuring. It will only hurt for a little while. This is familiar. This is the feeling you get when you shoot someone. You have them in your sights; you wait for hours…sometimes days…and wait, holding still, without letting them know you are watching. Your bones freeze. In the desert where the sands blow over you at one-hundred-fifty degrees, you still freeze. We are good at freezing, or so I've been reminded over and over again. Two years spent as an army ranger sniper before that hip shot ending my army career entirely…damn. The thing still hurts sometimes.

I was very good at my job then and I'm good at it now. Except, of course, Beth meant the most to me and I let her down. I knew it would shred my soul if I let her warm me. Every time she touched me, my body warmed a little more I knew eventually I would have to rebuild the cold. Damn if didn't feel like my soul was shredding now. If only for a little while, only for a minute, I thought the pain will stop. The absolute sense of failure has to stay. Britt was attacked, that is no one else fault. She should have been protected.

I walk through the room and realize that, this is what failure feels like. All eyes know what she said. She said I did it…she knows it was me. I messed up. I should have never let her know that pain. I have been a cop for a long time in a very busy city. I have seen this kind of brutality before. I have seen this before. I should have known.

Run, run…don't walk. Flinging open the door to the Sheriff's office, I exclaim, "You knew, you remembered."

"I am only surprised you didn't."

"How long were you going to let me worry?"

"Nothing we can do about it now. We have his DNA, I am sure of it. There was too much on her for it to not be his. Maybe this is the break we need." I'm going to kill him.

"You knew when you looked at her. Those serial rapes last year, they stopped…what? Six months ago with no sound from him again. They were every month for several months, then nothing. What gives? How did he get to her?" I had to know how he got into my club.

"I don't know, but the suspicion is that he is law enforcement or attached to it somehow. Only someone who had a detailed knowledge of forensics could know how to cover himself so well. He is educated and methodical. He knows how to cause permanent internal damage that won't be life threatening. Britt is the only one he knocked out and I think it is because she knows him."

"She does fit his victim type. She is single, educated, well off, and strongly sexual. Who is he, Luke?"

"He's one of us. I can feel it in my bones. I had to rule you out first. It damned near killed me when she said it was you."

Yeah you and me both. "Alright, so where do we start? Tapes…I will pull all the tapes for entire night, I will have Marabell give me second eyes...."

"No, I will come I will look with you. If we see something, I will get a warrant for all the video. Hell, I'm going to get one anyway. I was writing it up when you walked in here. Let me send it out and I will go with you."

"Come on; I will give you the grand tour, but you know you can't use any of it until that warrant is in your hands."

Walking into the control room, otherwise known as Marabell's room, I ask "Hey Marabell. What did you find?" *Please let her have all the answers.*

"Nothing, Graham. I got a big fat load of *nada*. There's nothing and no one. I had forensics check your locks though before they left. Both the outside and the office door were jimmied open. Guy told me it looked like a professional job."

"Okay. How did he get up my back stairs without you seeing him?"

"Camera was taken out; it took us less than five minutes to get it up and running. Your back door was locked up tight, so we figured it was a malfunction and didn't check. I know I messed up, and I will resign as soon as you get your replacement."

That bitch isn't going anywhere. "Don't be melodramatic. Yes, you did, but it was a mistake. Your guard checked the door, your other cameras overlap back there, and surely we got something."

"Yeah, we got a guy in a hoodie walking across the parking lot. He looks like a vagrant carrying an empty bottle. He keeps his hood up and head down. I have no video of him getting into the lot, of him looking to the cameras, nothing. Then the camera goes out, he is gone, and all is quiet on the western front." We designed this system themselves. There are no blind spots. I spent hours walking the grounds with Marabell to make sure every square inch was covered except my stairs, office, and apartment. I got her raped, my precious, small little

Britt. She trusted me and my perverse sense of privacy got her raped.

"Load it up and let's look at it again." I watch the Sheriff watch the video for a fourth time. He wasn't going to see anything new. The warrant has been received and is being faxed to me while we sit here, but it isn't going to give us anything. Marabell won't let the Sheriff even look at the video of the clients or Britt until the warrant is in her sweaty tired hands. She says she thinks there is something of interest and she really wants to show us,

"Marabell, you are driving me crazy. Please sit and pull up the video you want me to see. Let's look. Luke will keep his unwarranted eyes averted until the fax machine beeps." She must have seen something good because she relented.

Marabell pulled up a video starting with Britt walking into the bar from the kitchen. The time stamp shows it was just after she left my office at ten. She walks straight up to the guys at the bar. I know what's coming, I've seen it before. The woman puts on a hell of a show. Then I know where Marabell's mind is going. James lifts her onto the bar and my only thought is please not tonight, don't let her be doing the beer bottle show tonight. I've heard about her bottle show, but I've never seen it before. The camera view is directly at her front, including a full frontal of her and the beer bottle. Men and women line up to get a taste of her. This is not my thing, but I made a vow a long time ago to not judge anyone's idea of sex. The "What the--" behind him reminds me the Sheriff doesn't have my or Marabell's open mind about sex.

"Is she doing what I think she's doing? I am not really seeing this, am I?" He hands Marabell a piece of paper. It must be the warrant because she rewinds to the beginning of the show.

"No, Luke. You are not seeing it wrong. It looks exactly like it should. Your precious innocent little girl just opened her legs to an entire bar full of people for a taste. She is protected; just look at Danny on her side. He watches everyone and nobody so much as looks at her that he isn't in control of them. She belongs to Danny and he is damn protective. The bartender above her head, he too is watching her face, to make sure she's okay with it all. But Luke, look at the other guy, do you know him?"

"No. Should I? He looks disgusted. This was his idea, he put her up there. He wanted to make her feel depraved." The Sheriff seems to get the weight of the situation.

Marabell gets it. "He didn't though did he? She is beautiful and protected and loved by everyone there. No one is looking to hurt her or cause her pain."

"Beautiful, I don't know about that, but yeah I see what you're saying. It's a little rough for my taste."

"Well, you don't have to taste." Marabell is really rankled by him passing judgment. I have never seen her partake even a small amount in the entertainment here, but I know she will protect our clients with her last breath.

I am going to kill him. He is not taking care of her. She is his responsibility the minute his hands touch her. He took that on, and he is looking at her like nothing more than trash. "Luke the other guy is James Simmons. He's with metro." I knew something was wrong with him. "Marabell, have him–"

"Already done, boss, I sent you an email about an hour ago when I first saw it."

"You only saw it an hour ago?"

"Yes. All feed is monitored in a bank of monitors and there are two guys watching. They aren't watching for couples nuances. Those are done when there is complaint or the staff gets suspicious or edgy about a client." Marabell really was good at her job Graham thought. "I didn't know where to start, so I started at the beginning of the day. I had a lot of footage to cover."

"I want to see her taken to the office." They forward through, showing the bartender open the door for James on the way up and then again on the way down. James kept walking out, got in his car and left. Steve went back to the bar.

"Nothing…nothing else on any of them?"

"Nope, Sheriff," Marabell answered. "Danny stayed at the bar drinking for a few more hours, played a little more then went up, he stays almost every weekend. He's still here, said he would stay as long as you need him." She stood pacing again.

"You can have everything we have got. Your warrant says so, but we don't have *mierda*." Marabell was angry, edgy.

"Marabell, you need a break? How long have you been here?"

"Boss, I have a job to do. I will stay till your Sheriff gets everything on his warrant and then I will go to the hospital. I have to apologize; the poor lady was taken on my watch. I sat in the other room doing nothing while she was being hurt. Then I am coming back here and like it or not, you are getting cameras on your back steps and in the hallway to your office. I will know every hair you lose off your precious head. You bring a pussy up there, I will be able to gauge how wet her damn panties are from my office."

She was radiating rage and pain. This was why I felt that she wasn't a great cop. "Marabell, you did not do this, I was suppose to watch her, we were both duped by a guy who has been doing this for a while. His MO is in and out around security systems in some of the most secured buildings in town. Yes, let's get cameras in there…not in my office and or my apartment, but you can have the hallway lit up like Christmas, if you want." It won't fix what we broke.

"You bring women to your office often, Graham?"

The suspicion in his voice scraped on my skin. "Luke I am not a suspect. My sex life is none of your business. And no I don't." Only Beth had ever been in my office, in my shirt.

Graham knew the sheriff has something he was working in his brain, but he also knew he couldn't be let in on the secret. He wasn't part of the investigation into the other rapes and he couldn't part of Britt's. He would do whatever he could though. "Luke, what have you got? I can smell your brain turning."

"A lot of references to that Officer there, he looked pretty pissed at her, almost like he was angry because it didn't turn out the way he wanted, creepy cop."

That punch to my heart, I was trying to not think about Beth. "What did you say?" I have only heard that reference once. I could see her pretty face laughing in the bar, flushed standing against the car while we were making out like kids, sated in my arms at the bar that first night. Freezing, fuck, my body is freezing again.

"Creepy cop, it's something Beth said in the hospital. She said she was being stalked by creepy cop."

Now my rage was showing. I could feel it and I couldn't control it. "I know, she won't tell me who he is. What does that have to do with this? You think my Beth's creepy cop is Britt's rapist?"

"Doesn't fit; none of the other victims mentioned calls or stalking of any kind and Beth doesn't fit the pattern of victim because of the family. None of the other women had family to speak of."

Marabell, in her brilliant wisdom, said, "None of the other victims were law enforcement. Britt knows him personally. Britt's attack was too personal to not be someone she knows. This guy knows too much to not be part of security somewhere." She is so smart that I want to kiss her.

"You know who it is don't you Luke? You think you do, right. Get a warrant and get him." I have to protect my girls, even if they don't want me anymore. My body is cold all over, my Britt will never be so shiny and I don't want to lose her. Women don't come back from this kind of thing the same though.

My Princess...my sweet Beth is already lost. She wouldn't look at me. She honestly believed I could be this guy. I can never have her body wrapped around me, the light in her eyes warming the darkest part of me. Her laughter late at night when she is tucked up in her bed would slide through my body and remind me there are good things in the world. Because some monster was able to get past my defenses I lost it all. I deserve to lose it I couldn't keep one petite firecracker safe, but I know I will miss it the rest of my life.

Rising, the Sheriff put his hand out, "Graham, stay here. Don't touch the security footage, don't do anything. I can't stress it enough, stay out of the office until the guys are finished. I know you didn't do this. You have a rock solid alibi, but let's keep everything as spit shiny clean as we can. We want to nail this guy."

"Come on, Sheriff," Marabell was getting good and pissed "You know as well as I do that this will never go to trial. That girl gets on the stand and her credibility is shot. You saw what she asked him to do; do you really think that reflects a woman people are going to identify with? You know he is going to say she asked for it again. He is going to say she likes it rough, though that girl is a gentle as the day is long."

"Yeah, I know, but maybe, just maybe, if we can tie her to the other women we will have enough to convict him without Britt." Wow, that was wishful thinking.

"Luke, even you are not that stupid. All those women were promiscuous and heavily sexual. Every one of them was raped in some fashion she liked sex, one was strangled, one was raped with a whip. You've got a man that has a problem with strongly sexual women. That is going to be a brutal trial. Not one of those women was sweet innocence that can stand up to scrutiny. At least Britt will be prepared, though I don't think anyone is prepared for what a defense attorney will do at trial. You are screwed." Nothing will get the sick bastard off the street. I have seen cases like this before and there is never really justice for the rape victim.

"Again, I know, but we have to protect them. While none of these women are my cup of tea, none of them are doing anything wrong. You're right, however; it's not my job to worry about that. I have to get him off the street, let the District Attorney worry about keeping him off." He loves Britt, he will help her. Yup, help her right into a plea where a rapist cop

134

doesn't do time and Britt lives in fear the rest of her life. I won't let it happen, I can't. I have to protect them.

"Goodbye, Luke. I will call you tomorrow. Marabell, I am going to bed. My door will be locked if you need me call. When I leave I will come down here first and I will leave through the front till they clear my office." This was going to suck we were all going to be living under a microscope. I hope there was still a club to give Britt back when all was said and done. I hope I don't freeze to death.

Rebekkah Rogers

Chapter 11
Beth

"Come on, Britt. You have to get up and move again. You can't sit in this room forever." How was I going to get her out of this damned house? I was going stir crazy. Four days in the hospital, three at home, and we have six more weeks of limited mobility, according to the doctor. The doctor told her about the hysterectomy and all the other shit that monster did to her. She hasn't been the same since. I keep reminding her she won't get her period any more but she just sits in the dark pacifying me. "We are going outside to get some fresh air."

"Beth, it is a thousand degrees outside. I will stay here in the AC."

"Ok, I concede it is a furnace out there, but you need it. You love the heat remember we live in the desert for a reason. Now give me your hand." I have to get her out.

"I'm in underwear."

"We both are." We're both in boxers and fitted tanks, to be precise. "In this neighborhood, no one will care. They all know me and know not to set their expectations high. Now one small walk around the cul-de-sac and we are done. You can sit on the couch, have a pain pill, and watch trashy shows."

"Can I watch porn?" I don't know if she is joking or not.

"Will it get you out of bed?"

"It might."

"As long as you turn it off when the boys get home, you have full run of the pay per view." I'd do anything to get her out of the damned room and into the sun light. "As long as I can keep the blinds open, too."

This is the hardest thing. I have nursed tummy aches and broken bones, a concussion once, the flu enough times to be a pro, but never a broken woman. I don't know where to start. I don't have anyone to ask. My mind keeps going to Graham. I want to tell him about her. I need advice on the sexual stuff. She keeps bringing it up and I don't know how to respond to her. I thought most women would shy away from sex after such a trauma, but she seems to want to gain that control back in her life and I don't know anything about meeting her needs. She keeps making remarks like she thinks I can fix her. I don't have anyone to turn to because I went to Britt, Damn Graham, I wanted him so much. I should have known I couldn't have him. It was too easy. He was too good.

Getting her down the stairs I realize she hasn't bathed today, again. Oh well, we are getting out. The sun is almost blinding. It is like walking on the sun and we may both die of heat stroke before we make it back. But I need this...I need sunlight. I feel like I closed off my world when I closed off my heart. I can't let the heartache out because it hurts Britt to see. I know the boys are aware that something is up, but I have tried to keep them from seeing too much. They are smart though, eventually they are going to want answers.

It was in the news every night. "Child Advocate attorney who owns sex club was raped in partner's office. No comment from partner, although department officials say that it was her partner that committed the crime. No arrests have been made." I told the boys I would answer their questions when they had them, but I didn't want them going to Britt with them or calling Graham for any reason. They just nodded and walked out. My house has felt like a cold wake for the last week. No one is saying anything. We are just doing our stuff and avoiding all semblance of warmth. It is killing me. I need my boys. I need my girly to get better. I need Gr... no. I'm not thinking that, I can't have him. The Sheriff has been over several times to interview Britt. He calls to check in on her, I get the impression they have been close for a long time. He showed her surveillance footage of Graham at the station until twenty minutes before he called 911. She understands that he didn't do it, but she won't see him or let me see him.

I know he is not the one that hurt Britt but there is nothing that I can do, I still lost him. I turned my back on him and I can't get that back. I feel so cold. I just need the sun to warm my skin. Maybe it can clear my head and bring back my warmth.

About half way around the block, I hear the sniffles. "Wanna talk about it?" I know she won't, though. She just cries and doesn't talk.

"There's nothing to say."

"Alright, so here we are in the sunshine, in our jammies. No one is watching because all my neighbors work during the day. We are both on leave from work, and so we have nothing but time. I will wait you out, but you could just fix this and tell me what you need." Sniffle, sniffle is her response. Shuffle, sniffle, shuffle sniffle. This is the longest walk I have ever taken. "I love you, Britt. I am here to take care of you, you promised to submit, I don't know how to dominate your confessions out of you. I know you're in pain. I know your heart is broken. You blamed Graham and now you don't know what to think. The doctor told us that you probably used him to protect yourself. It's okay. I know all the shitty things going on in your body as well. I have been there for all the hormone surges and stuff as well. You need to tell me now how to help you fix you." Please, just give me a clue.

"Beth, I can't have kids."

I didn't think you wanted any.

"I know, Sweets, and I can't give them to you. Well, I can, if you want two grown boys that smell bad and never clean their bathroom?" All I can think is she needs the light back in her eyes.

"I didn't think I wanted kids. I see everyday how hard it is to raise kids and have a family. I see how good parents are screwed by bad ones. I didn't want that."

"But it was your choice to not want them, and this monster didn't have the right to take that away from you. Britt, you're probably too old anyway, but you had the choice. It was your life to live the way you wanted and someone came and made the choice for you." She finally looked me in the eyes and I could see the fear and cold.

"I didn't want them, but I think maybe I did. Maybe I wanted a baby to hold and sing the nursery rhymes I hear you singing all the time. I want someone to look at me like the boys look at you."

"I can't give that to you, but you know as well as I do that blood doesn't make a woman a mother and child look at you with love. That is something that is shaped and grown every single day with a person you choose to raise. That takes hard work and commitment not blood. You can have that still. God, if anyone knows the amount of kids that need homes and need someone to look at them with love and give them nursery rhymes, it's you. I don't think you have lost anything. I think you are gaining perspective on what you want in life."

Turning around and heading home, I feel like some of the sun has gotten into us. Maybe we will be okay, after all.

Then she says, "I want to have sex again."

"Of course you do and you know you can, because the doctor said it will be possible in six weeks."

"He told me it may hurt me for a while."

"No, no way. With patience and a gentle touch, you will enjoy sex again."

"It hurts to touch myself. Even my own hand hurts." God, I so don't know what to say to that.

"Britt, you have to give your body time to heal; it has only been a week."

"I have never gone longer than a week before."

"Really? Wow. After you have a baby or surgery, six weeks is the standard healing. Then it is still pretty tender. Give yourself time. You are not in a rush." Shuffling back, I know we have covered more ground in the last ten minutes than the last week.

"You promised me pussy if I needed it."

"God Britt, really, come on, give yourself a break. We are all trying to help."

"What if I don't want men anymore?"

"Then you will find a nice sweet girl and I will love her because you love her or I will scratch her eyes out because she is a bitch. You can have whatever you want."

"Except you."

"Yes Britt, except me. Sweets, I know you are scared that you won't be able to be with men, I know you are terrified that this has broken you, but it has not. Hear me well. You are not broken and you will be able to enjoy sex again" God, why won't she let up? Every day it is something new. At first, it was the same tease we have always done, but it feels like she is shifting, pushing. I don't want her to feel rejected. I want her to know I love her. "Come on, let's go in. I'll get you a pill and you can sleep on the recliner." I know she has used sex to heal her broken heart in the past. She is the biggest proponent of rebound relationships that I have ever seen. I thought she would be more reserved, but then I guess her personality doesn't really allow for reserved.

Walking back in the room, I see her curled up in a recliner remote in hand. "Jesus Britt, turn it down a little. The neighbors are going to think I am hosting an orgy." Handing her an iced tea and her pill I turn around to turn it down. Is she watching…? Yup, she is watching lesbian porn. I can't take my eyes away. My mind starts running to Graham. God, I was so ready to get laid. I needed to feel him hard inside me. I was ready. I never thought I would want another man after Marc died or that I would ever be anything but a mom again. I felt myself coming alive at the thought of just a kiss. I'm thirty-nine years old and would get all hot and bothered over a kiss. God, this is incredible. I am not sure I have ever really watched girl-on-girl porn before. It's incredibly hot and–wow, I just didn't know. I sit in the recliner with her. She wraps her small body around me and we watch. I can feel how still she is and that she is worried about me, but I am more concerned about her. I'm also hotter than hell. I feel myself stilling, not moving an inch, and holding my breath. I know she is acting out in an effort to regain her control, but I am not sure I want to be one that she does that with.

Her hands run along my stomach pushing my shirt out of the way. Her warm hand stills against my prickling skin. I can feel her hot breath across my neck, where her head rest on my shoulder, her other against my lower back. The women on the screen are eating at each other...kissing breasts and ...bodies grinding. I am so hot that I can feel myself soaking my panties. Her hand rubbing my stomach, soft slow strokes almost like I'm the wounded animal. I know what she's doing, but I can't stop it. Higher on my stomach, just below my breasts, I can feel how heavy they are. My nipples are throbbing in time with my heartbeat. My pussy is creaming and women are panting and moaning on the screen. Her hands are soft as one slides up my back and undoes my bra while the other takes my breast in hand and pulls at my nipple. "Eyes on the screen Sweets, I want your hard candy in my mouth while you watch her cum." I couldn't pull my eyes away if I tried.

"Britt I don't think we should do this, are you sure you want this?" I am so turned on, but I don't want to push her. She has all ready done so much today.

I feel my skin exposed to the air conditioning. Then the hot mouth softly pulls my nipple. I can feel the heat of her mouth to my core. Whips of lightning rush to my core. She pulls both hands to my breasts lifting them while her mouth covers one and then the other. The fire licking through my body, the heat...I need the heat in my bones, I ache for it. I arch into her hands, "So good, god you are so good." Her voice is a rasp against the heat pouring from her mouth through my nipples into my soul. I need this. I know I should stop her. I know if we do this there may be no return. I need to know I can be a woman. She needs this; I can show her how to be a woman again. I want her for this time, in this minute it is all about her.

Her hands start running down my legs, down the outside, up the inside dragging flames with them. The pressure on my knees draws my eyes to her, straddling me, "Let me in, Beth. Let me taste you." I know she can hear my moans. She has to know how close I am. She stands and drags my breasts with her. She pulls me to the edge of the chair and the edge of my reasoning. "Stand up; you need to take your pants off, now." There is sharpness in her voice that makes me shudder. Her hands run down my body and take my boxer shorts with her. The flames, the sounds, god the moans, mine, hers, the porn stars…each build in me like a raging fire ready to consume me. It is so erotic and strong in my body until I can't feel anything but her burning hands. Standing in front of her, she is much smaller than me, a slight bend at the knees and she is pulling my nipples into her mouth again.

My knees start buckling and I order "Down to your knees." She follows me to the floor. Kneeling before me, she starts laying kisses on my shoulders, the tops of my breast, little nibbles and bites all long the drop of my cleavage. Running her hands down my sides, she pushes my hips back to my feet. I sit on my feet with her breasts in my face. I have never kissed a woman's breast. She has small nipples, poking straight out. She must have taken her shirt off when I was watching the show so intently. My hands slide gently to her waist because I don't want to hurt her. She still has stitches. I lick out at her nipple and she moans, it is rock hard and tastes like honey and apples. I pull it gently into my mouth. The feel of it is hard on my tongue as I rub it against the roof of my mouth. I have to be so gentle when I touch her.

I feel her hands slide between my thighs, "Spread them, Beth. Open for me. Lay back and close your eyes. God, we need the blindfold."

"No, I will close them for you, Britt." I would do anything for her and she knows that. Lying back, I notice how open I am for her. My feet are under my ass, my back bowed as my shoulders rest on the floor with my dripping pussy pushed up into the air. Small kisses on my inner thighs have me dripping onto the floor. The heat is killing me. As she drags her warm hands through my slit, I know how wet I will be for her. She circles my clit, dragging her fingers through my short hair giving it just a slight tug I can feel in my throat. White hot heat pours out of my body.

"We need to wax this pretty kitty." Rubbing up and down from my anus to my clit with two fingers she is gathering my juices in her fingers. She reaches up and rubs it on my nipples and slides around to leave me open to the room. She takes my nipple in her mouth and with one hand on my other nipple she pulls at my breast. She moves down between my legs and pulls my clit into her mouth, rubbing her tongue across it. And I start coming. She pulls at my nipples, pushing her fingers in me pushing the orgasm farther and farther. Pushing in and out, I can feel her pulling on my sensitive walls, licking and slurping pulling everything I have out of me. The heat and fire kindling as wave after wave take me. "You are the hottest woman I have ever sucked. You respond so well." As I come down from my high, I feel her watching me, my skin now prickling from the sweat cooling in the air conditioning. My feet are tingling from being tucked under me and I pull them out.

"Oh, Britt, I don't know how to give you that."

"Don't be ridiculous. Of course you do. But you can't; remember no sex for six weeks. And I am already sore and tired." She overdid herself. What was I thinking? I can't do this with her.

"I, um, Britt, I'm sorry, come on; let's get you into your chair. By yourself and you can rest." Standing us both up and getting us dressed, I hand her the tea to wash her mouth out.

"Uh huh, I am not rinsing you away. No come on, I need to cuddle."

"All right, but let's watch something else." I can't stand the sound filing the room any longer.

"Read to me, please." How can she pull off what she just did and then sound like a little girl in the same five minute span?

I pull out the book I have been reading–it's some stupid murder mystery that really doesn't catch my attention–and I start reading. Before long, she is sleeping and I am pulling away. I walk to the kitchen and pull the bottle of wine from the fridge. I know it's only noon, but I need something to process what just happened. She was able to set my body on fire. I never thought I would want a woman, but she tasted sweet and soft. Britt was not like Marc, who was so spicy and musky. Graham's kisses were warm and hot like whiskey, but Britt's were–what the hell? I can't compare them.

This is too much to process. *Deep breath in and out.* What was I going to do? I can't do this with her. As amazing as it was, it's not what I want. I don't want a relationship with a woman. I don't want, oh no. Back to my wants…I can't have what I want, so now what? I can't have Marc back and that just hurts my heart to think about still. I can't have Graham and that just makes my body crazy and my soul ache. I don't want Britt. I love her, her teasing, her laughter and the way she always seems to get me, but I don't want a life with her. I don't know how to fix this. I haven't tried to call Graham. I know he won't talk to me. I don't deserve his forgiveness so I can't even ask. Every time my phone rings, my heart beats wildly. I can't get it under control. It's usually the boys wanting something, a ride or permission for something. Occasionally, it's even creepy cop. It's never the call I really want.

This time, the number is unknown. Maybe.... *No don't think it. It's probably just a telemarketer.* "Hello"

"I told you to stay away from her. I told you she was a dirty whore and would ruin you. I love you and you never listen to me. I am only trying to look out for you. I don't want you to end up like her. She got what she deserves because she is a whore. You and I both know you're not. What happened today, well, that had to be a mistake, right? You wouldn't corrupt our love that way." How does he know what happened today? My heart won't stop pounding. Ice runs through my blood.

"Why are you calling me again, Jimmy? I told you to stop calling. Are you watching me?" I need help.

"Oh, my darling Elizabeth, you are so innocent. Don't let her corrupt you and make you her whore. You deserve more. I will fill your belly with babies and make you a home. You send her away and I will come to you. Just say the word." Fill my belly with babies? No thank you, freak. What am I going to do?

"No, Jimmy, the answer is no. I am going to call your captain again if you don't stop calling me."

"They can't find me." He sounded like he was taunting me, "They have all been looking for me for a week. Only you know where I am."

"What? Where are you?" I find myself talking to dead air. I look around; sure enough, my family room curtains are open. I have a private backyard, so how could he see in? I need help. I can't do this anymore. I can't take it. He is getting worse every time I talk to him. He always calls her a dirty whore. I have never told her, but I am so tired of being scared. I can't call Graham, since he won't want to hear about my problems. Besides, I know he is retiring soon and he probably doesn't want any more cases. I don't know who else to call. Jimmy's boss told me to not worry about him, that he was harmless. Maybe that sheriff that interviewed Britt will help?

I dial the sheriff's number from the business card tacked to my refrigerator. At the receptionist voice I ask for the

Sheriff, I think I am on eternal hold. Maybe I will die on hold. Finally I get a terse, "What?"

"Um, Sheriff Carver? I am not sure if you remember me. It's Elizabeth Williams. I was with Brittany Morressey when you interviewed her, and you came to my house."

"I remember you, Beth. What do you need? I'm a little busy."

Big girl panties, I remember I am wearing big girl panties. It's something Britt always tells me when I am getting nervous. "I had told you that Officer Simmons was calling me all the time, well, he hasn't stopped, and he is starting to get really crude and mean. He mentioned today he was looking in my living room window. He told me...."

"The entire damn state is looking for that guy. Did he tell you where he was? Is he at your house? If you can't tell me, just say something stupid."

Something stupid, what is he talking about? "No, he's not here. He told me everyone was looking for him, and only I know where he is."

"Well, where is he girl?"

"How would I know? I called you to have someone come look in my yard. The police chief wouldn't listen to me last time I called him. I have privacy fences. Unless he was in my backyard, he wouldn't..."

"Yeah I get it. Someone will be on their way. I have an officer in your neighborhood as we speak."

"Why? Why is someone in my neighborhood?" This ominous feeling sweeps over me; this is going to be bad.

"Don't worry someone is on the way." And the phone goes dead.

All I could do was pace and wait and hope that maybe just maybe the deputy that comes will be–no, I can't think that way.

Not five minutes later the knock on the door startles me. My stomach was clenching and I knew who it was and how bad this was going to get. He knocked again. I didn't want to wake Britt, so I hurried to the door and pulled it open before he can knock a third time. "Stop, she's sleeping."

"Why didn't you tell me?" God, he looked good. He appeared tired and worn out, even if he hadn't shaved in a while. The urge to lick him almost forced my body forward.

"Let's sit out here." I flip on the mister on my porch. "Do you want tea?"

"Yes, please. It is hotter than Hades and I have been sitting in the sun all damned day. Let's sit inside. Your girl won't be asleep long. The entire police force is set to rain down on your house any minute."

"Why are you in my neighborhood?"

"I knew he would come back when he didn't get what he wanted. He is going to hurt her again. I didn't protect...." With a grunt and a wave of his hands, Graham continued, "Anyway, we knew he would come back here."

"You were using us as bait, just letting us be sitting ducks. You think Jimmy is her rapist? No, he is crazy but he's harmless."

"Is that why you called the Sheriff? Is it because you felt he was harmless? Don't be stupid, Beth. The man carries a gun and is threatening your friends."

"How do you know he is threatening my friends? I never told anyone. You guys are listening to my calls, aren't you? What else you listening to Graham? You guys have the house wired for sound? You listen to me cry at night?" Why did I say that?

"No Beth, god, no. We have recordings of him calling me and Britt's phones. He is threatening us directly." As he reached out his hand, I can't help but want to lean into him. No I can't. My heart is breaking all over again. His hand drops almost like he wanted to touch me, but can't.

"You? He threatened you? He's calling Britt?"

"He has been leaving her dirty voicemails. The sheriff took her phone the last time he was here. How did you not know that?"

"She has two–her personal one and her business. He took her business. I think I may be the only one that calls her personal."

"Her personal is the only number I have as well, but she won't take my calls."

"He threatened you?"

"He told me he planned to publically ruin me. He said he planned it so well that I would spend the rest of my life in jail for his fun."

"How did he convince Britt it was you?" Oh God, my heart is tearing. I bet if we were silent, you would actually hear it.

"I don't think he had to do much convincing. She probably thought it was me at first. I told her I would sleep on the couch. When he crawled in next to her, she probably thought it was me and started talking to me. He responded to her in the affirmative and then I don't know if he didn't make her say my name or something. The other women reported that he did that to them. He had them call him names of people they knew."

"Others? There are other women? How did he get away with this?" What the hell? I feel like I walked into a horror show half way through.

"God, Beth. We didn't know it was James. Do you think if I did I would have let him anywhere near Britt or you for that matter? He was standing over you, watching you the night we were in the club together. Several people were standing around watching, but he was there as well." Lightning streaked through my body as he pushed my hair off my shoulder, making just the faintest contact with my almost bare skin. Heat and lust from his proximity and touch warred with revulsion at the thought of Jimmy watch me with Graham.

"Oh gross–yeah, I guess that's my fault. Apparently, I am finding that I have no shut off switch. I would have recognized Jimmy in the bar, so how did I not see him? Britt was with him on the porch. That's why he didn't want to meet me." I really need to get my emotions in check. What the hell? I was leaning into him. No, he is not for us. I can't have him. "Graham, I am going to go get you some tea and wake Britt up so the noise doesn't scare her. You let in the cops."

As I turned to walk away, I heard that voice that feels like fine scotch on my throat. "You won't be able to run from me for long, Princess. You are mine and I don't lose." Fire courses through my body at his words. His? Like his little piece of property? I want to be his. I want to belong to him more than anything. But I don't know how it could work. I feel like I am going to lose here.

Chapter 12
Graham

She smells sweet like peaches and cream. It is taking every bit of control to not touch her, just to hold her hand and give her some comfort. She believes in me and she knows I didn't do it. "Mine" chants in my head over and over. It's not the sex; I have to protect her. She belongs to me and nothing can stop the force pulling us together. It's like gravity. My world is revolving around her. I have killed myself on this case by working day and night so I could protect her. I had to stop deluding myself—it wasn't about me or even Britt and my stupid guilt about her. It was always about my princess and keeping her safe. When I walked in that room, I saw Beth. She clutched her hand in mine as the doctor told us what happened and my gut told me that it was all about her.

A sleepy, slurry voice filled my brain and I couldn't process the broken little girl standing in front of me. "I told you that I didn't want you here."

"The Sheriff told me you didn't believe him when he showed you proof it wasn't me. God Britt, I would never hurt a woman like that." Why didn't she believe me? I need her to believe me I need her back in my life. "She doesn't want you, Graham. I will get stronger and I will take what was always mine. I am done playing games." Hers? Beth can't be hers. She's mine. I feel the cold leaching into my bones.

"Britt, she will never be happy with you. You can't give her what she needs." My cock driving into her is one but I know it's more than that. I should have been protecting them both. I lost sight of what was important and let Britt get hurt. I was so focused on Beth I didn't see what was happening right in front of me.

Her sleepy eyes keep losing focus she is fighting to just remain upright. "You can't have her."

"Britt, go to bed. Let me take care of both of you when you are awake and coherent. We can talk about this later." I need a strategy that will help Britt come to grips with who did this too her and I need a way to keep my focus around Beth "This isn't what she needs right now."

Tipping her head as though trying to assess what to do with me, like a parent to a child. "You would let a pussy you just met, what, less than a month ago, ruin your life? Take your club? I will ruin you if you come any closer!" Now she's the heartless attorney that never loses.

"How will you do that Britt?" Beth's soft voice envelopes us. How much had she heard? "I have heard so many tales of how people are going to ruin Graham. Please, Britt, tell me what's your plan?" At the sound of her voice Britt and I turn to look at her. She is vibrating tension and I want to hold her, to sooth her. I know if I touch her I would lose my hard earned control so I stand and watch.

"Beth, I thought you understood. I need you, I love you. You promised you wouldn't see him. Why is he here?" Jesus, had she committed herself to Britt? No, I won't let her.

She looks so sad. Her eyes are on the ceiling as though she is pleading with heaven for help. The swallow in her long graceful throat makes me realize that she is holding back her tears. "No Britt no, I love you. You are my best friend and I don't want to lose you, but I don't want a life with you as my lover. What happened today was a mistake I should not have made. You know that. You know it shouldn't have happened."

"You bitch…you have been teasing me since day one. You stood in that hospital and promised whatever I needed you would provide. Well I need you, all of you, body and soul."

Britt was angry, swaying on her feet and working up a good rage.

I wanted to take Beth in my arms, but I felt like I shouldn't move. I don't want to draw attention to myself. What happened today? Did they...? No, Britt is too hurt for that still. The tears in Beth's eyes just about break my heart. "Britt, you have all of me, but you can't have my soul. That's mine. You can't have my body, as it is not for possession." *Want to bet that body is mine? I can wait. I will wait.* "Britt, I loved Marc. I was able to commit to him because he was what I wanted in my life. A partner I believed in and that believed in me. Not one that wanted to possess me and lord me over other people. I can't be what you want, and you don't want what I need. I am not a toy for children to fight over." Now she was looking at me. "I want a man strong enough to slay dragons, but smart enough to let me do it when necessary,"

"Sweets." God, she looked awful. She was swollen and bruised still and appeared as if she was going to fall over.

"No more, Britt. Beth doesn't need any of us fighting over her. She is right. James is threatening her and going mad because he can't posses her, you are behaving like a petulant child because you can't, and I can only imagine the overgrown hormonal teen she sees when she looks at me. You need sleep, go to bed. I will wake you when the rest of the officers get here. Someone can take you home." How do I make this right? Beth has tears running down her cheeks but her shoulders are squared and she is not letting go. "I'm sorry, Beth. I don't, well, all I have is I'm sorry." I know she wants an apology and someone to understand she is hurt, but I didn't do anything wrong. I should have protected Britt and known that James was crazy. Still, I can't fix that. I can't make it better. I will fight here, even if it is unfairly. If she wants an apology, I will give it. If she wants anything, well, she's mine I will provide it.

She looks so resigned and defeated. I just want to hold her tight and kiss away the pain. I know I am what she wants. This week, I made plans that would let me be with her and be the man that she needs. She looks as she did the day her husband dies. Her world is imploding. I can only do what I know will help. Watching her walk away is always a treat, as she has the nicest ass. "Princess, where are the boys?"

She answers over her shoulder, "School, for a couple more hours." Good, at least they will be protected. I pull my phone from my pocket and call Luke.

While the phone rings, my mind keeps picturing the tears and resignation on her face. She looked so sure everything would not work out; she kept her shoulders squared but her eyes showed how much it hurt her that Britt was hurt. I know she thinks I blame her for not talking to me when Britt was in the hospital. But I somehow saw how it would play out and I knew even then I would not lose her. "Luke, you need to send someone to the high school to watch the boys. That's her weakness and I think he will try to exploit it." I walk into the living room and can feel eyes on me. "He's still here watching I can feel it."

"You should have backup in less than three and I'm five minutes out. Getting the chief of police to understand that we plan on arresting one of his officers was harder than it should have been." Of course it was, because it meant the bastard has been sleeping on the job. He told Beth not to worry…that James was harmless.

Heading up the stairs to make sure the windows were closed I met Beth at the landing half way up. "We need to talk." Then she walked past, nothing else, no emotion nothing but her sweet peaches and cream scent and my body, hard and frozen. I follow her into the kitchen I walked right into her back and wrap my arms around her.

Her heat raced from my hand through my body where I touched her. "Oh God Princess, are you okay?"

"Stop, Graham." She turns and pushes on my chest, although it's not hard enough to mean it.

I pull her closer and am not sure who needs the reassurance more her or me. "I can't stop, I won't let you go.

154

Now stop fighting me Beth and let me make sure you're all right." The door bell rings.

She acts like I was killing her as she shoots me a look filled with regret and pain that stabs into my heart and chills my body cold. No, she is not getting away.

As we answer the door and I start directing the troops of officers that are surrounding her house, the park behind her and into her neighbor's yard. I know it is going to be a while before I get to be alone with her again.

I feel like a planet in her orbit. I know where she is all the time and I feel myself orienting my position to hers. She doesn't talk to me again, she directs the officers from the city to me, but she never actually speaks to me. The entire sheriff's department knows me. I have been the lead investigator for the county for years. I listen for her voice, but really she is a glorified barista who makes coffee and cookies and runs up and down to check on Britt. I know we are missing something…the entire police force is missing something, but I can't put my finger on it.

I have pictures of James distributed, but he is gone. The police are watching his house, his haunts, and everyone he knows. Every cop knows his face, but still we can't find him. I have poured through his background. It's full of crappy arrests and complaints from citizens for his harsh behaviors, along with suspicions by senior officers. Nothing stuck to him. He's worse than "The Teflon Don". Finally, when the forensics techs leave having taken finger prints and foot prints of everything in her yard from the bunnies to the boys, there is nothing left to do.

I send everyone off and turn to her. "Everyone's gone" Tired, red eyes look up at me, so full of fear and pain and something else. Something I can't put my finger on…what is it? I can't wait any longer I know how to help her feel secure again. I need her to know I will be here with her. Two strides later and my hands are on her hips lifting her to the counter. My intentions of being gentle fly out the window when she grabs my hair and pulls me to her mouth. I know she needs soft and slow but she can't have it. Not today. I want to feel her around me, warming me. I feel myself grabbing the back of her head by her heavy hair and pulling it back. Her eyes clear void of all fear now, that something that is all her shining through, but no fear. As I lean into kiss her, I feel my whole self slip into her. She is going to kill my control. Her soft full lips opening for me, letting me in, letting me push into her mouth with force. I am taking not giving. She doubted me; she thought I couldn't take care of her. I need to show her I'm strong enough to take care of her.

She will learn to come to me first. Her first call should have been me, not Luke. She tastes sweet like the cookies she has been passing out all day. Her legs tighten around me as her mouth continues to eat at mine. She has taken control again and surprisingly I am okay with ceding control to her. The heat burns at my tenuous control. Her soft moan pushed me farther than I planned as I push against her and grind myself against her hot core. Her breasts are pushing into my chest warming my whole body. Through my undershirt, dress shirt and suit jacket I can feel her pushing those plump, heavy breasts into me.

I can't move my hands from her hair or head any more than I can move my mouth from her. I want to die right here, with her tongue in my mouth, her hands wrapped around my neck and her legs around my hips. When she leans her head back to catch her breath, I want that neck in my mouth. I want to mark her, show everyone she's mine and no one else can touch her. I feel her soft tender skin in my mouth and her vibrated deep throat moan when I bite down on that throbbing vein and pull the skin in my mouth. Her small yelp is such a beautiful sound of passion and excitement that punches straight into my body. That is how she will sound when I spank her ass for not believing in me. I soothe her pain with my tongue and my hands run down her back and up her sides. They lift her shirt to reveal large breasts smattered with freckles and large, dark-rose nipples so hard that they could poke an eye out. "Take it off!" She reached behind her with one hand undoing her bra, never lifting her head, watching me look at her.

"Graham, I don't think…"

"Shush, Beth we can do this, we both need this." Her legs tighten at the force in my voice, she is spectacular. Without removing her bra or shirt, I take both breasts in my hands. Feeling how heavy and full they are, I run my unshaven face along them to watch the skin pink and the nipples harden even more. Her harsh moan when I take her nipple into my mouth makes my hard on swell even more. I grind into her, pulling on her nipple and the sweet tit.

"More please, Graham. More." She is grinding into me, pulling my head closer to her. She grasps my hands that are trying to squeeze her breasts.

"Hands down, this is my turn. I have waited too long for you to rush this." With her tit still in my mouth, my cock grinding against her, I lift her hands to my shoulders, pat them once, and return my hands to her butter soft skin. The heat coming off her is enough to keep me warm forever. She is so hot and finally warming me. I can feel sweat pouring down my face, as it lands on the swell of her breast. Her hands slide under my jacket pushing it off my shoulders. I could care less that my best suit jacket ended up on the floor of her kitchen. I am so wrapped up in her breasts and her hands in my hair running over my head and down my shoulders that I don't hear the door open.

She must have heard it. She sits up straight and pushes me back so hard I have to catch myself. She moves like nothing I have ever seen. She is clothed and picking up my jacket before I even register that I still have hands.

"Hey Mom. P. stayed late to finish a chem assignment. His partner will bring him home." I register the voice and that this should matter but I can't put it together. Her son is home from school. It must be a mom super hearing thing. She was ready for him.

As he walked around the wall to the kitchen, she sticks her head in the fridge and from there, says, "J. you want a sandwich? Graham?"

"Well, duh, Mom."

"Yes Beth, please," I say not sure if I should correct the kid. No, it's not my job, and he is fifteen-year-old boy. "All right, Graham. I will make you a sandwich. J., you can haul your ass back to the door of the kitchen, reenter, and try again." Wow, look at her, so obedient, but no one's door mat. I love her. What? No, do I? My whole body is warm. Do I love her? I guess the signs are all there.

"Jeeze, Sorry Mom. Yes please, will you please fix me a sandwich if you are making one for yourself?"

He keeps his eyes on me but talks to her. She is so nervous that she won't even look at me.

"Hey, Joseph," I venture. "It's good to see you again." I know I need to be in good with the kids, not just to get her to want me, but because they are important people. They are going to be great men and they deserve the respect of someone who cares for their mother.

With a nod, the kid tosses his backpack on the table and starts unloading it. There are a lot of books. "Good to see you again, sir. I thought after what happened at the hospital that we wouldn't see you again." "You can call me Graham. Not sir, not Deputy, just Graham. Also, I wouldn't let a little misunderstanding come between your mother and me." Her little gasp had me looking at her. "Nothing, Princess, will come between us, ever. I told you that in the hospital." I can't help but put my hands to her face.

The way he clears his throat leaves me unsure whether to slap him or laugh. "Nothing Beth and no one with come between us again." She has to know that Britt is not stopping this. She can't. I am pretty sure that they had sex today. I could smell it on her and the conversation earlier was, of course, the biggest clue. I know Beth won't be happy without a man. She needs a dominate man, someone to take care of her in everyday ways as well as someone to make sure she gets her needs met. Britt could do it, but Britt would need more soon as well, Beth can't give that to her. It is a disaster of epic proportions just waiting to happen. "We will catch this psycho, and then you and I are going to take a long weekend away. We'll get to know each other without interference."

She pulled her face back to the sandwiches and commented, "Graham, I have to take care of Britt and I have the kids and no one to stay with them. Our family isn't even in this state. I can't leave them for the weekend."

"Pssh." It sounded like J. had sprung a leak. "That's bullshit and you know it mom. You can go have a weekend in Sedona with Graham. P. and I will be fine."

"Watch your language Mister, and *you* stole my car last time I left for the night. Remember the midnight call to Britt to get you before you got arrested? That was one night and I was just at the convention center downtown." Turning those chocolate eyes to me, I saw my life in her eyes. "I'm sorry Graham. That sounds like fun, but right now I have priorities. We can have a sandwich, you tell me what happens next with the investigation, and then I will call you later in the week or if I hear anything."

Is she kidding me? Didn't she just hear me? I can feel J.'s eyes on me as well. "No, Princess. You will listen because I will only say it once more. You are mine, and your priorities have shifted. You, your children, and then me...everything else comes second to us. No more killing yourself to take care of Britt. A nurse will be here in the morning to see to all of her needs. You are only going to be her emotional support as a friend. You are not her lover, her spouse, or her mother, and you will stop killing yourself trying to be. You are going to start getting out of this damn house, but that will be with me and only me until Simmons is caught. You are only to mother your children. You are my lover and no one else's and you *will* trust me to take care of you. I will protect you, I will provide for you, and I will not be pushed aside while you work yourself into the ground." I feel like I have just put on a show for them. Both mouths gape and I catch J.'s eyes. Respect and a glimmer of maybe hope? He knows she needs someone to take care of her. A strong man can see her needs a mile away.

Her eyes fill with tears, tears that feel a little like my soul is falling with each one. "Why? Why do you want me Graham, I can't be what you are."

What I am? What? "What am I Princess?"

Sheepishly, she ducks her head. She is so innocent sometimes. "You know "The Club", and the lady at the bar."

Speaking softly so her son doesn't hear what I say. "Elizabeth, I want you to hear me clearly. You are what I want. You are a grown up, mature and steady. You are so innocent it kills me at the same time you are so sexual. You are kind, generous to a fault and you are a perfect match for me." Leaning into her ear even closer, I can smell the sweet shampoo she uses, I focus and tell her. "You are so beautiful when you submit to me. But its more than that, you make me laugh you make me want more. " I then pull away because I can feel myself getting hard and it just wouldn't do to have a raging hard on with her son sitting there. "I think we should try. I have never had a real relationship like you want and you have never had one like I want. Let's meet in the middle and try." I keep reminding myself to make her feel like it is her idea, like she has a choice, but I can't. "I told you Beth, Mine." I growl into her ear and feel her twitch, her breasts lifting on the deep breath in. Yup, I have her, she is mine.

Sitting at the table, I eat my sandwich and ask J. about his school work. Wow…this kid is smarter than I could ever be. "Your mom says you want to go to Notre Dame?"

He nods but does not stop working or eating. "Yeah, it's what dad wanted for us. They have a great medical school and a great baseball team so I will be happy. If P. can get on the football team, he doesn't care what he studies. All he has ever wanted is to play football for Notre Dame. Dad wanted us both to play, but I know I can't play well enough to get on the team."

Wow, talk about pressure. "Hey I'm sure your dad would be happy just having you play something you love." What was I talking about? I didn't know his father. Maybe he was one of those pricks that had high hopes for their kids and didn't let them live down the expectations.

"Yeah, mom says I misunderstood him. She says he wanted me to get into football, as in watch it and support it. She says dad wouldn't want me to do something that I didn't love. I want to be a pediatrician and I can't do that if I kill myself playing football." Yeah, that is what I thought his beautiful mother would say to him.

Beth was upstairs feeding Britt, probably trying to mend their friendship. "So your brother is going to play though?" I am just trying to find something that will let me into her world. I will do anything for her.

"Yeah, P. wants to play he's a running back. He runs so fast. Mom gets frustrated because he says he has no other aspirations. He says that he will play for four years and then he will finish his MBA. He says he will come run my life and we can open a whole service wellness clinic. I will be in school until I die and then I will have to build a patient list. I just don't know if it will work the way he is planning."

Sounds like a great plan, really. I start thinking about things I have never thought about–student loans, SATs and stuff that really has nothing to do with me. It is so easy to get sucked into her world. As I watch him eat, study and watch me all simultaneous I hear the phone ring on the counter behind me.

J. jumps up answering it. "She has told you she won't take your calls." Going on alert I know who it is. "Yeah sure, maybe then you will get it, she has a boyfriend and doesn't want you calling anymore." J. hands the phone to me. "Creepy cop wants to talk to you." I am already scrolling through my phone, texting the Sheriff.

Caller ID shows unknown. I hold out the phone waiting a second. I am gathering my cloak of calm around myself. I want to reach through the phone and kill the sick bastard. The rage rears up on me like nothing I have felt since I was a teenager myself. I try to pull the ice back into my veins; Beth and this great kid next to me have melted me. I can't think about anything except protecting them all. It makes me sick to think he spoke to her son. He is an innocent, good kid that will be a great man one day and I don't want him tainted with James's freakiness.

I know I need to drag this out to try to get a bead on him. Her phones are tapped the call going straight to the station. "Where in the fuck are you?"

"Oh, come now, Graham. I have been living under your nose for years and you couldn't catch me. I use to watch you and think how stupid you were." J. was watching me with such intensity as though he was listening to the phone call through my head.

"Why? Tell me why you did it? I get that you're in love with Beth, but why Britt? She liked you and trusted you."

"*She's a whore*," he yells into the phone. I need to bring him down so I don't lose him. "She was going to ruin my pretty little love. She is so good. She's going to beautiful carrying my babies. She's an amazing mom." Carrying his babies…I almost choke on his idea.

"That she is, I won't argue that. What makes you think that after you brutalized her best friend, she is going to want to have your babies?" Yup, I just threw up in my mouth. J. is standing, rooted in his spot but I can see his brilliant brain processing what he is hearing. I know I should leave so he can't hear it, but I want him to know that I trust him.

"Mom can't have babies." J. whispers to me. I just nod my response to him.

"She'll see soon enough that the dirty whore isn't really her friend. She only wants to have sex with her and then she will leave her. She'll walk away like all the rest of the whores." Oh my god…Britt walked away from him and hurt him.

"When did Britt walk away from you? Who did she turn too? It's always been you for her."

"Like you don't know, I was supposed to meet up with her. I saw you driving away with both of them. I will kill you. Britt is a whore and deserves what she gets. She deserves your depravity, but my love will never be dirty and you have no right to touch her. She is mine." He must've seen us the night I brought them home.

"James, you know I only drove them home because they had too much to drink. I didn't sleep with either of them. I haven't touched her." I didn't want him to change his mind about her. If he thought Beth was dirty he would hurt her. J.'s eyes widen and his head tips as he rubs at his neck. He is trying to tell me something but I don't know what.

"I want to talk to her. I want to know you haven't ruined her. She better be the innocent she was when I last saw her. She is mine and you will not take what's mine. She is untouched and you can't have her."

He has lost his mind. She may be innocent and sweet compared to Britt, but this a woman who has two kids, and let me suck her pussy in front of a bar full of people while he watched. She is not untouched and naive. "You can't talk to her because she is sleeping. She and Britt had a rough day. You will need to call back."

"Then I want to talk to the kid, he will give her the message. I know he will because she raised him to be right. She told me adoption was the greatest thing."

"James, you can't talk to him, either. Do you really think these boys are adopted and Beth is a virgin? Is that what you think?" J. just about chokes on his tongue, he is still pointing at his neck, oh shit I get it. I marked her. She must have a hickey on her neck. I didn't notice it before she went upstairs, but J. must have.

"You can't ruin her. She is a precious innocent unlike the whores you surround yourself with. No wonder you can't see it." Finally my cell phone beeps. They have him, they have his location. He is in the house next door.

"Hey Graham, this has been enlightening. Remember, you son of bitch: you touch her and I will kill you." Then he hung up.

I was on the phone immediately holding up a finger to J. to wait. "You get him?"

"We are on our way." Luke said and hung up. I moved through the house out the front door with J. hot on my heels. Pounding on the neighbor's door for all I'm worth, there is no response.

"Graham, they are out of town." I turn to J. I feel like he spoke a foreign language. I am shaking the door handle and looking in windows, I'm debating whether to kick in the front door or not. "I said they are gone. You are going to set off their alarm."

"He's here." There is no car in the drive, nothing in the back. "They triangulated his cell phone and he is here." I look at J. he is holding out a set of keys. "What?"

"I take in the mail, water plants... you know. Use the key." He is shoving it into my hand. The door unlocked and I yell at him to stay put as I run through the house clearing room after room.

Nothing, he is not here. The slam of defeat nearly takes me off my feet. J. deactivated the alarm system but it was turned on and working when we got in the house. There are no signs of him. I look out the door and see Sheriff Carver and the Chief of Police Max Lancaster pulling up. Well, at least they are together. After shaking hands, I introduce J. and explain what I found...which is an ass load of nothing. I need to figure out how this guy knows where we are all of the time. How does he know every time we are getting close to him? I need to keep them safe. I need to get a step ahead of him. I need to think like him.

At the sound of the door slamming, I turn and see Beth walking towards us. If fury had a name, it would be hers. "What is going on here? Why is my son in the middle of the road with one, two...." And of course, she is counting cop cars. "Six! Six cop cars, and how many people?" She turns to me.

I need to calm her, I can feel her fear radiating off of her in waves, anger and fear swamping all her senses. "Mom, I'm fine it was so cool. Graham kept him on the phone until they tracked him here and then Graham went in with his gun drawn. Did you know he had a gun on his belt? He walked through the house clearing rooms. Creepy cop was gone but it was just like the murder mystery books P. likes. He is going to freak when he hears this." The kid kept going a million miles a minute. I tried to get her eye, but she only had eyes for J. It was funny; of course she knew I had a gun. She used it to hold her legs up and around me earlier. I didn't even think about it. Lust slammed through me, standing in the sun and I can see each bead of sweat on her brow and I know there is some running down between her breasts. I want to spend hours licking her.

Finally J. winds down, his hero worshipped is cool. I wonder if he knows how I feel about his mother. "Beth of course I kept J. out of danger. He let me in the door and stayed at the door until I came for him. I was introducing him around that's all. We didn't find Simmons, not even a trace of him. Can you think of anything we are missing?"

Shaking her head she looked so defeated and worn down. I want to wrap around her and hold her too me. Let her sleep away her hurt and pain. Taking a step to her, she turns from me and walks inside, "well come inside before you all die of heat stroke." Walking in the house, I remember how damned hot the desert is in August.

Britt is sitting in the formal living room and looking out the window when we walk in the door. "He's here isn't he? Did he call?"

I sit across from her and lean forward. There's a flash on a memory of me sitting like this with Beth when her husband died. My posture wanting to comfort, but keeping my distance so I don't scare her, when had I ever had to treat Britt like this? I won't. I won't lose Beth because Britt is wounded and I won't lose Britt because she made a mistake. I move to the couch next to her ignoring her involuntary flinch. I take her hands and see that she is so cold. "No, Britt. We didn't get him. He called. He knows we know about him and he gave me so much information about his reasoning. He is mad. I think he has finally just snapped."

"Did you get it recorded? I want to hear to make sure it's him."

I don't know the answer; I look to the Sheriff who is still standing in the door hat in hand. "We have it at the station as soon as you can get there, you can listen to it. I promise you, hun. It isn't pretty and I don't want you to hear it." He looks at her like a scared father, not sure where his place is in her life. At least she didn't lose him.

"I recorded it on our machine. Mom has us recording him all of the time now so she can show his boss how often he calls and when he says ugly things to her. I automatically turned it on when I answered it."

I wanted to kiss the amazing boy.

The Sheriffs asks, "You recorded it?"

"You have more than one like that?" asks Chief Lancaster

As for Chief Lancaster, I want to kill. He let it get this bad and had so many complaints that weren't looked into, even though Beth alone called him several times. He wrote them up, but never consulted James on them. He should have been fired, at the very least. "Well, let's hear it then." I hold my hand out for Britt as a peace offering...something to show I want things to return to the way they were.

She tucks her hands in her arm pits and stands wobbly but upright. "Let's go," she barks and throws me the coldest look I have ever seen. I look for Beth, but she has her face down and is curling in on herself. I follow her into the kitchen trying to get a moment, a micro second of eye contact. I want her to know I am here. She doesn't even register my existence. She only has eyes for J. and the Sheriff. She won't look at Britt either, but I don't know that that makes my case any easier. My fight won't be simply with Britt or with Beth's fear, but with the change in their lifestyle.

I had a feeling we were all going to lose Britt. I can't dominate Britt for long, as she needs too much I won't give her. I can give it to Beth. I can make sure Beth has what she needs, but I can't do that for Britt. I need to find someone to help with Britt.

We all listen to the phone calls that get gradually more and more aggressive until he is out right abusive. I can't figure out why she never told anyone he was calling her and behaving this way.

The chief asks what I want to know but her response baffles me. "You told me he was a good guy and if I filed a formal complaint, he would get in trouble. I didn't want him to retaliate worse than he was."

The words sink in as everyone is staring at the man that told her not to file a complaint against a man who raped her friend and has been stalking and harassing her for months. "Are you fucking kidding me, Lancaster? You told her not to file a complaint? *You told her that he may get in trouble?* Did you think to investigate it or to do you damned job? Britt got raped because *you* were too stupid and lazy to do your job! You are required by law to tell the IAB. I can't even think. I am just yelling and he is nothing but prey in sights, prey that needs to be taken down before someone else gets hurt.

"Graham!" I can hear Luke in my head telling me to settle down. I have never lost my control, not as an adult. I have never hit another man as an adult, either, but I really want to hit him.

Small hands wrap around my middle from behind. "Let him go Graham, we are okay. Graham, I am okay. Graham, let him go." The white noise fades and I look, I see Britt wrapped around me and bringing me back. Beth is crying, why is she crying? "Put him down now, Graham. I will see he is taken care of." I look and see I have the Chief of Police pinned to the wall with my hand around his neck. I back away, dropping him looking at my hands. What did I do? I never lose my control.

It's Beth's fault, she makes me crazy. I can't maintain control around her. I turn and walk out. I can't...I can't even look at her. Out the front door and I remember I can't leave, I won't leave her unprotected. I take off my tie and jacket opening my shirt and sit on the front porch. Her porch swing is nice...creaky, but nice. I could fix it for her if she let me, but I think I just ruined that for good.

Chapter 13
Beth

I think I opened the seventh ring of hell in my kitchen. I can feel tears slide down as I watch Graham and his self-control snap when he discovers that Britt was raped because the police chief didn't investigate the threat when I reported it. I am pretty sure he is mad because I knew it was going to happen and didn't tell him. I saw the wounded eyes. I saw the anguish I feel everyday reflected back at me. I didn't know he was going to rape her or that they knew each other. He had warned me against allowing my friends to push me into bad choices. I knew he was bat shit crazy, but I also knew he never said anything specific and he never said anything the police could use to force him to stop calling. Until we were at the hospital, I didn't realize that it was the same guy Britt knew. He calls himself Jimmy to me, James to her.

I feel like I should be doing something to calm everyone down. Britt had calmed Graham, not me. I couldn't do it. I don't know how to respond to that kind of anger. I probably would have ended up singing him stupid nursery rhymes. Britt was standing straighter and stronger than I have seen her all week. She found something in helping him. J. is just watching me waiting for some response I can feel his tension like it's my own. The Sheriff and the Chief are arguing in low murmurs and hushed voices. I wonder if Graham will get into too much trouble for his outburst. I would imagine it's a pretty big offense, although the Sheriff, his boss, didn't look too worried at the time.

I want to go to him. I want to crawl in his lap and let him pet me like a cat. I don't think it will help his nerves, but it would do wonders for mine. "J. Please finish your homework. P. will be here soon, I will send him in. Britt, back to bed with you, and no arguments! Gentlemen, I appreciate you coming over. Please take the answering machine with you when you leave and expect me in tomorrow to file a formal complaint. I expect you to investigate and you will be hearing from my attorney when she can get back out of bed. I will be on the porch as I hear that my swing needs attention. Show yourselves out." I grab two beers from the fridge and head out to the porch. I know they are going to have to walk past me, but I don't want to engage them.

Stepping on to the porch, I see his long legs spread and his hands on his head. He is looking at the chain holding up the swing up. "You know if you let me I can fix your squeak."

"Nah, that's how I know when the kids are out here, they all congregate on my porch because of the swing." I hand him the beer and curl up in the small spot next to him, with my feet tucked under my legs. He doesn't even move but to take a long swallow off the bottle.

"Thanks, sorry about that. I think it's your fault." Damn, he is so sexy...like a wild animal coiling back its strength.

"Ok, I'll bite. Why my fault? Not that I will concede that point." He slips his arm around my shoulders and I lean my head against him, sliding in close. He keeps the swing rocking and rubs my arm. It feels so good I want to purr.

He takes another drink, and it seems like he is planning his words for maximum effect. "I love you and I can't keep my head around you. I can barely think when you're in the room. I think that's love. But damn girl, you mess with my control something fierce."

Deep breath…in and out…in and out. Did he just say that? "You love me? But you're not sure?"

"Nah, I know I love you. I have never felt like this about anyone else. It has to be love…that, or indigestion." He chuckles as he pinches my arm lightly.

"I have Rolaids, so there's no need for you to suffer any longer." I can't help but pinch back. "Graham, I know what love is, I know it's about sharing your life, the stupid stuff, and the big stuff. It's about dreams as well as the nightmares. It's about having a partner to back you up, not do it for you. I have never been a submissive in a relationship. I don't know how to do it." My stomach clenches at the thought that he might get bored teaching me.

He takes another drink of his beer and a long, deep, breath. "Princess, you have always been a submissive. I just don't think your husband was a dominate." I don't want him talking about Marc poorly. As though he can feel my tension, he starts right in holding me tight. "Now hear me out. It's not a bad thing to not be a dominate. Not all men are, and not all women need men who are. Love doesn't require one be the other, however our relationship would have that as one of the many facets. Let me guess: you guys would argue about where to go for dinner, what to see on television, but always because you wanted the other to be happy. You pick his favorite places, him picking yours, right?"

"Yeah, sure, that's what you do when you love someone. You make choices that would make them happy, too." I don't understand what he is getting at and I am trying really hard to not get upset. His touch is going along way to soothe that. His hand is so warm on my arm and it sends little licks of flames through my body.

"No, Princess. That is how two non dominate people figure things out. A dominate doesn't ask a sub where they are going; he tells her. I may ask pizza or burgers; if you respond, I don't care. I will pick, not tell you to choose something. I am always going to listen to you, but you will always trust me to

171

take care of you. You are going to feel treasured and loved every minute of every day. You are going to learn to ask for what you want and need, but you will trust me to give it to you." His words send fire through my belly and make my heart want to tap dance.

"I didn't say yes, yet. I have kids I can't get involved in your club. I have Britt to take care of...." I don't even get to finish my list of worries before he pinches me again.

"Slow down. You remember when your husband died and everyone thought he was cheating and you sat in that living room convinced he didn't do it." He was such a dick about it. I remembered.

"You rolled your eyes at me. I thought I was going to slap you. It took everything I had not to do it." I said to him.

"Well, I wanted you so bad from the moment you opened the door, I was determined to prove that he was cheating. I wanted to come back and claim you and tell you not to mourn him he was a bad man. I dug and I dug, but he was so crazy in love with you he would tell anyone who would listen how great you were."

"He was an amazing man." The rock just sits in my gut, I didn't want to cry, but I knew Marc was good and right. I just didn't know he was that good and right. I knew he never cheated, but it was nice to have it confirmed.

"Yeah, he was lucky. That's all. I knew then I wanted what he had, not you as much as the relationship you had. I wanted someone to be proud of and to brag about...someone that made me never want to turn my head away."

"Graham, you can't step into his life. I am not the same woman I was with Marc. You can't think he never thought about cheating. He was a man...a normal, regular man. He left his socks on the floor in the living room and belched and thought it was funny and he was just a regular guy. But we were in love. You and I won't have that relationship. That is his and his alone." I don't know what else to tell him but he can't replace Marc.

172

"You misunderstand me princess, I don't want to replace him, and I come with my own set of issues as I am sure you do as well. I just want that devotion, and faith in a relationship. I don't want your relationship with him. I want you to teach me how to have one of our own. I love you and I want you for my own."

I can't stop the tears. They just come. Some are for Marc but most are for the man who just told me he loved me and seemed to know what it meant. I was so warm inside I felt like marshmallows were invading my brain. "I love you too, Graham, but I can't raise children around the club. I know it's important to you, but I can't and I have to think of them first."

His petting is become sincere now. I can feel him rubbing and stroking with intent and it is filing my body with passion. A passion I can feel suffusing me with heat and light. Still, he rocked and drank his beer and just thought. I felt like I was going to lose him and that it would kill me. I was losing Britt and I would lose Graham as well.

"You know I am retiring at the end of the month from the Sheriff's department." He said it like we just spoke about it this morning.

"Graham, you didn't tell me. You haven't talked to me." Which is, of course, my fault, but I wanted him to not take no. He told me he wouldn't. Even in my own head, I know I am all kinds of backwards for that round about thinking.

"No Beth, I haven't talked to you. I thought I would let you ladies cool off and come to reason. I see I was too late, and I should have been here sooner. But yes, I am retiring either at the end of the month or when this case is wrapped up." Yeah, that left me feeling all kinds of guilty.

I can't respond because I don't know what to say to him. "Well, Princess, I was thinking about hiring a manager at the club. I already figured you wouldn't want the kids to be involved or even around it at all. So, I thought I would move my head of security and bartender up and have them split my duties. I figure I will still do the books and oversee it, but I don't have to live there."

This is the first time it feels real, we could do this.

But what will we tell people, where will he live? "Where will you live Graham?"

"Oh Princess, you wound me. You move Britt right in, but me you leave out in the cold—or rather, the extreme heat. Why are we out here?" I can't help my chuckle.

I want him in my house, in my life and yes in my bed too, but I have the boys and I have to set an example for them. What kind of mom would I be if I just let a man move in without marriage? No I cannot think about marriage yet. "I can't move you in here. It wouldn't be right." He covered my mouth with hand.

"Say no more, I know having kids means no hanky panky in the kitchen." My whole body flushes and I can't help but dart my tongue out and lick his fingers where they are covering my mouth. My lower belly clenches and I feel my body get wet for him. "Stop that or we will have hanky panky in the swing Princess."

Fire lights my body and I want so much to keep him. "Can we?" I say on a laugh. I finally feel like I might get to keep him. His growl is his only response and he lays his head back pulling me tighter to his side. "Where are you going to live, Graham?"

"I still have my condo not too far from here. I will move back there." I can feel he isn't too excited about it, but I can't have him living here. I just can't. Can I? No, definitely not. I need Britt to talk to about this. She would help me figure out what I should do. I feel like I have lost her and I miss her all ready. "You don't seem excited; you seem almost resigned and pouty." I hope he doesn't get upset, because I really can't lose him.

"Princess, I am sexually frustrated to a level I have never been before, I am worried sick about you and Britt and the boys. We are discussing turning my life upside down and I am just a little worried about well, everything right now. This is so new to me; I am still trying to process the whole thing. I am still raging angry that Lancaster let you down and I need to find James so I can get him behind bars and actually start my life. I just want to spend time with you and no interruptions. "

"Well, since I left a house full of angry policemen, my teenage son doing his homework another pulling up as we speak, I don't think that is going to happen any time soon. But keep that thought."

"Princess, that thought never leaves my brain. I will get you alone and it will be soon.

White hot heat fills me as my body tightens. I want him.

I look down and he is hard. His suit pants are doing nothing to hide it. "Put that thing away. Here comes P."

He drapes his hand over his lap but stays in the same position as P. walks up dropping into the chair next to us. I give him a rundown of all that has transpired in his absence. He seems distracted and I can see a huge hickey on his neck right where his shirt collar meets his skin. "Peter Anthony Williams, what is that thing on your neck?" His hand goes to his neck and I feel Graham give me a big pinch and shake his head.

Who is he to tell me what to say to my son? "It is the same thing that is on your neck mom." And he stands up and walks in the house.

Graham is stifling a laugh. I am feeling my neck as though I could feel the mark. With my elbow to his gut to emphasize my point, I ask "Why the hell didn't you tell me?"

He's laughing out loud as though this is the funniest thing he has ever seen. I have never seen him laugh like this. I want to choke him for it. His laugh is a deep rumble that fills me with light. "You're too funny, Princess. I didn't tell you because you would have been self conscious, but I can assure you everyone saw it. Everyone took note and until there is a ring on your finger, the mark stays."

I stand trying to get a good huff on, "I can't go to work looking like a tramp with that all over my neck. That's just gross. No."

He is laughing so hard I can't keep a straight face, "Alright, not on your neck. I will figure out a better place. You will learn to love my marks. Wear them with pride."

"Buy a damned ring or pee on my leg. Just leave my neck alone." As I stomp in house he stands to follow, still laughing out loud.

His laughter follows me all the way into the kitchen. He wraps his hands around my waist from behind, "Aw, Princess don't be mad at me. I couldn't bear it."

"Fuck you," I say under my breath

He leans in close to my ear, "I wish" and lets me go.

I look around the room, notice everyone watching us playing. My boys seem happy about it. I realize the two policemen are still here. "I thought you guys were leaving." Can't they take a hint?

Sheriff Carver walks toward me and answers, "No you will have someone outside and someone inside at all times. We have created a joint task force to staff the security until Officer Simmons is found."

"Mom, it was the coolest thing. They called the mayor and he had to fund it and they told him Britt was going to sue the city. They worked out a rotation schedule to always have someone on site outside in a marked patrol car and inside in plain clothes. They didn't staff that, but they said they know who will do it. It was magic at work."

Graham is laughing at him now, quietly but I can feel his body shaking. I can't hold in my chuckle either. "No baby that is bureaucracy at work. If there wasn't so much red tape and stupid checklist and people to include, Jimmy would have been investigated from the get go. What you saw were two old men who have to run for office and don't want to lose their jobs. They are also hoping to appease Auntie, though they know she will still sue the city. And she will rain the shit of

176

Satan and all the fires of hell if Jimmy gets in the house and hurts one of you two; they're just protecting their asses, honey."

All eyes are now on me. Graham is still laughing but he has stopped trying to hold it in, Chief Lancaster looks like his going to pop a button, but the Sheriff nods. "You're right, Beth. We are worried sick something will happen on our watch again. The shit storm you so eloquently spoke of will not touch me if I can keep doing what I am doing but yes the city will feel the wrath of god if Britt gets in a court room. We are trying to cover our respective asses, but we are also trying to get this taken care of as soon as possible. As soon as this hits the news, all officers are going to be suspect to the public and we can't have that. Let's get him caught, and then we can worry about Britt. If he is still out there, she will leak this story and she will look so good on the television all torn up and bleeding while protesting how the police department had complaints and did nothing."

I turn to Britt who is sitting quietly, demurely drinking her iced tea. This is the scary Britt, the one that sits in a deposition and listens to the parents argue and then draws blood with every word said later. I have never seen her, but I have been told. "Aw, Britt, you wouldn't do that, would you? Stand in front of a camera and tell your story just to get headlines?" I know her; she isn't about notoriety. That's why she is in family court. This is about blood—hers being spilled and mine being threatened. The boys being worried and I would think even Graham's good name being dragged through the mud.

I watch her. She doesn't respond. Instead, she just slides the notepad she has been doodling on over to Chief Lancaster. He glances at her intermittently as he reads it. All eyes are on him and everyone is holding a collective breath.

"I have been receiving an amazing amount of calls from the press," she starts. "How they haven't found me is amazing, but they are all wanting my story. What you are reading is the story that will go out with copies of the rape kit pictures if he isn't picked up in twenty-four hours. I know I have no case in court. I know I will be crucified."

I can't stand it when she says that. "You don't know that, Britt. Stop giving up before the fight has begun." I know she is an attorney and has probably seen something like this. She can't let him get away with it.

"No, Beth. I am not giving up. I will fight. He will go to court. He may not get rape or attempted murder, but maybe he will get simple assault. I am not worried about that. I am concerned that he is going to kill you." Graham's arm tighten around me again as the fear that slightly abated came rushing back. "Your little cuddle fest on the front porch probably only pissed him off. The rest of the chief's plan is to keep everyone in the house permanently living in fear while the police chase one of their own. Don't mistake their simple minds for men who aren't out for blood. They will get him, but only after he shows his face. Meanwhile, you and I and the boys have one guard to protect us all. Your kids are to be pulled from school and your life stops today." I look at the boys and they are holding strong, but I can see the fear in their eyes, the knowledge that the world isn't safe. I have tried so hard to protect them from that knowledge after Marc died. What have I done?

Looking at Graham, I see resignation and knowledge. He knew that this was coming. "Why didn't you tell me?"

"Tell you what?" He holds me tighter, like he can't let go of me. "You knew you had a mad man after you, so I didn't think scaring you would help."

Britt stands up tipping her chair over and everyone rushed to her side. "Are you kidding me?" Britt starts yelling at Graham, "You are trying to protect her so she isn't scared? Shouldn't she be scared? Won't fear protect her? It probably will, better than you can. You need to leave her alone." She is shaking and yelling. I have never seen her lose her cool so completely.

"J., get her pills. P., grab her water. Come on, Sweets. Let's get you settled down." As I take her arm to lead her to the sofa, Graham's heavy footsteps stop so that he towers over her.

He takes her face in his hand and says gently, "I know I let his happen to you and that you should have been protected. I let him in our club and into our lives. I had no idea. I will get him…you can count on that. I don't scare her because she has nothing to fear from him. He won't hurt any of you again." My heart stops and I just watch as he scoops her up and heads towards the stairs.

The boys are pushing water and pills in my hand as I follow behind. She is petite, but he carries her like she is a child. With no effort at all he is stopping at the top of the stairs waiting for directions, looking around. I can hear Britt sobbing and I point towards the guest room where she has set up her life. The simple bright room has a queen size bed, large chest of drawers, small dressing table that is doubling as Britt's desk and shares a walkthrough bathroom with my office. I quickly pull the blankets down as he lays her in the bed. I had showered her earlier apparently missing the phone call. Handing her the pills and water, I can't think of a single thing to say to her. She can't blame Graham can she? That's like blaming your ass because you stubbed your toe on a chair. "Britt, you need to take a deep breath, remember strong, capable we are survivors." I start stroking her hair. I had someone come in and trim it up short the day after we got home. I look at Graham who is just standing over her watching us.

"She's right. I let her get hurt in my house and I let him get close enough to see in your windows. I can't protect you both." With that, he turned and left. I felt my heart being pulled from me. It had to go with him, it belonged to him. I watched the door willing him to come back and to turn around. His footsteps on the stairs are not deterring my desire to see him standing there looking at me.

I look down at Britt so broken and small and I can't fix her. I can't make her feel safe again. I didn't notice how scared she still was. I know she slept with the lamp on and that she was afraid of the dark. More often than not, she slept in my bed to keep her monsters away, but I didn't see how terrified she was during the day. I want to crawl in her brain and pull out all the thoughts that are scaring her. He had to have said something to her to make her feel like he was coming back. I'm angry that she didn't tell me and so pissed that she thinks Graham should keep her safe at all times.

Why is he responsible? Why do I have to be responsible? Why can't she just keep herself safe like the rest of have to? I know nothing could have stopped what happened to her. She couldn't control someone breaking in and getting to her. She needs to know no one could have stopped him. But it's my fault that he wanted to hurt her. I heard the recording. I know he is angry at me because he wants me to love him. I don't know how to stop him, but it's me James wants.

I watch her eyes flutter as tears still leak down her cheeks. I flip on her lamp. It is still light out and will be for a while. As I stand to leave, I walk over to close her window and see him, in the park. I know he sees me, he knows I see him. He jumps from his post on the cement block fence that separates the park from the school. He jumps down and is gone. I can't see him. Fear rushes up my arms freezing my heart.

I close her shutter blinds and leave. Her soft breathing is regular and strong. It lets me know she will be out for a while. I step into my bedroom to go splash some water on my face and Graham is sitting on the edge of my bed, my silk camisole in his hands. I didn't hear him come back up the stairs. I need to break the tension I feel pulsing off of him. He looks rumpled and so damned sexy. His hair is mussed again and his beard growth is just enough to show he hasn't saved in a day or two. His top two buttons on his wrinkled white dress shirt are undone though still tucked in his equally rumpled charcoal grey slacks. I want to strip him down and climb on top of him. I want to see the light in his eyes as he laughs again.

"Are you trying to kill me? You keep looking at me like that and I am going to take you where you stand." Oh god, I want nothing more. The lust grows from my belly wetting my panties.

I watch him take my tiny scrap of silk to his face and smell it. I slept in it last night then just laid it on my bed this morning to sleep in again tonight. Watching him with it against his face is so erotic. My head is swamped with images of him running his face along my breasts and between them. Shaking my head to clear the fuzz "You can't I have a house full of people."

Rebekkah Rogers

Chapter 14
Beth

"Your boys are the only ones stopping me. Shut the door and come here." The demand in his voice brooks no argument. Honestly, I wouldn't have one if it did. I push the double doors shut behind me and walk to him, all the while checking to make sure my curtains are closed. My heart is racing. I want this more than anything else.

"How does this work, Beth? You have to tell me. Is there no sex with kids in the house? That can't be the rule or people would never have more than one."

I'm confused and I can't think.

His hands grab my hips and pull them between his legs as he lays his head against my breasts. I clutch him tighter and feel him shaking inside. "Nah, you just have to be careful and damn quiet. You don't want to get caught because they aren't going to catch you doing it all vanilla with the covers around you." I feel his body laughing quietly.

"No. The way your luck is, Princess, you would have the entire police force lead by your two intrepid adventurers catch you getting fucked in the ass." The image of him behind me pushing me to the wall and holding me still with my hair while he impales my ass is too much. My whole body quakes with the lust pulsing through me. It's hot and ready to swamp me at any minute. "Like that thought, did you? I knew you would be fun."

I can't keep the small moan from escaping as his hands grab my ass tight and hard and lifts me against him. I want him so much I can't think of anything else. My focus is on him and his soft, thick hair in my hands. His mouth nips at my breast through my tank top. His hands streaking flames and heat through my legs as he pulls at me. I can feel my nails sinking in his shoulder as he runs his hands along the inside of thighs, not quiet hitting the spots where I want him most. My moan matches the pace of his deep throated growls and it feels like he is trying to pull me inside of him. I can hear our breathing and pants echo through the room and I know I have stop or something. I have to do something. "Music, Graham. Music is how we do this."

"I want to hear you. I need to hear you screaming under me. Now!" He all but growls his protest at me. His words are so deep and grave that they scrape along my nerves and make me hotter than I ever remember being.

"No, we need music so no one else can hear." I'm trying to keep my wits long enough to make sure my children don't hear us. He lifts my shirt over my head streaking lightening with his touch.

"I want them to hear you, to know you are mine." I just shake my head and step away, flicking on my music. I know what's in it. The woman's deep rich voice fills the room. Still standing back from him I slip out of my pants.

I stand in front of him in my panties and bra, both of which are simple yet durable tan lace. They are certainly not my sexiest underwear. I can feel my wetness on my thighs. "Graham, please. We have to hurry. I only have a couple of minutes."

He shakes his head. "I won't last long, Princess. I want to see you. I need to drink all of you in now. The minute I touch you, I will be gone."

My head fills with his words. His gaze is so strong I can feel it stroking me. I reach behind me to undo my bra and I can feel his deep breath. "I want to see you Graham. Please."

He stood up and unbuttoned his shirt painfully slow without ever lifting his eyes from me. I noticed tattoos in the club but I didn't get to see them for long. I asked him about them in our talks before, but I want to touch them. I want his hot hard body under my hands. He drops his shirt on the floor, kicks out of his shoes, and starts on the belt. I drop my panties and he stops just taking me in. I can feel the flames of his stare. I watch him as he slides his boxers off with his slacks and places his gun on top of his pants.

His erection springs forth, the head wet from the pre-cum. I have wanted to know what he tastes like. I want him. My blood rushes at the thought of his hot salty taste in my mouth. I drop to my knees where I am my arms out to reach behind his legs and pull him to me. "Oh yeah," he growls as my lips close around him. My fingers close around him and I realize just how large he is. I can't get my hand all the way around him. I can't take him all the way in, he's too big. He will never fit in me. He lifts my chin with one hand as he pushes my shoulders down to open my throat for him to slide himself down. I feel my eyes water, but I can take him. "Relax and take me. You feel so good."

With one hand holding him as hard as I can and the other holding his balls, lifting and stroking them, he keeps my head still and shoves into me again. It is the hottest thing I have ever done. With him deep in me, I swallow against him and he sinks deeper. I am completely at his control. I couldn't stop if I wanted. I feel my body clenching and my muscles pulsing. The lightning shooting through me makes me moan deep in my throat. "Have mercy, Princess. Don't do that. If you come with me in your throat you are going to get all of me. Don't cum yet." I don't know if he's talking to me or himself. I can't stop mine. I'm not the one in control of my body. Doesn't he know it's his? I feel him slip out my mouth, dragging him along my tongue. I want to bite, just a little nip. I pull my tongue back and pull him back with a scrape of my teeth on the bottom. "Jesus Christ Beth, oh fuck, you are incredible." He pulls me up by my armpits. I don't think I could move of my own volition if I tried. It's his body, his to command.

He lifts me higher as my legs go around his waist then higher still. His arms are under my knees as I sink down and he opens me to him. With one long burning thrust he is deep inside me, farther and wider than I have ever taken. My head arches back with my arms around his neck as he lifts me by my thighs and holds tight to my ass. Pushing me on to him hard and fast, I can't slow the erotic heat racing down my body. The white flames consuming me and I am trying to not scream out. His pants and grunts wrap around my soul. "I have wanted inside you for so long, tell me your mine." He is too big, the stretching and pulling on my sensitive skin, my whole core is on fire with the burn and I have never felt anything like this before. "Say it, be mine. Come for me now Princess, you feel so fucking good."

His hands slide to my pull my ass apart, only pushing against my tiny sensitive hole and I am burning, the pain of the fullness, his pressure on my ass, the hard hands holding me up. The scrape of his hair on my nipples, the hot gravely words. And my orgasm takes me over, swamping me. I know I am arching away and digging my nails in for purchase on his shoulders. He grabs me harder by digging into my body with his hard hands and I feel his hot heat surging inside me. He slams my hips up and down on him and the wet heat bathes my sensitive skin. "You're mine, Graham, only mine. I love you and I belong to you." He roars and pounds harder and harder to get every last drop out and into me. It is the ultimate in possession. There is no question I am his.

He puts his head on my shoulder still holding our weight. He is panting and grunting "Sweetheart, put me down." He just shakes his head against my shoulder. I can feel him softening inside of me. I clench my inner walls against him, because I am still pulsing and turned on.

"Oh, Princess, don't do that if you ever want to leave this room." He surges into me again and he is hardening again.

I can't keep the groan in. My body is so soft against his. His shoulders are hard and as I look I see they are bleeding.

"Graham, why didn't you tell me I was hurting you? Please, put me down. Let me clean you up." I slide my legs out of his grasp and he lifts me off him. I feel empty, he belongs inside me. He fills me completely.

I feel his cum running down my thigh, and see he is still mostly erect and dripping. I grab his hand and pull him into the bathroom with me. Wetting the hand towel, I start with his shoulders first. They are going to hurt soon. I didn't just dig in, but rather, I scratched long deep pulls on him. "Don't please, please leave them. I want to feel your mark on me."

I can't help but kiss his shoulders as I feel him wrap around me again. He places small delicate little kisses on my head. "I love you Graham, I really do."

His body shakes on a chuckle. "I love you too princess, now come on let's get you cleaned up. We need to get back down stairs." The kids, the cops there are too many people in my house. I pull my hair on top of my head and turn on the shower. Using the sprayer I wash my body while Graham watches me. "Why not the hair?" he asks when I get out.

"I washed it this morning, it takes forever to dry. I mostly just wanted to wash the smell of sex off so I can face the kids. You wanted to know how this is done; well here are the gory details." He slaps my ass as I walk by him. He is just leaning on the counter watching me run around the bathroom. "Get dressed, now".

He just keeps chuckling and it is the best sound in the world. "I feel so dirty princess. No woman has ever thrown my clothes at me and pushed me out of the room after sex."

I can't help it, but the stab of jealously goes straight to my heart. "No more women Graham, no one else right?"

Stepping forward with his arms out, he states, "No one can compare to you. That was the most amazing thing I have ever done, and I wouldn't jeopardize it for the world. No one but you Beth can have me ever again!" It's a balm to my tenuous hold on my nerves. I can only nod and step into a tight quick hug. I watch him get dressed. He looks younger, still hard and fierce, but softer in the eyes. I leave the music playing but turned down low it should play for hours on the continuous loop. He follows me out of the room I can feel his eyes on me burning to my soul.

I know the kids didn't miss us when we get down the stairs and I hear the J. yelling at what I assumed was P. until I walked in the room. The Sheriff, in his full uniform, is sitting on my couch playing video games with my teenage son. J. is yelling directions, but not anything I think either of the men playing should be hearing. "No, you have to hit the cop on the head and run. Kick his ass, kick him while he's down." I can feel my face heat as I look at Graham. Do I stop it? What do I say?

P. looks at me and asks, "Hey mom what's for dinner?" Then he turns back to the game and gives Chief Lancaster instructions very similar to what J. is giving if not just a little less colorful.

I can't wrap my head around what I am seeing. Grown men, old enough to be their grandfathers, listening to the boys teach them how to steal cars, kick cops asses and beat up hookers. Okay, no wonder our world is such a fabulous place to live. I'm going to kill Britt for teaching them this. "Is your homework done boys?" To the chorus of *yups*, I ask "Shrimp for sandwiches or pizza?" I know before they even open their mouths, but it is the men that surprise me with their joined echo of pizza. "Don't you guys have wives or families that need you at home?" Without so much as looking up from the game, I get *nope* from both of them simultaneously.

Graham can't keep his hands off me and I love it. Each touch sends little shivers of need through me. "Leave the guys alone, Princess. They feel bad enough as it is. They have assigned themselves protectors to the boys. I get to watch you and Britt, they will watch the boys. Nothing will happen on their watch I promise you that."

I am baffled; my children warrant the protection of these two powerful men. "But they are politicians, not cops."

Graham just shakes his head. "Luke was my partner when I was a rookie. He was a damned good cop and he really doesn't have anybody else. Nothing will happen to the boys under his watch."

I just nod my head and turn to walk to the phone. I holler out and ask what type of pizza everyone wants. I have teenage boys; I order a pizza each and I know it won't go to waste, no matter what the options are. Graham and I stand in the kitchen necking like kids while the boys play video games waiting for the pizza. I almost forget anything is wrong. For just a minute, I felt safe and right. I can hardly remember the last time I felt loved and cared for like this. My whole body was warm and surrounded.

Well, nothing lasts forever, I think, as the phone goes off and the door bell rings at the same time. I start to move to door when Graham says, "No let me get it," and walks away. *All right then*. Instead, I move to the phone, but the Sheriff is already there and giving me a steely hard look while shaking his head.

Well, I can set the table at least. I head towards the cupboard when I hear Britt scream. I am running up the stairs as fast as I can with the whole of the force of men behind me. She is sitting up in bed, panting and screaming. This isn't like any nightmare she had before. "He's here. He was in my room. He touched me."

I am on her and in her bed with my arms around her before anyone can react. "It was a dream, Sweets. Hush…it was just a dream." I'm rocking her and singing again before I even realize I am doing it. Just as Graham walks into the room and flips the light on, I notice something that gives me chills.

"Graham, her shutters are open. I closed them. I know I did. I turned on the lamp, closed the shutters, and then the bedroom door before I left her."

He is watching me as he is trying to absorb my words. "Everyone out" he yells. I see Chief Lancaster and Sheriff Carver each with a hand on a boy's shoulder.

"Come on boys, let's go eat." I hear Lancaster say as he turns them from the room.

I start to get up pulling Britt with me. "Not you; you two are staying here in this room." I see he has his gun in his hand and is walking corner to corner. He lifts and examines everything before him and clicks the window lock. I would have sworn it was locked earlier, but I didn't check the lock. Seeing my gaze, he comments, "You have shitty locks on your windows. It doesn't take much to get them open."

We should have had the alarm on while we were in the house.

He shuts the bedroom door and slides the chest of drawers in front of the door. He steps into the bathroom and locks the door behind him. He walks through to my office, moving things as he goes. I hear him walking through the house, clearing the upstairs. I hear Sheriff Carver yell cleared from downstairs, he must have been doing the same thing down there.

The whole time, Britt is sobbing. "Did he say anything, Britt?" Meanwhile, I hear Graham talking down the stairs to the Sheriff Carver.

Her only response is more sobbing and head shaking. She has been through so much. I want to wrap her in gauze and protect her forever. Graham walks back in and moves my furniture back in place. "The window was open. The room is different from the way it was before, but I don't see him. J. turned on the alarm so it will sound if you open windows or doors. Remember that and, well, just don't open anything."

"Graham, how did he get in my house?" I can't stand the thought that maybe he is still here. But I trust Graham when he says that James isn't in the house. "Why come in just to mess with us?"

"He thrives on fear, baby. That is why he just toys around. He could have hurt her again but he didn't." I want to ask why he didn't hurt her, why he doesn't just come out with it and then the plan forms. I know Graham won't go for it. I know he wants to protect us all, but I can't live like this anymore. I also feel Britt slipping back to sleep. Her adrenaline rush pushing her under as it burns out.

Laying Britt back down, I check her window again. It is locked and closed. I pull the dressing table under it and put a lamp in front of the window. I turn it on and herd Graham out of her room. The silence upstairs is unsettling. Something about it was niggling at my brain. I walk room to room and perused all the same things Graham checked. All the windows are closed and locked. It's a second story, so I can't figure out how someone could get up here. All the rooms are locked up tight. The boys will sleep with me tonight. Then this nonsense will end tomorrow.

Heading down stairs the noise is comforting, like nothing could touch the house. Graham's hand at the small of my back lends me some reassurance but I need resolve not reassurance. I know I have to protect the kids. I have to stop this and I know how. I want to curl up with Graham again. I already miss the intimacy of the porch swing and the feel of his hands holding me tightly in my room.

While I'm standing in the family room watching the boys play, Graham breaks my reverie. "They're fine. It's like nothing happened to them. Come in here with me. I want to sit in the dark, hold you, and make out like teenagers after Prom." I can't stop the giggle and the heat that fills my body.

He leads me to the couch by my front window. I see him look around. From here, you can see the front door, up the stairs, and Britt's door. Through the dining room, that resembles a study hall table and not the formal table it really is, I can see into the kitchen and part of the family room where the kids are. He picked a vantage point to watch the house. The house is lit like a runway except this room; only one table lamp that isn't turned on and the sun outside light this room. The sun is going down, but it is still pretty bright outside. He can see and hear everything from here. I'm comforted just knowing he is watching out for us.

I slide close to him as he puts his arm around me and pulls my legs across his lap. Sitting in his lap like a child makes me feel so safe and protected. I know he would never let anything hurt me. As I lay my head on his shoulder, I hear him whisper in my hair. "You will be getting spanked for this."

Heat floods my body and I can feel his marks where he held me so tight earlier. I have never been spanked, at least not a real spanking as I have read about. "Why?"

His chuckle bounces me in his lap and I can feel him getting hard again. "Because you should have told me he scared you. You should have told me his name and damn it, you were cruel in the hospital. You chose everyone over us. You owe me for that."

I can feel tears pool in my eyes; doesn't he know how bad I felt when he walked away? I know he isn't trying to hurt me, but it does. I feel so guilty for what happened between us. "Don't you know how bad that hurt me? I was so scared and I didn't know what else to do. I didn't think you would come back."

His deep exasperated breath makes me angry, but he holds me tighter as though he knows it will. "I know. That is why you need the spanking. I want you to remember it is me you come to, you don't push me away. I am yours and you're mine. You can't push me away anymore." His hand tight around my hip and his kiss to my hair are more reassuring than the words.

"Princess, you are going to look beautiful with your hands tied behind your back, on your knees with your ass in the air pink from my hand. Your body will be open and bared to me, dripping wet because I know you will enjoy it. I will sink into your pretty pink ass and feel all that heated skin against my hips as you buck wild against me."

I can't help it; I know I'm getting wet again. I am trying to hold very still so my body doesn't betray me, but the whip cord of desire is lashing me the more he tells me. His cock is throbbing against my hip and I know my body is betraying me as I press into it more just to hear him groan as he grinds into me more. "Do you think we can make it upstairs without them noticing?" I ask. I can't help it. I need him; I need what he does for me.

"I will make sure of it. You head upstairs. I want you naked and waiting. I am right behind you." I head up the stairs as I watch him walk in the living room, I hear him open the fridge and tell the men that he is going to sit up in the window upstairs to watch the park. I stand at the top of the stairs and listen as he orders them to keep their eyes on the boys. I am pretty sure everyone, including my two sons, got the innuendo, but nothing gets through to them when they are playing video football. I'm just happy they aren't beating up on cops anymore.

I hear Graham start up the stairs, so I quickly step into the room and strip off my clothes. And start the music again, surprised it is off. I thought I left it turned on. I am standing naked when he gets to the top of the stairs, two beers in his hand. He sets them on the bathroom counter walking right past me. "Stay there, princess," and I hear him walk farther in the bathroom, use the facilities, wash his hands. I'm standing naked and he doesn't even look. He kicks out of his shoes, unbuttoning his shirt at the same time. I realize this time because I am taking my time watching when he drops his pants. He checks his gun before he sets it on top and out of the holster that sits on his belt.

I can't take my eyes off the tattoos that cover his upper arms and part of his chest. He told me it was one big tattoo that had lots of smaller pieces. It's gorgeous. His chest is fair but hard and toned. Dark hair dusted over it leads my eyes to his enormous erection. He locked the door into place and looks so comfortable in my room. This is where he belongs. Following his gaze to the chest of drawers behind me, I know what he is seeing. Wedding pictures, me almost 20 years ago with Marc smiling, kissing and dancing. "I will move the pictures later, unless you need them moved now. I know he would want me to have you."

He just shakes his head "You were so beautiful. So happy, so in love…I want you to look at me like that one day." I can't help but step to him. Walking to him I hear him catch his breath. "Come here," He opens his arms and they are around me. His hot hard body against me, I lay my head against his chest as he holds me tightly. I am a little surprised when he pulls away sitting on the edge of the bed pulling me to him he says "remember spanking first before you get to come. But I want a little of that throat again. I can't get that out of my head. I want to come down your throat first. Now get on your knees." The idea of taking him again, of feeling him fucking my throat makes me almost come just standing there. He stands again.

I sink to my knees, this is what I want. "Princess, hear me and hear me good. You will not touch yourself and you will not come." Oh yes, I feel myself clench and my nipples throb. The heat builds in my body. I sit on my feet taking him in hand; he is so hard. I wrap both hands around him holding him tight pulling as a small drop of cum forms on the head. Holding my tongue out I lay it flat to catch that little drop tasting his salty musky essence. That one drop makes me flow more and causes my whole body to clench.

I know I can't come. I can't let that fire whipping through my body take me. His hands on my face open me up to him. He buries one in my hair holding it tight. Little pricks of pain from my scalp invigorate me as he sinks into my mouth. I tip my head back opening my throat and flatten my tongue to let him take my mouth as his own. Hard and fast and deep, I can feel my eyes watering and my body constricting on its self. I swallow when he is deep in me and feel his groan through my whole body. "Have mercy. Take it all." He is thrusting into me and waiting for me to swallow, then thrusting again. I am sucking as deep and hard as I can. I feel his balls lifting. I know he is going to come. His hands tighten in my hair as I moan against him and pull my tongue so he scrapes my teeth. I pull on his balls, pulling them down and holding him off for just a minute looking up I meet his ocean blue eyes. His hand softens on my face and his expression is so full of love. "So beautiful, God do that again." Another tug and scrape of my teeth and he is holding me tight again, pulling at my hair as he pushes harder into me. I feel the heat on my throat and it brings on my own heat, each swallow and grunt makes me hotter and wetter. My thighs rub together and I can't hold in my own moans. His dark gravelly voice slides down my back and commands, "No, Princess. You can't come yet."

He pulls himself out of me and stands me in front of him. I am running down my legs and have never been so turned on. He wipes at the tears that are running free. Bending to kiss me he still holds my face gently, but the kiss is anything but gentle and soft. It's consumption and need I feel him tasting himself on me. I want him in me somewhere anywhere. I feel my body moving too him like a magnet. He holds me back by my face with his rough hands and gentle touch. My moans are impatient and wanting I know he hears my need, but he doesn't touch me. He has to know if he touched me I would combust. I am so hot. My skin feels like I have been flayed open. "Get on your knees, Princess. Let me look at you open to me." His hand at the small of my back while he leads me to the bed is enough to make me moan and lean into his hand. On my knees on the end of the bed, he pulls my hands behind my back. His hands scrape down my arms sending flames through my body. I feel silk wrapped around my wrist. I don't know what it is, maybe my panties. He pushes my shoulders to the bed my ass rising in the air. He runs a hand through my dripping slit. I try to push into him but he won't let me. The need is going to kill me. The slap on my ass is like a sharp stab of heat straight to my pussy. It's harder than I thought, but the hand that rubs the spot turns that pain to heat. "Now Princess, when I slap, you count. I should hear one sir, two sir, and nothing else."

Oh, no. He can't think I am going to be able to count and think through this does he? Another slap and more heat the pain and then the slide of pleasure runs through my body. "I can't hear you, princess. Did you count?"

Another? Oh No, I can't take it, "Please let me come. Please, Graham." He runs his hands over my wet clit and around my opening while pushing into me hard and fast.

"Count them. We're on four." He lets out another brutal, punishing slap.

"Oh yes. Four, sir, please." Another rub of my pussy drags my juices across my clit and up to my ass.

"Princess, have you ever been fucked in the ass?" Another slap, followed by more heat and I feel myself clenching ready to orgasm.

"Five sir. Yes sir, I have." His groan is the only warning I get as he pushes into me deep. He grabs my hands pulling me back to him. I feel them freed and I am up leaning back onto him. I swing my hands up over my shoulders and around his head holding his hair as he drives into me. His hands run up and down my belly like he can't decide where to hold me. He takes my breast in a punishing hold, pulling on my nipple rolling it in his fingers. His other hand takes my clit and rubs and pinches in the same rhythm as my nipple. White heat takes over my body, his hand moves from my breast, sliding up my throat and over my mouth. His fingers slide in mouth to hold in my scream as my orgasm rolls through me wave after wave. His grunts and hot seed push me further and further over the edge. I feel him lay us down but my brain is full of white noise and my whole body is numb. He rises, but I can't focus on it. He is wiping me up and talking but I have nothing, nothing to give him in return.

The little kisses on my temple and on my nipple as he pulls it into his mouth and finally, I can focus on him. "That my naughty little princess is called sub space," he whispers against my lips as he lays little kisses on my mouth. "It is the place where a submissive feels safest, taken care of, loved."

"Can I live here?" I feel him wrap himself around me from behind, still laying gentle kisses on me everywhere he can reach.

"Sure. I'll let the boys know you won't be back." He chuckles.

"Thanks." I can't form any other words. I feel the cold bottle pressed to my lips as he lifts me.

"Drink," he says and I taste the foaming tangy ale on my tongue. This is really nice. I snuggle back into him and feel myself falling asleep.

Rebekkah Rogers

Chapter 15
Graham

I miss her already. I left her snoring on her bed forty-five minutes ago. She was worn out taking care of everyone else and she needs to rest. Looking around the room, I took in the comfortable surroundings and homey feeling her house had. The kids filled it though there were only two of them they were loud and large and knew how to occupy space. She obviously wasn't into posed portraits. There was one posed picture of each of the kids, probably school pictures framed and hung, but they were surrounded by candid pictures, both large and small, of a very happy family, on the beach, in the mountains, and in the snow. Pictures of the boys with their father dominated the walls. They looked identical to each other and were a perfect image of him. He was Mediterranean, maybe Italian very dark and very large towering over Beth in the pictures of them together. The boys were going to be taller than I am. They were already very tall and lanky. It would be nice to have this as a home…a refuge from all other places.

I know I have won her over, but I am not sure she is ready to see me as part of this picture. Would we hang pictures of us along side pictures of her children and husband? It feels like I would be imposing and forcing a layer over what was really the substance underneath. My grandmother used to tell me, "Just because you put cheese on shit it don't make it a casserole".

I don't want kids of my own. I never really have. I have seen the guys with the little ones and they are cute enough. But I came from the shit that couldn't be a casserole. I knew I would never do that to kids. I know I can't help her raise the kids, but I can't wait for years for them to go either. I won't wait and I want to be part of this. Watching the kids teach the old men how to play they are comfortable talking to them, teaching them and I realize they really are full grown men that just need their bodies and hormones to catch up.

Maybe they don't need to be raised. I won't get involved with them as long as they treat her right and they seem to be respectful of my princess. I want to go crawl in bed with her. She was naked and sated, warm and soft. I can't believe I am getting hard again. I have never wanted a woman like her and I know I won't be tired of her like all the others. The other women would grate on my nerves after a couple of weeks. Then the simpering and whining would start and I would be so turned off. My princess isn't that woman, she won't whine. If she wants something she will tell me or she will take it. She won't wait long. I am going to have my work cut out for me.

The boys have school tomorrow. It's a perfect of example of Beth getting her way. Everyone thought they should stay home, but she put her foot down and wouldn't budge. Her problems were not going to spill over and ruin the boys good time in high school. I don't how to remind them they are suppose to go to school, but it is getting late and I am sure Beth doesn't want them up all night playing video games when she was so adamant about it. Without anything from me they rise and head to bed. Following a round of *goodnights* and *see you tomorrows*, the boys troop up the stairs.

Soon enough, though, J. came running down the stairs. *Well, that didn't take long.* He just stood in the middle of the room looking at me. Well, I didn't dress her, but I made sure she was covered I am sure he already figured out what we were doing up there. Like a punch to my gut though his words rang through my body. "Where's my mom?"

I can't think I am on my feet and running up the stairs. "She was asleep when I left her, in her bed under the covers asleep. Did you check her bathroom?"

"Her window was open, all the lights off, and no, she isn't in the bathroom, the closet, or Auntie's room."

What?

As I enter the room, I notice first that the music she had playing was off. It had been on a continuous loop playing that slow jazzy blues indie rock crap that she liked. It had been on when I left. I had turned it down and turned off her lamp. I had not tucked her under the covers, but pulled her quilt up over her leaving her lying in the middle of the bed. I made sure the window was closed and locked with the curtains drawn. She has a big bay window in her room with a seat that would give her a view of the elementary school playground and surrounding neighborhood. It was full of stacked paperbacks, with enough room for one to sit among the pillows and books and an old rag doll. I had noticed earlier how cozy but actually organized it look. The books were now knocked over. The quilt was not on her bed and there was no sign of Beth.

I looked at the two boys, both of who now looked to be about four years old from the way they held hands, terrified. I have to fix this, I was supposed to protect her, and I was supposed to protect them. I don't want them to know this kind of pain. "I will find her. He won't hurt her. He thinks he loves her and if she is careful he won't hurt her." No, I will take care of these two kids with my last dying breath. They are her focus and now I see they aren't really men yet. They need comfort and safety. I catch the eyes of Luke, the man that taught me everything I know about following my gut. I call in the forensics and send the boys into Britt's room. While waiting for the task force and all the many people that will traipse in and out of here, I know I have to tell Britt and she is going to kill me. On my watch, she was raped and damned near died and her best friend was kidnapped. Maybe I can give her my gun and she can kill me quickly, rather than how she usually pulls people's hearts out, one little vein at time.

Britt is sitting up in bed wide eyed. Apparently the boys had stormed her room looking for Beth, and she was waiting for me. "He took her. I don't know how he is getting past her security system, but he did. I will find him before he so much as lays a hand on her hair. You, though, I need you to watch the boys. They are going to sleep in here with you. I don't want any of you leaving this room. Lock the doors and don't leave until I come get you. I will find her, I promise."

"No, we are going with you, that's our mom out there and we know what he does to women."

"Joseph, I completely understand your concern. I know what he is capable of, but I also know he is in love with your mother. She is smart and she knows enough to protect herself. She will pretend she is in love with him and that will protect her, I promise." Oh God, I really do hope we find her well. "Gentlemen we will be better able to find her and help her if I don't have to worry about you as well. I know you are smart enough to see the wisdom in letting the police do our jobs. We are highly trained and we know what we are doing." Yeah, I was calling in a dog to do my job. My first call was going to be for the K9 unit to get in here and follow them.

I can see the fury rising in Britt, but she holds it at bay and reaches out. "Come on, boys. I was lonely anyway. You guys can tell me scary stories and I will tell you dirty jokes." I watch the boys visibly relax as she puts her very small arms around the very large children and they lay on her like she can fix everything. An image of a queen holding court flashes before my eyes and I find I can see her maternal side as she strokes their hair and coos to them. Then the flash of Beth doing the same thing while riding in the back of my cruiser presents itself and I know Britt has learned how to do this from Beth which is why she's so good.

Chapter 16
Beth

My head is pounding...why is it so hot? The ground is hard and I can't open my eyes. My arms hurt. I feel drugged. I try and wrack my brain for a reason. I remember Graham giving me the beer, but I saw him open it and I just sipped it. He had lain by me, kissing me and holding me. It had been so long since someone held me and nuzzled me, a pang of regret and guilt had washed over me. I wasn't sure if it was okay to miss Marc, though I was well aware it was Graham I wanted and Graham that was with me at the time. I had pretended to fall asleep to get time to wrap my brain around my feelings and reconcile my heart with my head.

He had wrapped me up and left me and then I had fallen asleep. Where was I now? Pulling on my arms I realize they are handcuffed to some pipe of some sort. My eyes aren't covered but my head hurts too bad to open them. My mouth tastes tinny and dry. I am wrapped in blankets, but I think I'm naked still. Oh, no. This is not going to be good. I can feel the panic rising in my belly. I don't know what to do. There is scraping sounds and a door open.

In the brief glimpse I get of light I see I am in a garden or tool shed, but where? I am not at my house. I don't have one like this. I have no idea how long I was out or even how I managed to stay out. I fell asleep in my bed. I have to do something. I can't be stupid about this. I remember when Marc and I were first married he made me take a self defense class because I was taking night classes at the university and he didn't want anything to happen to me. I took the class5es and while I didn't really enjoy them, I do remember they told me no matter what happens, never stop fighting and never be quiet. You may get hurt, but you may not and you may scare them away or draw attention to yourself. I start screaming as loud and long as I can.

"No one can hear, you Elizabeth. You might as well save your strength. You are going to need it later when we have to fight them off." Oh no.

I have to catch my breath and he is probably right. If he isn't worried about someone hearing me then I probably should save my strength to fight him off. "Jimmy, where am I?" I have so many other things I want to ask but I remember Graham saying Jimmy thought he was in love with me. Maybe I could use that. "Please, undo my wrists. I promise not to run."

I can feel him coming closer and I don't know if this is a good thing or not. "I know you won't run. I know you wanted me to save you." He slides down on the dirty floor next to me. Oh yuck. He starts petting my face and I can't pull away from him. "I saw him fuck you. I saw him dirty you and use you. He left you naked like used meat. I am so sorry I didn't get there sooner. I had to wait for him to leave and get settled downstairs." He watched us? We had shared such a private moment and now I could only see it with him in it. "Did you know he was going to give you to the other men to use? I heard him talk to them about using you."

What is he talking about? "Jimmy, those other men are my sons. They wouldn't hurt me and they are no threat to me."

"My precious little innocent, I love that you have no idea how bad men can be. I will protect you from them. I know men like him and his plan for you. Sons grow up and fall in love with their mothers if they aren't taken away soon enough. He was going to show all those men how to use you." Jesus, I can't think to respond to that. He keeps petting my face stroking down my neck.

I know it is in my best interest to not flinch away, but I can't help it. "Please stop, Jimmy. I really don't like that."

The stroking stops and he pulls back. "Of course you don't. You have been used roughly tonight, haven't you?" Well yeah and I was starting to feel some of that yummy roughness in my sore body. But I would be damned if I would give him anything. "You should be treated better…loved and caressed. That monster treated you like a little whore. You are not a whore, are you, my sweet Elizabeth?"

He is twisted and the fear I think is making me nauseous. My head is pounding and I am going to throw up. "Jimmy, I'm going to be sick. Please, undo my hands." I start to wretch. I figure if I do, maybe he will undo me. If he doesn't, I will be covered in my own vomit.

I feel the click of the handcuffs come off, and I am curling toward him and I can't stop the wretch. I didn't eat dinner; I only had a little beer and nothing else. So alas, up comes the beer and something metallic. "What did you do to me?"

He backs away like I'm infected and grimaces. "They told me it wouldn't make you sick, just sleepy, if I only gave you a little bit. I figured you'd drink and wouldn't notice how much was in your beer. I gave you a little drop of liquid I stole from the hospital the last time I had an emergency."

"What was it?" I keep retching hoping to get it all out.

"How should I know what it is called? They give it to people who are having a breakdown to knock them out."

He drugged me and had no idea what it was. *Lovely*. "You fucker."

The pain registered first before I knew why I hurt. The entire side of my head was exploding in waves of pain. He was looking down at his hand as if it had hit me by itself. "You shouldn't call me names it's not nice." He sounded like a little boy.

I did the only thing I could think to get him back to my side. "I'm sorry, Jimmy. Please don't hurt me anymore. You're right; I shouldn't call you names." In my head, I am screaming every obscene name ever made.

He slides too me around my vomit, cooing to me in a sickly sweet voice. "My Elizabeth, I won't hurt you again if you behave. Okay?" Now I'm the child? Also, what is with Elizabeth? No one calls me that except telemarketers since my mother died ten years ago.

"How long do I have to stay here, Jimmy?"

He starts petting me again and I really don't know how to make it stop. "Just for a little while. I need to make sure we can get out and then we will leave Arizona. I have a cabin in Nevada and we can go live there. You will like it; it's so beautiful. Just off Lake Mead in the hills." Oh, hell no. He isn't taking me to the place where they based that story about the cannibals that ate the travelers is he? I had nightmares for a week and had to sleep with the lights on because Marc thought it would be funny to tell me it was based on true events. I have to stop that from happening. I can't let him take me away. I know I am close to home. He had to have carried me so I figure I can't have been far. I am not obese or anything, but I am not a small woman.

"You have a cabin, tell me about it. How long have you had it?" I have to keep him talking.

He just keeps petting me. I am feeling a little like one of the people in that movie, is he going to eat me next? "Well, it's more of a trailer than a cabin, but it is real secluded." Oh even better a trailer in the middle of the Nevada desert. Why didn't I think of that?

"Did you grow up there?" I don't know what else to do and I can't get away from him. He is all but wrapped around me. I'm naked and covered by my quilt from my bed. Its five thousand degrees and I can feel my heart beat in my temples. I am curled back into the corner as far as I can go and I feel a little like a caged animal. He keeps stroking me like he's hoping that I will come out. "Jimmy, do you have any water?" My mouth is full of metal and vomit.

He leans over and grabs a canteen and hands it too me, but he kind of spaced off. I don't know whether to drink or not, but I figure if I don't it will only be worse. If I do and I die, at least he won't have raped and tortured me or fed me to the cannibals in Nevada. I take a small sip of water. It tastes like the canteen or like the backyard hose, but it's clean. Finally, after waiting him out, I ask again, "So, did you grow up in Nevada?"

He just nods his head. I have to wonder what kind of childhood a man had when he turns into a serial rapist. I read a study once where they talked about how child sexual abuse was a leading factor in adult serial killers. At the time, I thought I couldn't have cared less. Don't we have to put the responsibility on the person who does the crime? Right now, I just wanted to get away from under James "Jimmy" Simmons, *suspected* serial rapist. I knew what he was going to do. I saw Britt in all her shiny glory. I also knew I was only putting off the inevitable.

I don't know what else to ask about? Obviously not his job or his expected time in prison, let alone how soon he planned to rape and kill me or why he thought I would want to go to Nevada for the pleasure of such a thing. "Tell me about your family."

"No Elizabeth. Tell me about yours. You still the innocent I think you are? Did your daddy touch you?" How did we get off the tracks so fast?

"No, Jimmy. My daddy died when I was in college and my mommy died not too many years after. I had a fairly normal upbringing. Girl scouts, softball, summers at the dam and the occasional vacation. My dad was blue collar, but hard working. I was the first to go to college on either side of the family." I don't know what else to give him .I want him to see me as innocent, because maybe then he won't have to hurt me. I know that much.

"When did you lose your virginity, Elizabeth?" I so don't want to do this; I know he is trying to get control of me.

He keeps petting me and I am trying to not cry though I think the tears are running. "Um, well I don't really want to talk about that."

"You still a virgin, my sweet little Elizabeth?" What? Didn't he just say he watched us have sex? I am a thirty-nine year old widowed mother of two. Nope haven't' been a virgin for longer than I can remember.

I don't, however, know how to answer him. If I say no he is going to be angry, if I say yes obviously he knows that a lie. I go with the only thing I can think. "Jimmy, how dare you ask something so personal?"

I really don't think it will work, but I don't know what else to do and apparently it worked. "Ah, Elizabeth, I'm sorry I didn't mean to offend you. I will try to not be so coarse next time. Okay?"

"Alright, Jimmy. Just please don't push me. I'm just not ready." I feel a little like I slipped in to Wonderland. Up is down and down is up; everyone is smiling and no one knows why.

"It's just that I want to know all about you. You're such a nice woman and you're so kind." Who is he talking about? Me? I don't think so.

"No, Jimmy. Why don't you tell me about you? We can share stories. You go first. Why did you want to be a cop?" I figured this was a safe topic. In fact, I think I had asked him this at dinner on our date.

Apparently, it was not. "No, I have no intentions of dragging up my drug addled father and whore of a mother for your inspection."

Okay, so apparently we weren't talking stable home life. Paint me surprised. I was just happy so far we hadn't slipped into rape Beth mode. "All right, we can talk about whatever you like. Do you like books?" I don't know what was coming out of my mouth. I only know I wanted it to stop but I felt like I couldn't. "You have to know I wasn't trying to judge you. I am just curious about you." There. I thought that might sound concerned.

His deep breath sounding like he was trying to get himself in control. "I suppose you are going to have to know about them soon enough. They are going to be your in-laws."

Confusion rang true here. "Who is going to be my in-laws?" I know my mother in law I already have is crazy, I can't figure out who he is talking about. Graham and I haven't talked about marriage and I know his parents are dead as well. Though I don't think we are talking marriage, I would really like to talk about it with him.

He started laughing, like a maniacal clown high and reedy. "My folks, when we get married they will be your in-laws. They are going to be so excited to be grandparents."

His folks, grandparents, what? Did he have my boys? "Jimmy, where are my boys?" I thought he told me he left them with Graham, but if he expected his parents to be happy little grandparents that means he needs my kids.

"I told you I left those men in the house. They are too old to be around women now. They were getting in bed with that whore when I went back to check on the house. Deputy Graham McDell," he said with such a sneer I couldn't hold back the gasp, "was telling them to get in bed with her, they were going to double team the little blonde whore that used to give it out in the bar."

"You mean Britt? Graham was telling my boys to get in bed with Britt?" Oh, I knew what that meant. Graham was coming to look for me and he was leaving them with Britt. I had every faith Britt would die defending those boys. Nothing untoward would ever happen to them. She was as much a mother as I was to them some days. She swatted asses when necessary, never missed a game if she could help it, and had no problem being there day to day.

He just nodded. "I'm sorry I know you wanted them to remain little boys, all mothers do, but you can't hold on to them forever. Eventually, they become men and I had to get you out before they did what men do and took what didn't belong to them."

Me? Did he mean the boys would take...? "What? Jimmy you can't be serious and think the boys would mean to do me harm. They are fifteen years old and innocent. I'm their mother."

He stopped stroking and grabbed my face hard. He was strong and I was sore where he hit me earlier. "You have no idea what boys think. You think those boys are innocent but at fifteen, they want nothing more than to shove their dick in your throat. I saw Graham do it to you; I know you know how unpleasant such an experience can be." I was so floored, I don't know if I should vomit at the thought of my boys and dicks, or if I should tell him that I quite enjoyed Graham and all he does too me.

I was holding very still trying to catch his eyes in the dark, but afraid if I do he will see my fear. I don't want to say anything to him. "Beth, men will push your boys into growing up, the men who came to your house are the same kinds of men that came to my house when I was their age. Men like that don't take no for an answer."

I have to hold it in to not pull away and shout in protest. Graham and Sheriff Carver are not like that. "Those men...." I start to say and he just shakes his head.

"I am a man. I know what men do; they will show them. They will start with teaching them how to please themselves. They will start with videos. I already saw the games they were playing with guns and violence." I wondered how long his rant would go on and I tried really hard to not picture this stuff happening to my children. I knew they were safe and not all men were twisted and sick. They had Britt, too. "They will touch them; I don't want to put thoughts in your head, my sweet little innocent. You have to know what men do though. They will shove their dicks in the young boy's asses." I can't stifle the gasp,

"Please, stop. Those are my children. You don't have to tell me." I can't stop the tears, though I know nothing is happening to them. I know they are okay, but I don't want to play this game anymore.

He just shook his head at me like I was so naïve "You have to know. They are going to fuck them until they are well trained in how to please a man. I suspect they are already at that point and that is why that whore was taking them to her bed. You have to know if she wasn't there they would expect you to take them. That's why I had to get you out of there. They were going to ruin you and make you take them both." I can't stop the vomit again. I tried, I really did try to keep it in and keep from showing how badly he was shaking me. "That, my princess, is why I had to take you."

What did he call me, no he can't have that. "Don't call me Princess. I don't like it and I don't want you to call me that." I can't stop the flow of words I just need him to stop talking. His voice is grating. His unwashed body and the drugs are doubling up on me and I can't stop my words, I can't stop my tears, and I can't stop the vomit. I dry heave for what feels like forever. He pats me and tries to sooth me, but he only makes it worse. Heave after heave, I was wishing I had the strength or knowledge or something to kill him.

"Jimmy, you have to take me home. I'm sick." He just keeps touching me. He starts trying to rub my stomach but that just makes the heaving worse. "Stop touching me, please. I need to breathe and I can't do that if you're touching me."

I know I have pushed too far. I regret the words as soon as they are out of my mouth. "You bitch I am trying to help you. Even if you don't want me to I will protect you. No one will hurt you again." Doesn't he know what he has done to me?

I can't focus enough to get my thoughts straight but I know one certainty, one truth that makes all of this livable. "Graham is going to kill you. He will find me and he will kill you for taking me." He starts that frightening maniacal laugh. I don't remember that laugh from our date. But I guess it was there, hidden under the layers of normal.

He reached for me with a twisted smile on his face and the panic drives through my body. I don't know what he is going to do, but he has me backed into the corner and I don't know how to get out. I don't even know how I got here. "You're wrong. He won't kill me. He will look for you for a while because he has to, but eventually you will become a cold case. Do you know what they do with cold case? The storage…they go into a large storage room and they are never looked at again. You, my sweet innocent, stupid girl, are going to be a cold case in a week when something bigger and badder comes along."

Even I know he's right. This is a large city and they aren't going to waste a ton of resources on me when there are more important things to do. I know they will continue to look for me at least until the next big headline. However, I know that Graham will look for me. Britt won't let them stop, when she is at full strength I think she could muster the hounds of hell if she needed. "You can't keep me Jimmy, I have to go home and take care of my kids. They have school tomorrow, or today. I have to be there to make sure they are taken care of. That's a mom's job."

I don't even know what I am pleading for, but I know I have to fight and I can't do it physically. He is huge and I could never overpower him. I need to out think him. He just keeps looking at me like he is trying to figure me out. "No, you aren't going back there. I know you think they won't hurt you but I have to protect you. Maybe it's time to show you what I mean."

I know what that means. "No, you don't have to show me anything. I know what you do to women. I was in the hospital with Britt."

Tsking me through his teeth, he rasps. "She is a whore, nothing like you. She wanted what she got. Did she tell you she asked me to shove that bottle in her twat in front of the whole bar? She let the whole bar take turns fucking her–now just look at what you made me do!" *Crack!* Stars exploded in my head as his hand connects with the side of my face. "You made me use that ugly language that we know isn't meant for you. Now stop being provoking. Your slut of a friend didn't get punished or hurt. She asked for it and I gave her exactly what she likes." My face is throbbing and I think he broke my whole damned head.

I can't stop my tears because he caught my nose and I think he may have broken it. "You can stop being a crybaby. It won't stop what has to happen. You have to be protected. You are not like those other women. The ones that thought fucking a cop even a lowly patrolman would secure them a happy life. They wanted to be handcuffed and slapped and one even wanted to be choked. None of those sluts got anything they didn't ask for."

Trying to hold back the sniffles I can't even look up or my head spins. "You don't know me, so why do you think I am so innocent?" I can't help it I know I shouldn't bait him, but I am at a point where I need something to happen, anything. "Don't you think that after fifteen years of marriage, my husband I did things that would be considered terrible to others? I have two kids, so obviously I'm not all sweet and innocent. Graham told me you watched us in the bar. I know that you know I am not what you need." Maybe he will just kill me and get it over with. I have to get out of this corner, though.

I start pushing out and forward in small amounts. Jimmy backs up, allowing me space. "I think you have always been hurt and I don't think you intended to let those men hurt you. Your husband was a terrible man that slept with his secretary and then you were forced to have sex with him. I don't think you understand. I don't think those boys are yours. They don't look like you at all."

Is he crazy? My boys are identical to their father and his father and all the way up the line? There are some strong genes in that line.

Another small slide, more space conceded by him. Doesn't he see what I am doing? "Those boys are mine, I delivered them. I was awake the whole time and they handed them to me. They look like their father, as all boys should. My husband was a good man and he did not cheat, *ever*." I can take a lot. He can talk about Britt being a slut, well, because she kind of is, and he can talk about Graham because he's strong and I know he can defend himself. Graham is going to kill him. He will not talk about my children or Marc. They are innocent and can't defend themselves.

He leans in and it takes all my strength to not pull away and back to my corner. "You are so stupid. They are men and you really shouldn't trust men. He was cheating with his secretary; that is why he was shot. Graham fucks every man and woman that comes in the bar; it's his job to try out the merchandise before he sells it. You are just too stupid to acknowledge it. I didn't realize you were so stupid and I have no room for stupid whores in my life." I know I shouldn't do it, but I slide closer to him.

"No, Jimmy. You're right; you are. They are all out to get me I just have to pretend to myself so I don't get scared at night." What am I saying? He smells and I can't think straight. My stomach is still heaving and I need to get out of this corner. I have to move closer to him again.

He puts his arm around me. Well, wasn't that smart? "I know, I know you just can't know what they had planned for you. Your husband put it all in the works and Graham is just going to finish it."

Ew, gross. The pain in my head is throbbing in time with my heartbeat and my thoughts are jumbling. I slide forward out of his arms and out of the corner.

Something pokes me in the back. I can't tell what it is, but if it hurts me maybe I can use it to hurt him. "You said Graham tests everyone who comes to the club. Did you have sex with Graham?" Yeah right, like I don't know the answer to that one.

Maybe I don't. The answer sat on my skin like a cold slime. "Of course I did I had to in order to get in the club." I know Graham doesn't do men. We talked about it. Some of those late night phone calls were very enlightening. I had worried about his sexual past and present. He had been very open, probably because he had a detailed history on me in his desk drawer. "Graham told me he never slept with men. He told me he had threesomes where the woman was the focus of the sex. Were you part of that?" It's the only thing I can think.

The shake of his head and his twisted smile, that I can see only because there is light coming in through under the door, is so demented and off it looks like a bad mask. "You really think he is going to tell you the truth? He makes everyone who walks in the door have sex with him in his office. That's why he has the pull out couch up there. That's how I knew there was one there to use with that whore."

I am so confused, and my throbbing head won't put the thoughts in order. I feel around to find out what is the long thing poking out and find it's a rake that tipped over, the metal kind used for playgrounds. We must be at the school. I have spent hours sitting in my window watching the kids play on the playground and then the maintenance staff cleaning the sand every evening. There is a tool shed next to the building, but how can we not be heard and not hear the kids? Today would be a school day, Wednesday. It's too bright out to not be middle of the day.

I need the other end of the rake. I can't stab him with this end and I am not sure I can hit him hard enough to knock him out. I won't really have room to line up my swing. I can't sit here and die, though, and I will eat nails before he takes me off to live with the hillbilly folk who raised him.

I adjust my blanket to look like I am just trying to keep myself covered. There will be no way I can run wrapped in a giant quilt. It will have to stay and my dash across the school yard will give the young boys something to think about for years to come. Yeah, I loved this quilt. I bought it at a craft fair. It was nothing special, but it matched the drapes and it and has seen a lot of years. The kids used it for forts, Marc and I wrapped up in it talking about our futures that never really happened. Most recently, Graham wrapped me in it when we finished making love. Maybe it's time to get a new one for him and me. I know a lot of things are going to have to change around us and I hope the kids and he are ready because I'm done with this fucker.

The rake is almost all the way out but covered in my blanket. Jimmy is just staring, like he is trying to see into my head. I can't think of how to distract him. I am not sure I am going to be able to stand up once I hit him. My head is throbbing and I know when I get a migraine walking is hard and those are nothing compared to what I have going on now.

I get my feet under my body, but I have to distract him. He can't see me pull the rake out or my swing won't be hard enough. I have practiced baseball with J. enough to know how to swing a bat hard. I even played a little in high school myself. I know I have one chance and a rake is long. I can't feel anything else and I am as far away as I feel he will let me get. I can't think how to get him to move his eyes from me. I was told to watch the shoulders to see how someone was going to strike; you can always see what's coming. Maybe if I distract him from my shoulders. I pull the blanket down just a little exposing the tops of my breast as though it was just a little slip. I shivered and saw Jimmy's eyes drop to my breasts. No way he can watch my shoulders if he is watching my tits. Another whole body shiver that made my head pound and the blanket slid just a little lower catching on my nipples.

Talk about focus…his whole body is oriented at my chest. I can see he's holding his hands back with sheer force of will. On my knees I stand as quickly as I can and swing as hard as I can. I forgot to think about the spikes of the rake. He apparently wasn't as stupid as I thought, but he wasn't as fast as he needed to be. The rake embedded in his shoulder and I couldn't pull it back for another swing, but neither could he get to me. I ran for the door with his roar in my head.

216

As soon as I stepped out of the shed, the blinding hot sun hit my head and I went to my knees. My head was exploding in pain to the point where I had to close my eyes to run. I had no idea which direction was the best. As my body settled into the run, I had to open my eyes and saw I was on the opposite side of the school, across the playground and away from any houses backed to a wash. I knew the best way out was through. I ran as fast as I could for the school.

I hit the doors to the school before I took time to look back at the shed. Jimmy was fast on my heels. Blood poured from his arm. He's screaming filthy obscenities at me. Someone must have seen me through the window because the doors open wide before I can get too them. School security officers start pouring out of the school. Stark naked with my head pounding, I am lead to the nurse's room. Thank God they have scratchy blankets it is something to cover me. I called Graham's cell first and he didn't answer. The nurse dialed 911. I figured the police though they were probably just school security would have done that already. I just want clothes and Graham. I called Britt and got P., my sweet baby.

"Mom, are you ok? Where are you? We have been worried sick. What happened?" I can hear the tension and tears in his voice as well as J. going crazy behind him.

"P., you have to calm down and I will tell you. I'm okay. I'm at Valley Ridge in the nurse's office. I know you are worried about me, but stop it. I am going to be fine. Did Graham leave? I really need him." I can't keep the plea out of my voice.

"No mom, he's not here. He went to look for you I think. He told Britt to look after us and cleared out as soon as he found you missing." I can't help but be crushed he is the one I want.

"Ok, tell J. to get my car keys and come get me. I can't walk and I think I need to go get my head x-rayed, oh and P., have him bring me some clothes." The tears are burning, but making my head pound.

"All right momma, we are on our way. Aunty is getting dressed."

"No, tell her to stay. She can't be up and about." I could hear him talking to her and I could hear her response very clearly.

"Tell her I love her too and I will see you guys in a minute." The nurse is looking at me like I'm crazy.

I hang up the phone and lay back on the little bed that is obviously designed for children half my size. "Don't you fall asleep, you hear me? You need to go to the hospital; I already told them to send an ambulance."

"Oh no, I am not leaving without clothes first. I don't need an ambulance. My son can drive me to the hospital where I will get x-rays. Please tell them not to send the ambulance." I see her call again and explain the situation.

She just keeps shaking her head at me even as I walk out with one boy on each side finally dressed in a summer dress. No bra, no panties, but hell I've got my ass covered and that is all that matters. She did give me an ice pack for my face that hurts like hell. I think my nose is broken but I can't tell my kids that. I'll wait and tell the doctor.

After sitting in the emergency room forever, I'm given a clean bill of health. My nose isn't broken but still hurts like little demons are banging on it. My cheekbone is broken however. I have a hairline fracture in my cheekbone and in my head. Jimmy had hit me hard. The officers that took my statement couldn't tell me where Graham was and after several attempts to contact him I stopped asking.

I was walking from the garage to the house, when the door swung open and Graham stood there looking fierce. "Where have you been?"

How dare he? I couldn't even look at him. I tried to walk past him but he wouldn't let me by. He just stood there with his hands on his hips. "Graham, you need to let her through now." Oh my sweet J. He was going to defend me to the end of my time. This had been rough on my boys and they needed to feel like they have done something to protect me.

I just stand there waiting for him to let us all in. The garage door closes and it's just us, the boys, Britt and I standing in the garage waiting for access to my house. I don't owe him anything and I will be damned if I am going to explain myself. "I already gave the police my statement…several of them, in fact. Now let me in, I need to lie down"

He looks so angry but as I watch fear and hurt streak across his face. What the hell does he have to be hurt about? He steps aside and lets us troop in the house. I head up the stairs without ever slowing down. I know the boys will eat left over pizza. I can't take care of Britt and Graham. They can go to hell, for all I care.

I can hear the footsteps following me and I just didn't care who it was. My head was still pounding, my face burned and my heart well. It didn't factor today. "You can't ignore him."

"Leave me alone, Britt. I don't care right now. I just need to be alone." My room was dark and cool. My bed didn't have a cover on it, so I lay on the sheets and closed my eye. I know it had been a long day for her as well, but I just couldn't rouse myself to care. I needed a break.

I could hear her puttering around and huffing. The cold cloth on my face felt good, but I just didn't want it. "I said leave me alone, please, both of you."

"I didn't know you even knew I was here. You haven't acknowledged me since you walked in the house." He was pissed at me?

"Four hours, I was at the hospital. Four hours, I waited for you and nothing. No one knew where you were, no one could reach you. Check your cell phone, Graham. I called you first. I did my part. Now get the fuck out of my house. I am done here. I need a nap, I need to recover, and I don't need your wounded bullshit. Both of you leave me alone. I looked up to see not only Graham and Britt, but the boys standing there too.

"I was hauling out your trash, Beth. I was at the police station questioning your kidnapper. Remember him? Remember my job? I tried to get away and when I called I was told you wouldn't talk to me. I was told you specifically asked me to stay away." I knew full good and well what he was talking about. I had finally after several cops had questioned me told the nurse no more. I didn't want to talk to any more cops.

I can't even think to explain to him. "Just go away right now. Can't we do this when my face isn't broken and my–well. Just go away." I don't want to think about all the things he could have done to be there and didn't. I don't want to think about why I blamed him for leaving me and never coming back.

Even though the boys woke me every couple of hours I didn't get out of bed for two days. My whole body hurt. Something about adrenaline crashes and muscle cramps. My heart hurt. I hadn't seen Graham again. I guess I really did push him away. Even my sarcastic bitch inside was hurt. I hadn't seen Britt either and that confused me. The boys brought me food and woke me up and then left. Both said very little, but never forgot. I ate a lot of pizza and sandwiches; I guess it's time to teach them to cook.

On the way to the shower, I averted my eyes from the mirror. I could feel the swelling on my face and I really didn't want to see it. I really should have showered earlier. I don't know how even my children could stand to be around me. Once I was washed and while I combed my wet hair, I stood in front of the mirror and took stock of myself. My hair is fine, though my head still hurts. I was told I would have a headache for a week or two. I am sure coffee will help. My face is swollen and I have a great big purple and black eye, but nothing else is wrong with me. My broken parts aren't on the outside.

My heart isn't visible. I don't know why it hurts so badly. I don't even know what is wrong with us. Did Jimmy break us? I didn't think that was possible. I was so confident that when I got out Graham would be there to put his arms around me. I waited at the hospital but he never showed. When I came home he didn't want to see me, didn't want to talk to me. It has been too long since I have done any of this and I just don't need it anymore. My heart hurts because I really want to miss Marc, but I just don't. I miss the thought of Marc, the idea that if he were still here none of this would be happening, but really I miss Graham.

Once dressed and felling mostly alive I headed downstairs. I mostly wanted coffee and to see if my house fell down around our heads. I was expecting a kitchen full of dishes and sullen teenagers sitting in front of the television. I found only a spotlessly cleaned house that was not cleaned by *my* children and silence. I stood in the kitchen expecting something, but got nothing. I headed to the coffee maker coffee first then I would find the kids. I knew they were here I saw them a few hours ago. Then I heard them…I knew where they were. I finished the coffee, comforted by the sounds of the splashing. Cup in hand, I headed out to the deck. I loved my back yard. We had a large pool with a wading deck that I could sit in a chair and keep my feet in the pool and my ass out. I also had a full living room and kitchen space out there. It was far and away the nicest part of my house. I very much wanted to curl up and watch the boys play and sip my coffee and regain myself.

I should have heard the boys when I was in my room as it overlooks the pool, but I was so focused on me I must have missed it. I didn't however miss the quiet conversation that stopped when I walked through the door. Well, that explained the kitchen. "I thought you guys left."

I couldn't have kept my heart from leaping even if I tried when Graham rose and turned to me. He was afraid and I didn't know why. "I told you I wasn't leaving, Princess."

"When did you get here?" I don't know what is happening but I can't do it. I can't fight with him.

221

He steps to me and I instinctively step back, the hurt flashes fast across his face and then it's gone. "I got here Tuesday morning. Don't you remember?" Of course I remember him getting here Tuesday, but that was days ago.

"Yes, but today…when did you get here today? I didn't hear the bell ring." I had a feeling that Britt didn't leave. I could hear her puttering around in her room, I thought, but I had no idea Graham had stayed.

He steps closer again. This time I don't retreat. I feel like prey being stalked. "I told you Princess, I love you and we are making this work. If you needed time, then you have it. But you will remember you belong to me and I don't share or give away my toys just because someone else wants them."

His hands settle on my hips, my coffee between us and I can feel all eyes are on us. "But you didn't even…" I didn't get to finish when he stopped me.

"I didn't come up and check on you? No you're right I didn't. I let the boys do that and report back how you were. You weren't ready for people. I should have pushed my way past your security at the hospital, but I was worried about scaring you worst than you already were. I saw you called, but I was on the radio so I didn't check my cell phone. I don't know why the officers you spoke with didn't radio me, but I meant to be there for you."

I put my hands on his lips to stop the torrent of words. First, I don't need them, and second they are hurting my head. "Forgiven, now you say it."

"Oh God Princess, you didn't do anything wrong. There's nothing to forgive. You were right to be angry." He leaned into my ear and pushed my coffee against my chest. "You are going to get a spanking for thinking I would leave you or those kids in a lurch." He pulled back and kissed my forehead softly. "I love you, Princess, now and always."

I could feel the tears and my head hurt, but I loved him, and I needed him to know it. I set my coffee down and leaned in close to his ear. I bit the lobe and whispered. "I will spank your ass for thinking I wouldn't want to see you." Pulling back from him, I slid my arms around him there was safety in laying my head on his chest. "I am a bitch, a really big bitch sometimes, but you have to know when I push you away I don't want you to go. That's my crazy. I get upset and push, but I don't always mean it."

He cocked head and lifted an eye brow at me. "Yeah I know, I'm crazy, I admit it fully. You should ask around. I never told you I was sweet and kind."

"Aw Princess, you taste sweet too me." And he lifted my chin to his mouth for a kiss that was definitely sweet.

Rebekkah Rogers

Epilogue

The panic washed over me "What if they aren't okay?" I know he is tired of comforting me. I know he probably wants to smother me.

He just strokes my arm and pulls me close "Princess, they're fine. They'll call you every Sunday morning and any time during the week they need to speak to their mommy. They are together and they are excited. Let them have this."

I look at my husband. He is really gray now. The lines around his eyes multiplied the night I was taken and again six months later, when J. wrecked his brand new truck. I knew I loved him, but watching him take care of everything when J. was hurt drove home how well he had settled in our lives. The broken leg healed; the truck was totaled, though, and Graham was never the same with the boys. He hovered almost as much as I did. He became openly affectionate and drew them to him with his strength.

The boys respect him and ask his opinion and actually listen to him. They never listen to me, because I'm just the mom. Graham never moved out, either. He shifted from the couch to my bed that first day I immerged and he never left again. Britt still needed help, though not as much, and she had stayed another week.

Britt is finally doing well, but I can't think about that now, I am trying to get something out of Graham.

"Graham, I want to call them and make sure." He just shakes his head at me.

"No darlin'. You promised."

"But Indiana is so far away!" He just chuckles at me. He is always laughing at me.

"Princess, this is what you wanted for them. They both got scholarships to the most prestigious university in the catholic community. They are going to be fine. It has only been two weeks." He leans down and nibbles on my neck. "Now I know how to take your mind off them and put it where it belongs."

Oh man, did he ever know how to take my mind off of my troubles! We have been married for three years and every time he touches me, I still feel the same leap of passion. I expect eventually our sex life will slow with age and time, but Graham assures me that isn't the case. His hands rub my arms taking my hands in his and pulling them around his head. I bury my hands in his hair because I love the feel of it. He keeps it just a little longer than he should because he knows I like to hold on to it when we have sex.

He pushes me back and slides the sandwich fixings into the sink as he lifts me to the counter. "I have better ideas for lunch." As I wrap my legs around his waist, I lift his shirt searching for the hard expanse of chest that turns me on just to see it. He is darker now, albeit only a little. He spent the entire summer in the pool with the boys. Never hovering, but grilling burgers for their friends and I know he bought them beer on the sly.

His hands go to my shirt as well. Lifting my shirt, he takes my nipple in his mouth through the lace of my bra. He knows I love the visual of that. I watch as his hands wrap around them and his teeth sink nipping into them. The heat is a slow build now, starting in my heart and working its way out. He is lifting my hips and sliding my yoga pants down before I can register the actions. I grasp at his swim trunks pushing them down his hips with my feet. He is hot and hard in my hands as I stroke at him and pull him towards me.

226

We have never used a condom and never had to. He has told me is a freedom he loves. He is in me pushing my shoulders down and holding my hips up to him. "Princess, you are as hot as the first time. I love your pussy."

I can't catch my breath and my body is coiling ready to burst. He knows I love when he talks dirty to me. He plunges hard and fast, slowing when he feels me start to orgasm, backing off to hold me at bay. It's a game he likes to play. He slows, pulling me back up kissing me. The kiss is slow and sweet, soft and filled with love, but it's not what I want. I bite down on his lower lip. "Fuck me, Graham. Harder! Now!"

His growl in his throat and hard nip on my neck are the only signs he heard me. He keeps it slow and easy, killing me with each hot deep stroke. Until I can't take it anymore, I lie back on the counter and lift my hips for him again. He takes me hard and fast. He slides in and out of me until I can't feel anything else but him. Hot jets of him push me over the edge.

His pants and little kisses on all the little bite marks as he stays buried in me are mingled with his words of love and I can't help but melt against him. I love him. He lifts me from the counter and takes the lunch fixings out of the sink to finish my chore as I stand with my back to the counter sated. I wonder how I can fuck with him again. "Hey, honey. Now that we got that out the way, can I call the kids at school?" His little frustrated growl and a slap on the ass are the only response as I run away, giggling all the way to the bedroom.

Acknowledgements

Chris you know I think you hung the moon and stars. It is my honor to have you by my side. Without you this would not have happened and it is as much your accomplishment as it is mine. Thank you.

Stephanie you do beautiful work and you were ever so patient with me. Thank you.

My family is the greatest; I have received more support that I ever thought possible. Thanks guys!

My Beta Readers are the greatest women to ever live! Thank you all!

About the Author

Rebekkah Rogers has been writing in secret her whole life. It wasn't until she met her super hero and he dared her to make her secret known that her debut novel Breathing was finally put to paper.

Residing in a suburb of Phoenix, Rebekkah is usually reading two or three books at a time and writing at least one. She is a member of several writing groups and remains active in them by beta reading, providing critiques and reviews as well as troubleshooting ideas for new and established authors.

You can follow Rebekkah at the following sites:

www.facebook.com/rebekkah.rogers

www.goodreads.com/goodreadscomrebekkah